The Mother Fault

Kate Mildenhall

HarperCollins*Publishers*

HarperCollins*Publishers* Ltd
1 London Bridge Street,
London SE1 9GF

www.harpercollins.co.uk

HarperCollins*Publishers*
1st Floor, Watermarque Building, Ringsend Road
Dublin 4, Ireland

First published in the UK by HarperCollins*Publishers* 2021

This paperback edition 2022

1

First published in Australia in 2020
by Simon & Schuster (Australia) Pty Limited

Selected Poems by Gwen Harwood, Text © John Harwood
First published by Penguin Books Australia 2001
Reprinted by permission of Penguin Random House Australia Pty Ltd

A catalogue record for this book is available from the British Library

ISBN: 978-0-00-843029-0 (B-format PB)

Typeset in Baskerville BT by
Palimpsest Book Production Ltd, Falkirk, Stirlingshire

Printed and Bound in the UK using 100% Renewable Electricity
at CPI Group (UK) Ltd

It is not for my children I walk
on earth in the light of the living.
It is for you, for the wild
daughters becoming women,

anguish of seasons burning
backward in time to those other
bodies, your mother, and hers
and beyond, speech growing stranger

on thresholds of ice, rock, fire
bones changing, heads inclining
to monkey bosom, lemur breast,
guileless milk of the word.

from 'Mother Who Gave Me Life'
Gwen Harwood, 1981

'. . . but no one bothered to read the terms and conditions.'

Professor David Carroll,
The Great Hack, Netflix 2019

1

Mim runs hot water in the sink, plunges her hands beneath the suds and gasps at the scald of it. Ben is particular about knives. She has to handwash them, even with the restrictions. She runs the blue cloth up and down each blade, feeling the smooth heat of the steel.

Missing.

He is missing.

Your husband is missing.

'Mum!'

She turns to her daughter leaning over the kitchen bench, scowling. Still in her soccer gear, she is long-legged and ponytailed. It is untenable how much longer she gets each day.

Essie holds out her screen. 'The Friendship Project – you haven't signed the form.'

There is always something else. 'You sure I didn't sign it already?'

Essie sighs. 'No, you didn't. Everyone else got to start uploading today and I didn't. 'Cos *you* haven't signed the form.'

Mim takes the screen. Apologises. Swipes her finger in a squiggle across the flashing rectangle.

'*Thank* you,' Essie says, taking the screen back and muttering, 'Wasn't that hard, was it?'

'Careful,' Mim says, trying to keep her tone light. 'Tell Sammy bath time, can you?'

Since when did eleven-year-olds have so much attitude? Ben will laugh when she tells him.

Mim puts one hand on her sternum, thinks she will vomit.

Keep it together.

She washes each knife. Pulls out a clean tea towel and dries each blade, sliding them one by one into the wooden knife block in the corner.

⌣

'What do you mean – *missing*?' she had said when the phone call had come that afternoon. She had been distracted by the kids tumbling their bags in the door ahead of her, trying to get her earplugs in to hear the call properly.

'It appears Mr Elliot has disappeared from the mine site at the Golden Arc. GeoTech have confirmed this with us.'

'But he's due back in a few days. Couldn't he just be on his way home?'

'We don't believe so.'

Essie called from in front of the open fridge. 'What is there to eat?'

Mim had frowned, pointed to her earbuds, turned away.

'Why am I hearing this from you?' She had tried not to raise her voice. There are ways to speak to the Department.

'We're working closely with GeoTech. Protocol, Mrs Elliot, on foreign investment sites, you understand.'

'But how can he be missing? He's chipped. Can't you just geolocate him?'

They had ignored her question. Asked if they could send someone around. She had asked again, but there was nothing they could tell her.

She had pictured the grey SUV parked in the driveway, the white concentric rings of the Department logo, the faces behind the curtains in the street.

'No, thank you,' she had said, 'we'll be fine.'

'You'll let us know if he makes contact?'

As if they wouldn't already know. 'Of course,' she had replied.

~

When the kids are in bed, she pours wine. Tries to think. She should call her mother. That's what you do when you have stressful news. But what can her mother do from up there at the farm? She'd only worry, call Mim back endlessly until there was an answer. And she's still so tender. Michael, then Dad.

'Call Ben,' she tells OMNI, even though she knows what the result will be. OMNI has a woman's voice, a soft, slightly clipped accent. The feedback from previous operating systems all pointed to people having a higher compliance with female voices. It was traumatic for the kids when they updated. Sam had only ever known SARA. OMNI took some getting used to.

'Unable to make contact.'

It's not unusual. She hasn't been able to call him onsite the entire time he's been gone. He could make scheduled calls with the rest of the crew from the IT room, hardwired in, so at least they get to see his face. They laughed before he left about what they should and shouldn't say. It's a well-known secret what the flagged words under the Department are. They can only imagine how many flagged words there are under China's security services.

She thinks of the last time they spoke, and realises she can't remember the specifics.

'OMNI, call GeoTech.' It's the kind of company they would have laughed at together in the past. Big money.

'Calling GeoTech now.'

It's after hours so she's not really expecting anyone to pick up, but what else can she do? She drums her fingers against the stone benchtop.

She leaves a message and rings off. They'll call. It will all make sense.

She gulps the wine.

What the fuck, Ben? Where are you?

She puts the glass down, and it clinks violently against the hard surface. Maybe he's just been delayed on the island. Her theories begin reasonably, but as the glass empties, she imagines him with a drink in his hand, then drunk, sitting with his back against a wall in a dark lane. Then in a hotel room, where there is skin, pulled sheets, the heavy groan of illicit sex. A mangled taxi, suitcase thrown against the traffic. A foreign emergency ward.

The glass is empty. Another glass means another bottle. Maybe it will help her sleep.

She scrolls the feeds for news from Indonesia. But there is nothing about a missing Australian engineer. Nothing but apocalypse stories, or that's how it reads. The equatorial region is beginning to really sweat it, the patterns of climate refugees marking trails like new currents on the maps as they swarm to higher, cooler, ground. Ben was mad to go there, but the money! The fortunes to be made there before the whole region swallows itself. Plus the danger money. Thanks to the ever-increasing frequency of seismic activity. Quakes. Aftershocks. The suck and spill of tidal waves. For people like Ben, like her to a lesser extent, there was a thrill in that. The added frisson of knowing how the earth worked, or thinking they knew, anyway. There was a need for people like Ben to extract the wealth from the fault lines before tectonic movement, the spluttering, violent earth, made it impossible. He had promised it'd only be another couple of years, then they'd be set. He could work less, she could take the helm, if she wanted, and they'd be secure, financially at least.

She missed work. The brain stretch of geology. That's why she was so keen to take Heidi up on her recent offer. Being out in the field, even being back in the front of a lecture theatre, would be thrilling. She was pretty sure that she was the one who suggested she give over her tenured position. The groundwater project needed someone who could work fulltime and she couldn't go back with Essie so young, but she wishes she hadn't. Wishes they had made it easier for her to stay. It's not just the brain drain heading back to their countries of origin after graduation – it's the ones who are wiping bums and pureeing organic fucking vegetables, too.

She keeps scrolling. She no longer reacts to the images. They are all the same and she has no feeling left. The stories are the same too. And who knows if what they say is true.

The world shifted slowly, then so fast, while they watched but didn't see. They weren't stupid. Or even oppressed in the beginning. Let the record show that. There were no assassinations. No riots. The people invited the new government to take charge at the ballot box. The two parties had consumed themselves. Left the system wide open for a third option. Reasonable, populated by diverse public figures, backed by both big money and big ideology. On a platform of innovative and economically viable responses to the climate emergency, a rehaul of the health, housing and disability schemes that would see the most vulnerable members of the community cared for, and a foreign policy that miraculously spoke to fear of the other *and* fluid borders ideal for capital in and capital out, the new party was humbly triumphant on election night. Simple, elegant. No need for finite portfolios and the bullshit of bureaucracy (their words, appealing to the everyday Australian). Centralised power was the answer: One Department for One Nation. The Department of Everything. A party who promised a different way, a better way, and a populace who needed to believe them. Like geology, history repeats itself. Sometimes it's just hard to see.

And then, within their first one hundred days in office, their greatest test. Mim didn't personally know anyone at the MCG on the day of the attacks, although, by degrees of separation, there were a few. Someone shoots that many footy fans in a city like Melbourne during a preliminary final and everyone's going to know someone. Likewise, the bank hack didn't affect them directly. She didn't go through the months of hell of getting the administration of their life back on track. But, like everyone else, they did bear the pain of soaring interest rates.

And then the bio-threat. The government tried to keep everyone level-headed, at the start at least. There were protocols in place for the media by then, supposedly to counteract scaremongering and division. So for a while they only knew that security at the MediSec facility outside of Geelong had been compromised. Eventually it got out. Two security officers and a virologist were dead. The terrorists had known what they were doing. They only took one frozen vial. Only needed one. Enough terror in that particular strain to last a generation.

So that's what they lived with. The knowledge that nothing was sacred, and nothing was safe. Not their money, not their health and not their football games.

After that, the government changed the terror laws again. People could be detained without charge for six months while investigations were pending. A new Treason Code. The punishment for violations? Loss of citizenship. The offender *and* their family. Loss of all assets. Stateless. *You bring terror to our nation, you don't deserve a nation.* No one could argue with that kind of rhetoric.

The ensuing authority creep hardly caused a ripple. In this, the lucky country, the land of the lackadaisical larrikin, no one demanded you jumped on board the new system. No one legislated. No, it was much more powerful than that.

You got a chip to protect a mate.

You got a chip 'cos you had nothing to hide.

Because we are all in this together.

The publicity campaign was a triumph. Rumour has it that they paid 5 million to one influencer alone to livestream her own chipping through her social media feed. Football clubs got chipped together. There were cross-cultural chip days in the inner suburbs – even the most strident of small L liberals on board.

And all in all, it seemed a rather small price to pay. It seemed increasingly likely that there might be a moment when you would like to know that your loved ones could be located in the blink of an eye. Less.

They were all doing it anyway, more or less. Geolocating their every move in exchange for Points! Rewards! (conditions apply).

You want to know where your people are when the world becomes a shifting, wild, hungry thing. When there are mass evacuations at least three times each summer on the outskirts of every city, tidal floods up the mouth of the river, a wave of eco-terrorism – bombings at a proposed radioactive waste repository site, and that storm – they couldn't call it a hurricane on an atmospheric technicality but anyone within fifty kilometres would say it was.

When they brought in the legislation she was heavily pregnant and had to wait until she'd given birth before she could get herself chipped. And Essie. *Easier to do it now for her*, the smiling nurse had said, *she won't even remember the nick*. Mim – leaking, weeping, feeling like she had been torn asunder – said, *Yes, of course*.

They did Mim first, a click, pearl of blood, nothing compared to the blind vortex of pain she'd just endured.

And then her tiny daughter, Essie, another click, a scream, eyes squeezed shut then open – the treachery of it! Of what she'd let them do to her. The nurse soothed, *Now you'll always know where she is. Doesn't that feel wonderful?*

She had grown this child, had been attached. How would she ever not know?

I will always know where you are, she had whispered.

∽

By the time Essie arrived, the Department had started rolling out the estates. She remembers watching it on her feeds while she nursed Essie late at night, and feeling hopeful that there was finally a solution to some of the problems that had plagued the city. The residents of those first estates were homeless women, crushed by poverty, violence, and the market crash that ensured their already minuscule super accounts crumbled to dust. Their children went too, of course. The overworked and underpaid former Human Services workers collectively breathed a sigh of relief. The Department had this in hand. Children in safe and secure housing with equitable access to education, adults in work and re-training programs, their healthcare and finances all overseen by the high-tech, omniscient eyes of the benevolent state. BestLife, they called it. No pun intended.

There was some unease, of course, there always is. But, how could anyone argue?

It wasn't until later that the gates to those estates became one way. And by then it was too late.

～

Her head spins slightly when she stands.

'Lights out, OMNI.'

'You are still in the kitchen zone.'

'Lights out.'

'As directed.'

The lights fade to dark around her, punctuated by the green and white glow of her networked kitchen. She stands at the bench, wondering where her husband is, trying to remember to breathe.

～

In the morning the school traffic is heavy and Mim is on edge as she waits to find a gap. She has two days before the kids expect Ben home. She suggests casually that there might be a delay.

'But can we call him?' Sam asks from the back.

She hedges. 'We'll try after school, huh?' Essie catches her eye in the rear-vision mirror, but Mim looks away. Tries to remember the last conversation she had with Ben but still can't make out any specifics. They all feel the same when Ben is away, the space behind him, even when it's a cramped comms room, seems to expand infinitely. After they sign off she can't help but imagine him, standing, stretching, walking away, back to work, his brain, the pulse of it all, to quiet perhaps, to solitude even. She accelerates, pulling out to get into a tight space. She cranes her neck to see what the hold-up is, but there is only the line of cars ahead, the smooth contours of all the hybrids. Keeping up with the Joneses is a competitive sport in this neighbourhood.

'Maybe there's an accident?' Sam says.

The familiar flash of lights in the mirror.

They all stare out the window as the grey SUV rushes past on the kerb, siren wailing, followed by the white van emblazoned with the block green font of the BestLife logo.

'What do you reckon it is?' Essie says, her voice low, even though Mim and Ben have been so careful not to scare them. Children always know.

'Must just be someone who needs some help,' Mim says.

Essie grunts, unconvinced, and slides back in her seat.

The BestLife squad don't even try to block the view as the traffic slows past the scene and the commuters rubberneck. High visibility is part of their effectiveness these days. So effective in its messaging and consequent public compliance, in fact, that they hardly even bother with the farce of the judicial system anymore.

A man is on the ground, his hands already cuffed behind him. He does not look especially dishevelled, although it's been a long time since she saw anyone looking that way. And even though they are already painting over it, the graffiti is still easy to read. Wide and pink across the concrete wall: *RESIST!*

Sam sounds the word out. 'What do you reckon it means, Mum? Resist what?'

'He's probably not well, darling,' she says, the words bitter, traitorous, in her mouth. She is glad they cannot see what she sees when she looks back in the rear-vision – the medic moving in, the flop of the man's body as they drag it into the van.

It is better this way. She and Ben had decided together that the kids did not need to know the details of the society they were growing up in. Not yet. Did not need the specifics of what BestLife had become or how it operated or how their uncle had come to die under their watch. Essie could not even remember him. But fear has its own signature, and even with their careful sidestepping, the kids know, joke in the playground – *You'll be sent to BestLife* – understand that something is being hidden from them, and they want to dig it up but keep their eyes closed at the same time.

The graffiti will be gone by the time she drives home.

All the same, she'll know it is there. Underneath.

Resist.

That's what her brother Michael had once said, too.

∽

Arriving at the school, she swipes to get through to the drop zone, watches the kids tousle in the line to hold their palms to the security pad as they enter the grounds. They run from there and they don't look back. She sees Essie point towards some of Sam's friends, the way she touches her little brother's shoulder before he runs off to join them.

Michael used to do that for her. Her eldest brother Steve never did. But Michael, just two years older than Mim, and gentle, so gentle (*Soft as the inside of a strawberry Freddo*, she once heard her dad say, not kindly) that his own eyes might glisten if she ran to him, crying at recess, with scrapes and tales and squashed sandwiches. The way the protective shadow of his arm enclosed her closest friend Heidi too. Until later, when they'd had to turn around and protect him.

She shakes her head, trying to loosen these images of her brother. There is no time for this now. For pain and guilt and what-ifs. For the treacherous voice whispering that she is a coward, that she has let his death go unremarked, that she has not stood up, that she has been found wanting.

The screen on the dash lights up. Incoming call. Unidentified. She answers quickly, hope high in her chest.

'Miriam Elliot?' A woman's voice.

She slumps back in the seat. 'Yes?'

'My name is Raquel Yu, I'm a journalist with *The Advocate*.'

'Sorry, I can't –' Mim goes to end the call.

'I'm an Australian based in Canada,' the woman continues, undaunted. '*The Advocate* is an independent news organisation peopled by correspondents from around the globe and funded by citizens who want the truth.'

'Sorry, I'm in the middle of something. If you're looking for donations –'

'No, no.' She laughs. 'It's not that, although if you're offering . . .'

Mim grits her teeth, annoyed at her inability to just hang up. 'Sorry, I really have to go.'

'I'm actually after your husband, Ben? Are you able to give me his contact details?'

She startles at Ben's name. 'What's this about?'

'I'm currently looking at the Golden Arc project and the unprecedented Chinese–Australian collaboration on the mine. I'm keen to speak to Ben about his work there with GeoTech?'

Mim doesn't speak.

'Are you there, Miriam? Have I got that right, GeoTech is his employer?'

'Mim,' she says, 'and yes, GeoTech, but he's not . . .' She thinks that perhaps if she doesn't say the words they can continue to exist somewhere else, a place of parallel possibilities. She wants to refuse the reality of them.

'He's not working there anymore?'

'He's missing.'

'Sorry?'

'They called me yesterday. He's gone missing from the mine site.'

'Oh, god, sorry, is that . . . ?'

Mim's voice is tight. 'Probably nothing to worry about, I'll get him to call you when he gets in touch. Ben's not one to give up a chance to get his face in the news.' She attempts to laugh but the sound does not work.

The woman says she'll send all the contact details, apologises for calling at this time. She had no idea, she says.

'It's fine,' says Mim, but her stomach flips over as she hangs up. Why is a journalist poking around the Golden Arc project? The international controversy was all over years ago once China acquired the island. And the domestic row was over before it began. 'Unprecedented investment opportunity for Australia.' Everything was unprecedented by then anyway. *Keen to speak about Ben's work there* — but what was so special about Ben's work? Mim rakes back through the messages, the conversations, that last video call in her mind. Had he seemed more stressed? Secretive? The calls were always monitored so it's not like he could have told her if anything was wrong. She shakes her head, separates the two events in her mind. She is conflating them for nothing. Coincidence that the woman called today, that's all. Strange and unsettling, but nothing more.

Ben will be home. Ben will be home and everything will go back to normal.

2

There is a grey Department SUV parked outside her house. She brakes suddenly, breathes, then guides her car into the garage, buying herself time to calm down before she greets them.

'Mrs Elliot?'

'I said I didn't need a visit.'

The woman's face is pleasant, not pretty. She ignores Mim. 'Okay if we come inside?'

Mim sees Kevin across the road peering around the edge of his curtain.

'Of course,' Mim says and swipes them in.

~

She makes them tea. Alexis and Ian. Ian introduces them, is obviously the soft to Alexis's hard.

He takes the cup and thanks her. 'How are you feeling? What a shock, huh?'

'Yes, I suppose, it just, it hasn't really sunk in.'

'Of course. And the children, how are they taking it?'

Alexis has a screen out, tapping, but keeping her eyes on Mim. Warm and wary. It's a well-rehearsed look.

'I haven't told them yet, Ben isn't due home for another couple of days, I'm just waiting for some more information, I mean, is that what you – can you tell me something more?'

Ian sighs, smiles almost sadly. 'Not at the moment, but what we can do is work with you to put in place a bit of a plan for the next little bit.'

'A plan?' Mim furrows her brow. 'To find him?'

'That's not our area. We leave that to the professionals, don't we?' He looks at Alexis and she nods.

'Sorry, what is your area?'

'We're in Asset Protection.'

'Right.' *What's the asset?* she wonders.

'So, it's our job to make sure you and your kids aren't hassled by media and are given a chance to tell your side of the story, if and when that's appropriate. We look at all the options available to you and advise you on the best way forward.'

'The best way forward?'

'That's it.'

'For who – me? For Ben? The best way forward is to find Ben, right?' She pushes her hands across the table in agitation. 'Sorry, I don't understand why there is anything else that needs doing right now.'

'Obviously we want to find your husband, Mrs Elliot, and the Department are doing everything they can to make that happen.'

'But,' Alexis says, 'in the meantime, it's our job to leverage public interest for the best case scenario.'

'As in putting the story out to help find him?'

'More nuanced than that. We've got a whole team of experts working behind the scenes on stories like this every day.'

Ian presses his fingertips together as if to accentuate the seriousness of the situation and Mim feels like laughing at his theatrics.

'If word gets out,' he says, 'you'll have the media all over you. No one's made contact with you?'

Mim thinks about the call register on her system. Raquel.

'No,' she says, 'why would they? How could anyone know?'

He smiles. All teeth. 'We just want what's best for everyone.'

Alexis hands the tablet to Mim. 'So there's just a couple of things we need you to sign.' She points with the stylus: 'Just here and here.'

Mim takes the pen but Alexis keeps talking, leaving no space for questions.

'These are the terms and conditions outlining our requirements of you while we manage this case. Basic things – exclusivity with media outlets, image permissions, approval of narrative etcetera, all really standard clauses.'

'Can I take a minute?' Mim gestures to the screen. She wants to read it, to try to understand, but Alexis is still talking and Ian has taken out another screen.

'We'll just ask you a few questions to build a better picture of the case.'

'While you're skimming through that.'

Mim glances up, back down. 'Sure,' she says.

'Has Ben got any family, friends, acquaintances he might be with in the region?'

She looks up. 'In Indo? No, I don't . . . no.'

'He's a regular visitor to the area with work. He's never led you to believe he visits anyone?'

'No.' Frustration flickers now. 'I just said that. He works at the mine, he does his job, he comes home. He would tell me if he was visiting someone. He wouldn't −' she searches for the word to articulate it, 'scare me like this.'

They both smile at her. 'Of course,' Alexis says.

'Why, where do you think . . .' she trails off.

Alexis and Ian exchange a glance designed for her to see.

Ian takes a gentle tone. 'Look, we don't normally tell people classified information, but in your case, we see no reason not to, it's just that −'

'Sometimes −'

'Rarely −'

Alexis delivers the blow. 'When we have cases of FIFO workers going AWOL, it's often because of indiscretions.'

Mim cannot read the words on the screen now, she just frowns in confusion.

'Marital indiscretions. Often with local women.' Ian lowers his voice despite the fact that there is no one else in the room. Mim would laugh if she wasn't so floored by the suggestion.

19

'You think he's left me?'

They both rush to shake their heads.

'No, we don't think that.'

'At all.'

'Not at all, in this case.'

But she cannot concentrate now. They've planted a fucking seed and they're watching to see if it'll take.

'So, just so we're on the same page, you've not told anyone as yet?'

'No,' she says.

Alexis performs a sad face. 'Not even family?'

'I don't want to alarm them yet.'

'Wise move.' Ian is nodding. 'You seem to be handling this all really well, Mrs Elliot. Can we call you Mim?'

She nods. Checks the time. Wants them out.

Ian goes on. 'Know that we are one hundred per cent behind you. We have a range of support options for you, if you feel you need?'

'Like?' Mim asks, thinking a food delivery service wouldn't go astray right now.

'For instance,' Alexis says slowly, 'we can arrange care for the children during this stressful time.'

A nanny, even better. 'So you'd send someone out?'

Alexis smiles. 'It's a residential service, actually. Temporary accommodation in one of our facilities.'

'In a BestLife?' Mim tries to keep her voice level. Wants to scream.

'As I said, it's one of a range of support measures you have available to you.'

'Thanks,' she says, evenly, 'I'll let you know.'

Ian gestures to a highlighted box on the screen in front of her and she signs her name with her index finger, skim reading as fast as she can through the dense wording. 'And here,' he says, flicking through the screens while Alexis continues to talk.

'And the final thing is just that we ask you to remain at this address until we've resolved the matter.'

Ian adds, with a smile, 'Just so it's easy for all of our teams to get in touch with you at short notice.'

'Of course.'

'Part of that protocol is handing over your passport for the duration of the matter, really simple, no hassle, we just hang on to them, update yours and the children's chips, and then put it all back to normal at the end, when it's done.'

Mim nods but doesn't move. Brain moving slowly now.

'So . . .' he looks at her expectantly.

'We'll take those now, thanks, Mrs Elliot,' Alexis says firmly.

The passports are in a leather document wallet in the safe at the back of the study. She had laughed at Ben when he said he was getting one.

'What do we need a safe for?' she'd said.

'Everyone has one.'

'Bullshit!'

'Well, I think it's a good idea.'

She had mocked him as he set it up. 'What are you going to put in there, huh? Your gun, our piles of cash?'

'Piss off,' he'd said and laughed. She'd let him sort the little pile, hard copies of their wills, the passports, the marriage certificate, the deeds for the house. Hacking being what it was now, there was a move back to storing the originals.

'At least all the important stuff is in one place,' he'd said when he was done.

She'd kissed him then. 'You're a fool, Benjamin Elliot,' she'd said.

He'd kissed her back, quick and hot, and they broke away laughing when Essie walked in and squealed.

Now she doesn't know where Ben is, and she is opening the safe he bought to keep things secure, and she is going to hand over her passport and those of her children, and in every single part of her this does not feel right, but what is there to do?

Refuse? Run? Pretend she doesn't know where the passports are?

Like they said, it's not as if she's planning on using them.

'Any problems, Mrs Elliot?'

'No, all good,' she calls back.

She watches them leave with the passports, with her signature. *You are a fool*, she thinks.

After school, she sits on the bench at the edge of the soccer field and watches Essie drill the ball up and down with her squad. Sam does flips on the small playground with one of the other little brothers, but Mim has moved herself away from the other parents. She feels brittle. The small talk could snap her into pieces.

She is unnerved by the Department visit. There is too much that doesn't add up. A scratch in her mind, snippets of Ben's voice, coming out into the kitchen late one night and seeing him there, in front of his screen, his head in his hands. That time, last month, he got ridiculously drunk, then angry, then maudlin, lamenting the weakness of his own dad, long gone.

'He was piss-weak. Never went out on a limb. Never took a stand.'

She had humoured him. To be honest she wanted drunk sex, the uninhibited kind they hadn't had for years. 'Come to bed,' she'd said, quietly.

But he'd wanted to talk. 'You've got to do what's right. That's all you've got in the end, isn't it? Huh?' He'd touched her face and she'd thought they might get somewhere, but he'd opened another bottle of wine and she'd gone to bed, pissed off and sober and horny.

People don't disappear accidentally. You do it yourself, or someone does it for you.

What did she sign? Why the fuck did she hand anything over? What other choice did she have?

She picks up her phone. 'Please call Raquel at *The Advocate*,' she enunciates slowly.

A beep to indicate a recorded message: 'You have called *The Advocate*. Please be advised this line may not be secure. If you would like to leave a confidential lead please go to our website and follow the links to the encrypted messenger service. If you would like to speak to one of our staff, you will be redirected now.'

Then a voice, 'Raquel.'

Mim stumbles, feels stupid. 'Hi, it's Miriam Elliot here, you wanted to speak to my husband . . . at Golden Arc.'

'Yes?'

She almost hangs up, feels the humiliation swelling in her. 'Sorry, I just, he's still missing and I wondered if you might be able to –'

The journalist cuts her off. 'I'm sorry, Miriam, but unless you're able to provide an update on the situation –'

'No, I –'

'I'm sorry, I can't help you.'

Mim notes she does not sound sorry.

'Get in touch via the website if there's any new information. Good luck.'

And the line cuts out.

'What the fuck,' she says under her breath, and then, *'What the actual fuck?'*

Her phone buzzes in her hand. A message from an unknown number.

It takes a moment to register what she is seeing, scribbles on paper.

She holds the screen closer to her face, using one hand to shadow the sun.

Don't call again.
Get out of town.
They will come for you.

From across the playground, Sam calls her name and she tears her eyes from the screen to wave and smile at him.

What if, instead of looking for her husband, they come looking for her?

~

Her mother's voice is so familiar it startles her.

'Mum! Hi.'

'Hello, darling. I was beginning to think I wouldn't get a call this week.'

'Sorry, it's been busy.'

'Of course it has. How are the children?'

'Good, we're good. Sorry, Mum, I'll be quick.' She needs to babble out the idea before she changes her mind.

She rushes on. 'Remember how I told you about that job? With Heidi?'

'At the university?' Her mother stretches out all the syllables. She's like that, old-fashioned, a bit of a snob. *My daughter, working at the u-ni-versi-ty.* Never mind that it's an underfunded regional shithole. It bears the same name as its big city sister and that's enough for her mother.

'Yeah. I'm going to come up to meet with Heidi about it. We'll be up tomorrow. That okay?'

'Of course. Ben coming with you?'

His name, so normal, the sting of it.

'Nup. Maybe later, he has to work.' It is a version of the truth.

'I'll get the rooms ready.'

'No fuss, Mum, okay?'

'None at all.'

She ends the call as Essie runs towards her. 'See that, Mum? See what I just did?' She holds her screen up in front of her to capture a selfie with the soccer field behind her.

Mim smiles, dazed. 'Yes,' she says, 'amazing.'

⁓

When the kids are in bed, she pours herself a glass of white. She wants Ben. Feels fear gripe in her guts. In the toilet, she shits liquid and feels relief for the light-headed emptiness in the wake of it.

They will come for you.

Fuck, Ben, what have you done?

She imagines opening the door of the bathroom and turning in the hall and into their room and seeing the bulk of him there in the bed. Pulling back the covers and sliding in next to him and feeling the weight of his arm go around her. Even in sleep, that sour warmth, the recognition of skin on skin – like sleep itself – as familiar as that. She can smell him. She feels as though she can conjure him up through the force of her need.

〜

In her memory, that first autumn they were together is blown with light, wind and fingertips creeping in to touch skin under t-shirts. She is constantly distracted by the thought of him. She drops coffee cups. Overfills pots of beer. Thinks that she had better pull herself together or she will have a car accident. Sometimes Ben comes and sits at the corner of the bar where she works and when she knocks off they do not make it home; he pulls her against the dark wall around the corner, or in the shadows of the playground at the end of the street and they are all hands and mouths, frantic with desire. It is unsustainable, she knows, this fire. It will burn itself out. In some ways she is relieved by this. If it continues she will not be able to get her head straight. They do not speak about what it is, because it just feels as though it should be. They are cocooned in the blinkered way of lovers. No one has ever felt like this.

〜

Sam calls out in his sleep. She wipes herself. Washes her hands. Pads down the hall to his room. The sheet on his bed is pulled back, and even when she squints against the darkness she can see there is no one there. Her breath catches. She switches the light on, says his name, steps into the room, then rushes out and opens Essie's door with both hands.

There, in the bed, the two of them.

Sam's blond tufts tangled in with Essie's dark hair. Mim stands over the bed and is astonished to see how, in sleep, Ben's face appears to be growing out of the children's bone structure. The arch of Essie's eyebrow, the length of space between nose and lip, the curve of it on Sam. She feels as though she might commune with her husband through the shadow of him in their faces.

And then? What would she say?

You stupid fuck.

I hate you. I need you. I love you.

Mim wants to lie down and curl herself around her children.

She remembers putting Essie down in her cot, the rituals of protection. Tucking her in under organic flannel sheets pulled tight to the edge, no toys, so there is no way she can get caught, tangled, smothered. A sensor pad will sound an alarm if it cannot pick up the regular movement of Essie's breath. A camera in the bear on the bookshelf, a monitor to test the air. Mim dutifully records her daughter's feeds on the FeedApp, which syncs with her FitApp and posts daily records of how much Essie has grown and the rate at which Mim has failed to shrink. There can be no surprises, and if there are, the data will be logged and seen and corrected and all will be well. In this way, they stumble through.

Safe.

But always, from the very beginning, that throb deep inside, what had been part of her is now outside of her. The terror of what is beyond her control, the first moment of clarity: *I will feel like this forever.*

3

It's a ten-hour drive from their home in the suburban fringe of the city to the farm, barrelling up the highway, cutting clean across the wide brown northern reaches of the state and crossing the border to dip down into what was once the fertile plains of the food bowl of New South Wales. No one calls it that anymore, of course.

It takes an age to leave the fringe, extended as it has to meet the fringes of the regional centres coming towards them. At least they generate a shitload of energy. All those roofs with all those solar panels, nothing shading them. No trees at all but for the very last of the river red gums dotted sporadically, monuments now to the lives that were lost trying to protect them in the years of eco-terrorism. Native grasses do well. Succulents. The genetically modified perennials designed to attract the genetically modified bees. There was no collapse in the end. Not the kind they expected, anyway.

She knows there is a BestLife estate out this way. Not the one Michael was in, that was in the west.

She remembers the visit. They must have had better water allocation on the estates. Blossoming eucalypts clustered at the edge of the front gates, almost camouflaging the glass gatehouse. The gates, imposing and yet aesthetic, rustic iron hinged onto enormous hunks of sculpted sandstone. It could have been a peninsula winery but for the uniformed guard, who cheerily directed Mim to place her hand on the screen. It looked exactly like a ticket dispenser to get into a parking lot, except this time she didn't get anything back. As she drove through, she noticed the cameras, the black bulbs of them under each of the architecturally designed streetlights. Who the fuck did they think wanted to get in here that bad?

Michael had agreed to her visit. She supposed that's why they let her in. But still, she hadn't spoken to him beforehand. It just came through as an alert on her screen: *Approved visit to BestLife, Bacchus Marsh.* It took her an hour and a half to drive there. Her breasts were swollen and hard and her left was beginning to leak. She needed to feed Essie.

The estate looked no different to the sprawling new suburbs that had multiplied cancerously in the paddocks on the outskirts of the city when she first moved down. Cookie-cutter houses with imposing front doors and drought-tolerant front yards. There were blocks of townhouses, double storey only, so that the whole place had a country estate feel. A sign ahead told her she was passing a *Learning Sanctuary: a safe place for your child to thrive.* A canopy of lush trees peeked from behind the high fences. She lowered her window and could hear the kids squealing, a green ball popped high in the air above the fence. For all she wanted to mock it, to be suspicious of the immaculate spin of it all, she thought perhaps they really had done what they said they would: changed the trajectory of people's lives, given them a second chance.

Michael's townhouse looked just like the rest of them, heavy door flanked by the ubiquitous black bulbs of the cameras. She thought about poking her tongue out at them but didn't. She could have used the capsule to bring Essie in but she wrapped her in the sling instead. For her brother's approval. She thought he might change his mind if he saw that baby Essie was so clearly part of his sister. Tethered to her. That Mim was using old ways to be a mother. Doing it consciously.

He opened the door and he was, for a moment, himself. An eagerness, delight even in his eyes, his mouth. Later she thought he was high, he was just high.

'Hello, Mim,' he said and leaned forward to usher her in, peering curiously at the package strapped to her chest, the little fist that had escaped and was resting against Mim's shirt. 'This is her?'

It was so good to see him. He looked better than he had in years. They must have been making sure he ate, it must have been part of the deal. Fuck, she had missed him.

'My boobs are gonna burst,' she said, instead of hugging him fiercely, letting the last nine months go unspoken. 'Let me inside so I can feed her, then you can have a hold.'

On the couch she unswaddled her child, unclipped the maternity bra, pulled across her shirt. He looked away at first as she held her daughter's head firmly, squeezed the tender points of her jaw to help her clamp her hungry mouth against her darkened nipple. The sound of it, perhaps, was what made him look, the gulping slosh of the milk being sucked from Mim's ducts and into the tiny body.

'How does she do that?' he said, face open in astonishment.

'Ferociously,' Mim said and snorted. 'And cos I'm what is keeping her alive.'

'That's . . .' he shook his head. 'I didn't . . .'

She looked at her brother's face, saw that this might be the thing to sway him. But she was suddenly engorged with jealousy, that his tenderness was all for her daughter and not for her.

'It's been really fucking hard,' she said, and he looked up, surprised perhaps at the bitterness in her voice.

She told him, some of it anyway, and he listened and Essie slept, milk drunk, against her, and for an hour or so it was something like it used to be. The room was small but new and bright and clean. She was glad for her brother, thinking of some of the dank places she'd gone to meet him when he was deep in the clutches of ice. He was mellow, too much so, she thought at one point, and she asked about the clinical trial. What it involved.

It was cutting edge, the pharmacological team were just ironing out the last glitches in the prescription doses. He said he was feeling optimistic, like this was his chance to really get somewhere.

'I'm a new person,' he said.

'Maybe you could come and stay with us for a bit when it's over?' Mim said, thinking about keeping him safe, helping him to stay clean.

He looked surprised. 'Oh, I can't leave.'

'Sorry?'

'It's in the contract.'

'During the trial?'

He shook his head. 'It's how I get the house, the payments, all of it.'

She guffawed. 'What, you signed a contract to say you'll stay here forever?'

'Yes.'

'You're fucking kidding me, right?' Essie squirmed on her chest, grizzled.

'It's okay. It's what I want. This project will change the way people treat addiction all over the world, change the way drugs are regulated, save hundreds and thousands of lives.'

'You sound like a fucking mouthpiece.'

He shrugged, that gentle smile again. Now it was irritating.

'I'm happy, Mim. You don't have to worry. The Department know what they're doing here. I trust them.'

'Bullshit! You've never believed in anyone in charge!'

A knock on the door. Mim looked up in surprise, instinctually cradling Essie's head in her hand.

'That'll be Elwin. My coach,' he added as Mim questioned him with her eyes.

Elwin made it clear that it was time for Mim to go, and Michael didn't disagree. She tried to get him on his own as she changed Essie and packed up the nappy bag. Said she could go for a walk and come back when they were done.

'That's okay,' Michael said. 'Maybe next time.'

'You didn't even have a hold,' Mim said and let the hurt sound in her voice.

He said he would next time and cupped the baby's head for a moment at the door. Mim took the opportunity, despite Elwin hovering in the hallway behind.

'You can call me, right, any time, it didn't take that long to get here, I can come whenever. I'm a lady of leisure now, right?' She laughed, but it was too high, too brittle.

'It was good to see you,' he said, like a script, and his eyes were skittery tired. She gripped him hard on the shoulders and didn't want to let go.

She felt hollow as she approached the gates of the estate. What had happened to her brother? She'd thought that nothing could be worse than the dark days of his addiction but maybe darkness insinuates itself in other ways. There was a black SUV ahead of her and Mim slowed to a stop. A female guard was standing by the window of the SUV. She appeared to be listening. Her face was pleasant, relaxed. Mim wished she could hear the conversation. Then the guard shook her head, still the pleasant smile, and after a moment, the SUV did a U-turn around the small grassed roundabout. Mim tried to see the driver's face as the car passed, accelerating slightly. It was a woman, her face set, and there was a child in the back seat.

Mim's chest was tense as she approached the guard, waiting in front of the closed gate, discreetly holding up her screen to check the numberplate. The guard held out the screen and Mim hesitated before remembering, holding out her hand to swipe her brand-new chip. In the back, Essie mewled.

'Just a moment, please,' the guard said and Mim had to brake because she had already begun to move off at the sound of the woman's voice.

'Sorry?'

But the guard was stepping quickly towards the gatehouse, one hand behind her, palm splayed, telling Mim to stay put.

Mim could hear her blood swooshing in her ears. In the rear-vision mirror she could see Essie's little leg kicking out from the capsule, her face in the mirror Mim had installed so she could always see her, eyes scrunched, mouth stretching.

The gate was very solid from this angle. She could see now that the artistically wound iron, as pleasing as it was to the eye, was impenetrable. She wondered what force the front of her car could withstand. The speed required to break a gate off its hinges. She closed her eyes and saw the other driver's face. Was it blank? Or terrified?

Beyond the iron gate she could see the service lane to the highway, could imagine the coloured swish of other cars, driving back and away from here, on the outside. She thought she was going to hyperventilate. She pressed down on the handbrake, slid her foot to the accelerator. Wondered if what they say about airbags is accurate. Essie's face, her kicking foot.

And then the gate was opening.

'You're good to go,' said the guard as she tapped the door and stepped back.

Not until she was out on the highway had Mim truly begun to breathe. She lowered the front two windows, took great gulps of air, turned the music up loud and whooped in relief.

⌒

Mim shakes her head. She needs coffee, albeit the shitty stuff they'll serve in one of the big highway stops. Dry paddocks, dumped rubbish on the shoulder of the highway, every now and then a hybrid that's run out of juice of both varieties, waiting for a city owner who didn't comprehend the distances out here, to come back for it before it's nicked or torched. Sometimes, the sporadic gruesome splendour of a floral highway tribute to a loved one who's become a tangled mess on this stretch of road.

The road signs are screens flashing info on kilometres, times and hazards onto the data screen in the car, always updating according to the road conditions. She remembers the old signs indicating the kilometres to a destination with fondness, the guessing games they'd play on the way to the beach, seeing who was closest in kilometres to their final stop. Steve always won. Of course. Now the signs give news updates too. The Department had decided everyone needed to be across a small and specific amount of news. Everyone's curated news had become so filtered that people had started unknowingly driving straight into bushfires and flood zones. Or turning up at the airport to fly to a country whose democratic leadership had just been deposed. The new legislation had introduced a mandated minimum of news stories everyone was expected to know.

Up ahead is Clarke's Pass, a mass of hills that rise up out of the flat pastureland, eons old, a dead volcano. She's always loved the feel of it. Measuring the earth beneath her as the car shifts gear to accommodate the incline. She crests the rise and the lowlands stretch out before her.

Jesus fuck, it gets drier every year. The good earth of the plains, beneath which the aquifers pulse with their riches, drier now than it's ever been. Fat pipes worming across the fields from the north, pumping some of the deluges that swamp them every wet season down to the drought-stricken south. At least they've stopped pumping it out of the ground. If the science hadn't convinced the powers that be, the series of increasing tremors that cracked the foundations of industry from the west to the east soon did. It's not a permanent halt, but it gives the earth a moment to recover.

⌒

She can see the neon signs of the service station in the distance.

Essie stays in the car with her screen on, but Sam is quick to jump out and hovers while she plugs in.

'Can I get something, Mum? What can I get?'

'There're rice crackers in the car.'

'Yeah, but . . .'

'We'll see.'

She swipes her hand over the payspot on the charge station, waiting for the quick ping of the verification noise. It doesn't come. Instead there is a buzz and the light flashes red. *See attendant*, the screen flashes.

Mim tries swiping her hand again, but the same message flashes. She sighs. Knocks on the window and motions to Essie that they are going inside. Essie nods, looks back at her screen.

At the counter she tries again on the machine. The attendant is young, bored, smiles thinly.

'Sorry, that's declined. Did you want to try choosing another method on the touchpad? Another account perhaps?'

Mim is out of the habit. She just knows that there will be funds, there has never not been. Ben's wage goes in, does all the things it's supposed to – mortgage, bills, a little aside for the emergency account, and the rest in the transaction.

'Right, yes.' She swipes her hand again, sees the options come up and selects the emergency account. She tries to remember the last time Ben told her what was in there. She squirms that she does not know.

'Mum, can I get one of these, I'll get one for Essie too?' Sam holds up a flip box of chewy mints.

'Hang on, Sam. Let me do this.'

She selects the account, holds her breath while the machine thinks.

'Muuuum! LISTEN!'

The attendant raises an eyebrow, scowls at Sam. He is starting to scrunch up his face and she can see the telltale pink creeping across his collarbone. She feels exhausted already at the prospect of a meltdown.

The machine pings approval. Her hands unclench.

'Yes, whatever you want.' She takes the boxes from Sam and slides them across the counter, relief coursing through her.

She makes the call outside the car, knowing Essie will be all over it if she hears. 'GeoTech, how may I help you?'

'It's Miriam Elliot here, I need to speak with someone in management.'

'Sorry, Mrs Elliot, no one's available.'

'It's urgent.'

A pause, Mim prepares to go hard.

'I'll see what I can do.'

She waits, steadies her breathing.

'Mim, it's Di Benton here. I'm so sorry we haven't spoken yet, I've just been flat chat trying to work out what's happening.'

She's met Di before. Knows she's only second in charge. Can't be that bad, then, surely. Or maybe they think a woman will do a better job of smoothing things over with Mim.

'Have you heard anything about Ben?'

'Not as yet, but we have everyone here working on it. Is there anything I can do?'

'I'm sorry –' She feels like she is sixteen, asking the bar manager at the footy club for her pay. 'I'm just having trouble with our accounts. Have you stopped paying him?'

'Stopped paying him? God no, why would we do that? Hang on, let me just check with Chelsea, you poor thing, are you stuck somewhere, I can send a car over?'

Mim almost shrivels with embarrassment. The ridiculousness of big business. She imagines one of their former university departments offering to send a car and almost laughs out loud. 'No, no, it's fine, I just couldn't work out – I mean, I suppose if he's not working, if you don't know where he is . . .'

'Give me a second, Mim.'

The line clicks and Mim paces beside the car, smiling briefly at Sam when he taps on the window and eyebrows a question.

'You there, Mim?'

'Yes?' Mim stops pacing.

'It's not a problem at our end. I've checked.'

'So?' The anger fails in her throat. 'So what does that mean?'

'I don't know, a bank thing maybe? Leave it with me, huh? In the meantime, are you sure I can't send someone –'

She cuts her off. 'No, no, all fine. Really, it's okay. I just want to know where he is, Di. I just want him home.' Her voice cracks. Shit. She didn't want that to happen.

'Of course, of course you do, we all do. I'll be in touch, you look after you, yeah, and the kids.'

'Who was that?' Sam asks as she starts the car. 'Was that about Dad?'

'All good,' she says, turning out on to the highway and avoiding Essie's eyes in the rear-vision mirror.

4

Before the border they begin to see the ravages of the latest fires. Unprecedented, again. The word has lost its meaning. The hills on both sides are still black. But it's what's underneath that's the biggest problem. The fires burn so hard and hot now that they crucify the seedbed beneath the soil. All that grows back is scrubby acacia, ready to burn again. Flora extinction rates rocketing. Thank Christ for the seed vaults. Mim flips her glasses down. Up. Disaster makes her tired. She opens the window a little.

'Mum, that's too windy.'

'Sorry, Sammy, just need to wake up a bit.'

Essie's serious voice, the one she uses to chastise, to educate. 'You should pull over if you're tired, Mum.'

'I'm okay, just want to get there now, only a couple of hours to go.' She eyes her daughter in the rear-vision mirror, staring out the window at the squares of yellow suddenly appearing in the black.

'Do they grow canola in Japan?' Essie says.

'Not sure.'

'Why?' asks Sam.

'For the Friendship Project, with our sister school.' She holds up her screen and clicks. 'No one else from my class will have fields of canola.'

'Have you got any pictures yet? From the sister school?'

'Nup.' Essie shakes her head.

'Maybe they'll send a pic of an earthquake drill? Do you think?'

Essie is non-committal. 'Maybe. It's meant to be intimate pictures. A real slice of life. Not something we can ask Google.'

'But you can ask Google anything,' Sam says and Essie whacks him on the arm.

'Mum! Oww!'

'Stop it, you two,' she says and changes tack. 'It'll be good to take some pictures of the farm.'

'Yeah, and then Dad, he hasn't been in it at all yet.'

'Of course,' Mim says, flipping her sunnies down again as the sun sinks lower on her left and the glare shoots across the dashboard. She opens the window a little lower so that the wind gushes in, and makes it difficult for the conversation to continue.

~

When they hit the turn-off, she tells the kids to put the screens away. Even in the dark, she wants them to be paying attention, to mark the significance of this homecoming with her.

In front, an orange streak in the headlights, green flash of eyes.

'What's that, Mum?'

'Fox,' says Essie.

'I thought the foxes were all gone?'

There is a part of Mim that is glad the eradication programs were never one hundred per cent effective. 'Too smart for that, foxes,' she says.

'They are *the* greatest contributing factor to the extinction of small marsupials such as the eastern quoll,' Essie says.

Mim nods seriously. Essie doesn't react well when she feels like Mim is patronising her. 'You sound just like your grandpa.'

'Was he a fox-hater too?' says Sam.

'He didn't like them much. I remember when he shot one once, your uncle Michael went searching for the babies —'

'Cubs,' says Sam.

'Yeah, cubs, and he found them, and one was still alive, and he kept it for ages, secretly. But when Dad found out he was so mad.'

She remembers the sound the cub had made, curled up against Michael's t-shirt in the makeshift nest he had made from old rags and cushions, while the two of them hid out behind the decommissioned digger in the big shed. It was like all those movies where ducklings think a human is their mother — the cub adored him, stuck out its hard little tongue to lick him, nuzzled at his armpits and groin.

'It's growing pretty quick,' she'd said, because sometimes Michael needed reminding of the world outside himself, the notion of cause and effect.

He'd ignored her, strummed his forefinger over the russet neck of the cub's fur, smiling indulgently. 'A survivor,' he'd said.

Which of course, it wasn't.

Steve made sure of that, following Michael one day because he'd got suspicious of the fact he couldn't be roused to fight. Mim had got there too late. Her eldest brother was standing over Michael, sneering at him.

'You fucking kill it, or I'll tell Dad.'

'I'm telling Dad,' Michael had sneered, false bravado, trying to humiliate his thirteen-year-old brother.

But Steve could be as clever as he could be cruel, and he knew that telling Dad would be a win-win.

∾

'What'd he do, Mum?' asks Sam.

'He shot it,' she says flatly, because the memory still hollows her.

'That was the right thing to do,' Essie says quickly.

Mim makes eye contact with her daughter in the rear-vision mirror. 'You're so like your dad, Ess.'

Essie raises her eyebrows in challenge. 'In what way?'

'So sure of yourself.'

∾

She leaves the car idling at the gate while she gets out, the crushed rock crunching under her feet.

'Can you two help me with this?'

Neither of them answers.

She could do this with her eyes closed, in the dark, the smell of the paddocks, the scatter of stars across the distant ranges, the way they seem to pool in the valley, the dense dark of the gums and the knotted green of the blackberries around the creek at the bottom of the track. They'd tried every year to get on top of them. Never worked. In daylight, she will look across the valley and see the great hunk of the landscape they took out. The bare wound of it. Even now. Despite all their platitudes and saplings and community consultations. In the end it went ahead anyway, cracking earth and family in its wake. She remembers Michael, standing astride the front gate in front of the cameras, his face defiant, his sign, DON'T FRACK OUR LAND, painted on the back of a real estate sign he'd nicked. Dad's humiliation, that his own kids, his two tearaways, not his eldest, would embarrass him like this. Mim was fifteen when she went to her first protest. An age that had shocked her, seemed to come upon her all of a sudden. The thrumming energy that infuses the blood, a kind of violence almost, in thoughts and sensation, all the ways in which the body betrays you. Anger and desire and a concrete belief that the world began at your own birth, that you alone are the keeper of all wisdom.

She had blood in the game, or property at least. It felt like blood. Felt entitled to her indignation, furious at the thought that anyone could just waltz through the front gate and dig in the earth her own family had worked for three generations and take something from under it. She extended her righteous fury on behalf of the traditional owners of course, the nuances of the politics of her own entitlement not yet making her ashamed.

She and Michael joined other unhappy locals. Tree-changers, the hobby farmers – outsiders who weren't even welcome at the pub anymore – who had formed an unlikely alliance with some of the farmers. During that time a lot of farms had *No Trespassing* signs that warned you'd be shot on sight if you entered, and everyone understood that to be true. There were A4 flyers up around town, and a group you could join online. They had plenty of information to serve at her dad across the dinner table while Steve sneered and Mum tried to keep the peace.

Dad listened. She had to give him that. He had all the paperwork from the fracking company, plus the stuff the Gate Closers group had dropped off. And then he had the bank. And the cumulative years of drying. Of seasons where the earth scorched and then, if rain came at all, it came in deluges that washed the topsoil into what was left of the river and deposited it on some other lucky bastard's farm. Mim heard the conversations at night. Him and Mum, even him and Steve – because, of course, by then he was already at ag college, reckoned he knew everything there was to know, primed to take over. Mum made half-hearted attempts to get Dad and Steve to take it all more seriously, but apparently you don't get more serious than the bank.

There is a roar that still vibrates in her chest, all the things she'd like to say, to have said before Dad was gone. She will not call it grief, even if it is. It's like a hunk of gristle she can't swallow. It won't go down, won't come back up.

∿

She unhooks the chain. No swiping palms against panels for auto-entry here. She relishes the work of it, the muscle pull as she guides the gate back, jumps back in and drives through.

'You two. Remember this? Look at it. It's beautiful.'

'It's dark, Mum.'

'You can still see.'

'I'm hungry.'

'Grandma will have cooked something. Ess, can you jump out and do the gate?'

Mim sees the roll of her daughter's eyes in the blue light of her screen, but she shuts it off and opens the door. Closes the gate behind them.

'Geez, cold here,' Essie says at the window. 'Can I run down?'

'It's a bit dark.'

'I'll run in the headlights.'

Her daughter's legs are long as she swerves potholes and rabbits crisscrossing the track. She slows for a startled kangaroo which bounds across in front. There used to be hundreds of them, and then, at their peak, thousands. They stopped needing to cull in the end. The dry did it for them.

'Look!' Sam hangs his head out the window.

She would have laughed at her own kids if they had rocked up in town when she was young. City kids. Wouldn't have a clue. She would have felt the strange seesaw of power, knowing she could drive a ute across the paddocks by the time she was thirteen, but didn't know how to get on a tram. Things change.

It's a mistake to come back here, she thinks, even as they pull into the house paddock, as the floodlights come on, as she sees her mother, grown smaller still, come through the screen door of her new unit and wave them in to park.

⌒

There's a white ute pulled up at the front of the sheds. Her brother is there, leaning against it, and another figure in the pool of light off the shed.

Sam yells out 'Grandma!' and jumps from the car, running over the grass already gathering dew as the night falls.

Essie is leaned over, breathing steadily, stretching out her quads.

Mim offers her a bag. 'Take this in?'

'I can take another one, too,' Essie says and hoists the bag to her shoulder.

The figures at the shed are moving towards the front of the unit where her mother is already bent down to hug Sam.

'Hello,' Mim says, reaching to put her arms around her. Mim holds her close, chin on her mother's shoulder because suddenly, *God, no, not now*, she thinks she will cry. She squeezes her mother's shoulder, brusque, business-like. 'How're you going, Mum?'

'Oh, you're a sight for sore eyes, the three of you. Come in, come on now, you hungry?'

'Yes!'

'G'day.' Steve steps fully into the light now. Something in his face has grown harder, older. He could be her father, shirt buttoned down, the slight paunch beginning over his belt, work jeans, hair cropped close because she'll bet it's thinning at the temples, just like Dad's had.

'Hi, Steve.' She has to step towards him to get close enough for a kiss. This is the way Steve plays it, collecting up each tiny win.

She turns to the other man and realises who it is, Jay Owens, Steve's age, from the farm that shares the back boundary.

'G'day, Jay,' she says, neutral as she can.

He nods. 'Mim, how's things?'

'Good, thanks. How's Sal, and the kids?'

'Yeah, all good, can't complain.'

'Say hello from me?'

'Will do.'

Oh, I know you will. And Sally will lean in and want every detail, how she looks, what the kids are like, the stories will race like wind in the crops all the way into town and everyone will know Miriam Franklin is back at the farm.

Steve claps his hand on Jay's shoulder. 'Thanks for that, mate. I'll drop it back in when I'm done.'

'No worries, no rush,' Jay says. 'See you then.' He nods at Mim as he leaves.

Steve turns to Mim. 'See you in the house for dinner in a bit, yeah? Mum's got it all sorted, bit late for our kids, but Mum wanted us to wait.'

She watches him head out into the darkness, breathing in the smell of the place and imagining the air pulsing through her blood, connecting back with her marrow. A place can be home, can feel like it's part of you, and yet you can want to run from it.

5

Mum bustles out the door with a tray of potatoes in her mitted hands.

'Come on then,' she calls to them. 'Don't want these getting cold.'

They traipse across the turned earth to the farmhouse, and Mim feels strange to see it from this new angle.

'You liking the unit, Mum?'

'Oh yes,' she says, 'so easy to clean!'

Mim thinks she is lying. How do you go from being the matriarch in the big farmhouse, the one where you've raised all your kids, lived out every day of your marriage, to being sent to the granny flat round the back? The one within calling distance in case you're needed to mind the grandkids. Anger flares in Mim and she swallows it back. This is not what she is here for.

At the front door, she hesitates. Everything is the same, and yet it is not. The sound of the wood contracting as night settles, the light that emanates from the kitchen at the other end of the hallway, travelling down the spine of the place and spilling through the red and blue stained glass of the door.

She can hear the baby crying. How can this be her home, the smell, the feel of it knitted into her matter, and yet feel so alien? She wonders if belonging can feel like two opposing forces.

'Go on, then!' Her mother comes up behind her, the dish of roast potatoes hot between her oven mitts. 'You don't have to knock for goodness sake!'

Mim knocks anyway, uncommitted, sliding her knuckles across the timber as she reaches for the handle. Then she pushes open the door and ushers her mother and the kids ahead of her.

She hardly recognises the toddler, Hamish, who is freewheeling down the hall towards them. It's been over a year since she's seen them. Two years now since Dad's been gone. They'd all met in the city with the lawyers to finalise the titles and Jill had been neat and glowing with the beginning of her next pregnancy, Hamish content to be jiggled on her knee. They'd been composed, a quiet style about them that Mim had always found elusive. People would look at them and know they were landowners, Mim had thought, and they would be right. And I am not.

'Down here!' Jill sticks her head around the doorway at the end of the hall, and Mim kisses the boy and leaves the kids there to negotiate playtime with their cousin.

It was one of the only issues where she found herself agreeing with Steve over Michael. Kids. Michael had always been clear he wouldn't have children.

'It's irresponsible,' he'd told her during one of her visits back here. 'You of all people should know that.' He'd been clean for a couple of months then, and she was excited to be introducing him to her new boyfriend. She and Ben were still plump and blushing with the newness of it all, the legitimacy of the visit home, the frisson it added to their sex.

She'd laughed. 'Maybe, dear brother, but there's also something incredibly right about it.' She'd touched Ben's thigh on the couch next to her and he'd gently pushed her hand away, laughing, not entirely comfortable in her family home. But later, that night, giggling in her old bedroom, he had nuzzled her neck and run his hands under her t-shirt, quickening to get her clothes off her.

'I want to have babies with you,' he'd whispered, and the effect had been shockingly physical.

'Why is that such a turn-on?' she'd whispered back and kissed him, hungry.

But she shouldn't have been surprised when Michael had not been impressed with her news years later. He was back on ice, staying with a mate in town. Perhaps there was some part of her that imagined her own life-changing news might change his.

'Overpopulation,' he'd said down the line, 'the greatest burden of our times.'

'Are you serious? That's your congratulations? I'm pregnant, you dickhead, it's family. You'll be its uncle.'

He'd hung up. And she was so angry she didn't call him again for the rest of her pregnancy, and then, by the time Essie arrived, he was already in BestLife.

～

In the dining room, there is a highchair at one end of the long wooden table, and her father's chair opposite, heading the other end. Mim lays out the plates and remembers Ben here. His hand reaching for hers under the table and squeezing as her father had bristled at her. She can feel a headache coming on. She is suddenly unsure why she has come here. Why would she put herself in a place where she feels so entirely untethered? It was a mistake. She can hear Steve's voice loud in the kitchen.

'Let's get them fed.'

Her mother's voice, 'C'mon, kids, up to the table!'

It's like a harem, Mim thinks, as they all tumble in around her brother.

～

Essie is quiet at dinner. Ben's absence has been made visible at the table and Mim can tell Essie is thrown by it. Sam ploughs on regardless.

'And so it's going to be released simultaneously around the world, that means at the same time, so like it could be at two o'clock in the morning here!'

'Goodness!' Her mother listens and serves Steve potatoes next to her. Jill has been relegated to the other end next to the highchair, Charlotte grabbing and babbling beside her. Mim wonders if this is what it is like every night.

'And how's school for you, love?' Her mother turns to Essie.

'Okay, I guess.'

Jill leans back from the highchair, trying to be involved. 'What's your favourite subject?' she asks.

'Sport.'

'You still playing soccer?'

Essie's face changes, energy shifts. 'Yep, Saturdays, next term maybe the Friday night comp, too.'

Mim tries to catch her in this moment, this normality. 'Oh, really?' She smiles.

'Dad said it would be okay.'

Mim sees the look on her daughter's face, backtracks fast.

'I'm sure it will be.'

Essie pushes her fork around her plate, then moves the thin grey slices of lamb to the side.

'Eat up then.' Steve nods his head towards Essie. 'Cost us a fortune to get some real meat to serve.'

Jill frowns. 'It's fine, Steve.'

Mim watches her daughter's head drop, her shoulders go completely still.

'Sorry,' Mim says, 'we're not used to it. Haven't eaten meat in ages. Ben's not into it.'

Steve scoffs under his breath.

'Really, dear,' says Mim's mother, and it is unclear who she is chastising.

Essie stands up and pushes back from the table. 'Excuse me,' she says, and hurries from the room.

'Bit sensitive,' Steve says.

Jill shakes her head at him. 'Honestly,' she says quietly.

Inside, Mim seethes. It's his catchcry. She remembers hearing it behind her as she ran to her mum, arm stinging with a Chinese burn delivered with fervour. Steve saying it with scorn as he stood over a doll he'd run over with his quad bike.

'Eat up, Sam,' she says as she gets up from the table. 'Sorry, I need to check on her.'

She can hear them murmuring as she goes down the hall.

'Ess?' She pushes the door to the TV room open. 'You all right?'

Essie is curled up in the corner of the couch, remote in her hand. The screen is on, but the volume is muted. 'I'm fine.'

Mim sits beside her, puts her hand on Essie's back, who shifts, but lets it lie. Mim goes to say *You sure you're okay* or *I know it's hard* or *You miss your dad*, but she bites them all back.

'Your uncle was always the grumpiest.'

Essie makes a hmmph noise in the back of her throat.

'When we were little we used to have to stay at the table until we'd eaten everything on our plates, and then we had to wait till all the grown-ups did too.'

Essie shifts her head slightly towards Mim.

'And if Dad's mum was over, my nan, gee, she could be fierce. We'd have to say "May I leave the table?" And she'd say "If you've had sufficient", in this plummy voice like she was the queen, and then we'd shuffle out silently and kill ourselves laughing once we got to our room. And sometimes later Dad would pretend to be cross that we'd been so cheeky but he'd have this look on his face like we were secretly on the same side.'

Mim reaches out and uses her index finger to pull the hair back from Essie's face and tuck it behind her ear. She can see the blotchy skin under her eyes and she resists crumpling her face in sympathy, even though all she wants to do is pull her daughter into her arms and cuddle her. If only she would let herself be cuddled, soothed. It is fragile, this new ground, eleven years old.

'Is that why we don't come here very much?'

'No.' Mim takes a breath to buy herself time. 'It's just a long way.'

Essie looks at the screen. 'But, still,' she says.

'Sometimes it's hard being back home. For me.'

'Cos you miss Pa?'

Emotion swells in her. God, how come they know exactly where to get you?

'Yeah.' She rubs her hand on Essie's back. 'Yeah, I do. And Michael, I get sad about my brother, too. Even though it's been so long.'

Now Essie turns to her fully. 'When can we talk to Dad?'

Mim nods, holds Essie's gaze, tries to organise her thoughts.

'Soon. Maybe tomorrow, we'll get through then. If he's finished with his work.'

She hears her own voice, the coolness, the absolute certainty of it.

'Can you not get angry at him?'

'What?'

'Just,' Essie shifts her head slightly so that her hair hides half her face, 'just don't fight about it. Him not being home on time. Or whatever. I hate it.'

Mim pulls her daughter in. This gigantic girl she grew, who's got so big and thoughtful and worried. A whole person. Half Ben, half her.

'It's just what grown-ups do, my love.' She runs her hand over the back of Essie's head, smoothing the hair there. 'We fight some-times. Even when we love each other. And we do, very much. And you. We love you both. You know that.' These, she knows, are the words mothers are supposed to say.

Essie nods against her chest, hugs her back and Mim is relieved, grateful she could say the right words this time, even when they leave a taste, like grit, dirt between her teeth.

∽

Later, with the cousins under a doona in front of the screen and Steve with a screen at the dinner table, the women clean and tidy, following the script of this house. Mim is tired, she can feel the long drive in her joints, her bones. She's also drunk too much wine. She stops with two empty wineglasses in her hand to look at the photos on the dresser. Jill has left them there. For now. That's nice of her. There they are, the three of them, Steve and Michael and her, posed against the fence in Nan's hand-knitted jumpers, the dark of her hair against the blond of her brothers. She's maybe Essie's age, her smile the after-math of a laugh, Michael too, they would have been cracking a joke.

Probably at Steve's expense. He stands over them a little, older and wiser and infinitely more serious. There's Nan's eightieth, Steve and Jill's wedding, Michael's graduation – that one catches at her, she knows now that it already had its hooks in him by then, not that any of them knew, a first taste of shard at the footy club, the feeling of being more himself than he ever had been, as he later described it to her, appealing to her to understand. A smaller frame of her and Ben at their wedding. They are looking at each other, laughing, exchanging pencils. She'd chosen the photo as a subtle up yours to her dad. It was a geology joke. Diamonds are just rocks yearning to be graphite. Graphite is the more stable substance – the one they laughingly said they aspired to in their vows. It was supposed to mean something about permanence and impermanence and deep time and fusion. It strikes her now as out of place among the other photos. Like they haven't captured the expected tone. She looks at Ben's face, younger. God, in her guts, that pull. She misses him. Being here, being home has pushed back the other feelings: the fear, the worry. For this moment she just wants him to be here with her, to be on her side, to get it. It is a physical ache for the familiar.

She moves to the last photo on the end. The whole family on the beach at Eagles Nest. They are end-of-summer brown, she's wearing a green one-piece and she is astonished now at the length of her, she must be thirteen, already crossing one arm over her chest, her breasts that summer, all of a sudden, and the way it changed everything, the way people looked at her, how that made her shudder with embarrassment and excitement both. Her dad has his arm around Mum, there is an esky. She wonders who took the picture. Even Steve is smiling. She remembers the hot sand, the salt crunch of fish and chips out of the paper on the pier. Two weeks every summer they went. They had an arrangement with the neighbours, the Turners did their place, then when they came back they did the Turners' farm for them. Later, when they were older, that first taste of sweet cider in the dunes with the other kids from the caravan park. And the last two years. Someone playing a guitar, the local boys, the smell of pot, hands, that boy – Nick – god, the gut wrench of all those memories.

'So, Mum said you're doing some work up here?'

She turns towards the table. Steve is still looking at his screen but she can play this game of disinterested conversation, she has played it before.

'That's the plan.'

'With Heidi Fulton?'

'Yep. You see her around?'

'Sometimes she does the rounds with Bruce. She's good with the animals.'

'Always has been.'

Heidi had loved coming out to the farm when they were kids. She wanted to play with the dogs, the chooks, the three sheep they kept in the house paddock. Mim tolerated her obsessions because it was bliss to have her friend there. To be able to spend whole hours under the shade of the peppermint gum. Before the heat forced them inside. Trying out big ideas on each other. Possible futures. Unpacking the social nuances of school. Actually, Heidi had mostly just listened to those bits. She couldn't really give a stuff about what went on at school. Mim was still trying hard to please.

When school finished Heidi went to Sydney, Mim to Melbourne. They both said they wanted to end up in the same place, but maybe they didn't at all. They wanted space to grow into a different version of themselves. By the time she drove up to Sydney on semester break, Heidi had sharpened her edges. She seemed to know exactly who she was now – hanging out with her new tribe, versed in queer politics – while Mim knew only what she wasn't. Heidi seemed to have sloughed off her former self expertly.

But not quite completely. She still, thank Christ, had time for her old friend.

The recent call had lit something up inside Mim.

'Mim Elliot. Hydrogeologist. Aquifers, EPA. You're the woman I'm looking for.'

She'd laughed, they'd exchanged the words – *It's been too long. How are the kids? What's happening?* Mim hadn't been entirely surprised when Heidi said she'd gone back to town. Her mum always let her know the town comings and goings.

'You interested in some work?'

She'd tried to play it cool, but yes, god yes, she was interested.

It was a six-month project. Mim would only have to be onsite three or four times, initial inspections, setting up the testing, monitoring results with the student team. There'd be a report at the end, but even the thought of that made Mim salivate. Work, brain-stretching, grown-up work. She'd said yes before Heidi had even finished giving her the details.

～

She sits down at the table now, pulls over the bottle of red and pours a small glass. She notices Steve's mouth flicker, perhaps distaste. She holds the bottle out, raises her eyebrows and he shakes his head.

'Few people not too keen on the idea of the study Heidi's involved in.'

'No?' she says and leaves it at that. She won't help him out. *Go on and fucking say it, big brother*, she thinks, *remind me how badly I fucked it all up*.

'Can't see how it helps anyone. It's done. In the past. Not going to stop anything now.'

'Who says anyone's trying to stop anything? It's just a study, Steve. Her students are just analysing some samples.'

'You can see why I would think that, though, can't you?' He slides the screen away.

'Not really.' It's dangerous to play this game with him, danger-ous and childish. But he always pushes her to it.

'C'mon, Mim. Don't be a bitch about it.'

'Jesus, Steve, I'm hardly being a bitch.'

Her mother's voice from the kitchen. 'Everything okay? Anyone for a cuppa?'

'Please, Mum, thanks,' Mim calls back.

Her brother ignores the question. 'Just don't come in and cause problems. We're all just trying to make a living out here. Trying to look after the family farm.'

She laughs thinly. 'Not really the family farm anymore though, is it?'

'Don't. You didn't want in.'

'Did I have a choice?' She can hear the child in her voice now, the blur of tears being held back.

Steve leans back in his chair. 'You broke his heart, Mim.' He shakes his head. 'It's no wonder . . .'

Mim watches him bite back the words.

The wine makes her mean. 'What?' She leans forward and hisses. 'Go on, say it. It's no wonder he got sick? Is that what you want to say? With fuck-ups like me and Michael for kids? Well, it's lucky he had you to look after everything, isn't it? Lucky he had reliable Steve. To kick his fucking mother out of the house she's lived in for forty fucking years.' Mim stands up, pulsing with fury. Steve's face is red and she can see his hands clamping into fists on the table. She wants to push him, she wants to make him explode, the way she could when they were kids.

She breathes heavily. 'I don't know why I thought it would be any different, coming here.'

Her mother comes in, carrying the tea.

'I've got to put the kids to bed. I'll have it at the unit, Mum.' Mim pushes her chair in, picks up the empty glasses.

'Yeah,' says Steve, 'I don't know why you thought it would be any different either.'

～

In the spare bedroom in the unit, she squishes into the double bed with her children.

'Shh, shh,' she croons and runs her hand over Sam's head, smooths his hair, his cheeks, so soft still. She lets her fingers brush his arm to his wrist, the tiny raised pimples at the back of his little bicep, the elastic skin of his elbow, forearm grazed with scratches, the almost imperceptible lump of the implant in the flesh between his thumb and forefinger.

She imagines the invisible rings of radar rippling out from her children's chips, her own. Who is watching?

Surely no one, not even the Department, could begrudge her this time at home while she is under such stress? She is prioritising caring for her children, she is going back to the workforce, she is keeping it all together. Surely, surely, she is doing everything right, everything they ever asked of her?

Maybe it's what Ben has done?

Once, one of the engineers ended up in an Indo prison for six months on some trumped-up charge because he was carrying an unverified drone. Not even the Department could get him out. Ben had laughed darkly about it.

'Don't know what's worse,' he'd said, 'Indo prison or being in trouble with the Department.'

'Don't even joke about it,' she'd said, but she'd laughed too. 'Either option is fucked.'

The first disappearances had been a shock, but were quickly and deftly rationalised. The Department could only now reveal that the extremists who had been detained had myriad links to international crime syndicates that were threatening our very way of life. The few remaining independent media outlets stopped reporting on them after a while.

Then came the app. Dob in Disunity. A gamified security hotline with rewards. Even kids could join in the fun! The dropdown lists of reasons for notification grew longer with every update.

It is simple to read a series of events in rock. Even a child, the most amateur and curious geologist, can look at a highway cut or the beachside cliff and point out the strata, each layer of history. They may not know what happened there but they can read the cumulative effect – this is how we got to where we are.

And so it was that when Mim first saw a protester outside one of the banks tasered and pulled into the back of a BestLife van, she didn't blink.

Nor did she when it became normal to see reports of CEOs dragged from their offices into the ubiquitous vans, corporate espionage stamped all over the reports.

Once, her hand even hovered over the send button in the app after Essie had come home from school with a new coding toy from Michelle's dad, who had brought them back from China for the whole class. She drank a bottle of wine that night, crushed the toy under her shoe and got the whole way through filling out the details in the app before she threw the device across the room.

They'd got the engineer out of Indo in the end. It had been a close thing, but as terrifying as they were, the Department could also ride in on their diplomatic white horse and bring home your loved ones. Damned if you do, damned if you don't.

～

Sleep doesn't come. She waits. She thinks of Ben. Imagines it is his breathing she can hear on the other side of the bed, that if she stretched out her arm she might touch him. She mouths his name in the dark, imagining his grunted reply, the way he might wrap his arm over her, letting it fit where it always does, under her breast, fingers tucked in around her ribs. She puts her own hand around herself to keep the fear away.

6

In the morning, she leaves the kids checking on the cows with Steve and walks out through the gate of the house paddock and across to the dam. The form of the land is recognisable, the dam that was dug over one hundred years back and has been full and dry and full again, this time though with recycled water through the north–south pipeline. The shift from livestock to high yield grain had started decades back. The farmers used to be seen as backwards rednecks by the educated city folk, but they had to start paying attention when most of their politics began to align. So many of the neighbours sold up. Whole regions did. It was a line on the map that saved them. That and luck. Their zone was the third option for the route of the pipeline, but a very lucky sighting of a lizard everyone had thought was already extinct in the zone of option one, and the bankruptcy of the Indian firm behind option two meant they were the region that ended up with the water.

She used to wonder if the alterations to the GM sorghum crop were visible to the naked eye. Whether there might be a strangeness to the way it moved in the wind, an unreal quality to the colour or the bulk of the heads of grain. But if there was, she'd never noticed it.

She squats in the clay at the dam's edge. She remembers being there with Ben when she was pregnant with Sam, five-year-old Essie being doted on by her grandmother back at the house. Ben had sat behind her, his fingers laced around her belly, round but not yet huge. It had felt okay to voice her fears across such an expanse of land and water. She had spoken, low and tremulous, and Ben had waited through it all, even though he had heard those fears many times before. What if it happens again? What if this is a mistake? How will I cope?

'If it happens again, we will cope,' he had said. 'Together. We will get through it together.'

She had rested her hands on his, knowing that his words were only platitudes. He had not seen inside her head. Had not been there on the days she stared blankly at Essie, the plump baby, then the toddler, then the running, jumping pre-schooler, and thought, *Who are you? Where did you come from? What have you done to me?*

A gust of wind scurries across the surface of the water. She'd spent whole afternoons here with Steve and Michael, floating on the inner tubes all hot black sticky in the sun, the itch of the mud, shin-deep in some places, where the cattle had worked it all over on the edges. Frisbeeing cow pats into the middle, seeing how far they could get them, how long they'd float before they sank below the surface. It hadn't all been a shitstorm.

Around to her right, slinking out of the thatch of scraggly acacia, is the creek, still feeding the dam from the spring further up in the scrub. She doesn't want to think about the trace elements she'd find in there if she brought her test kit up. The wells they didn't stop. The leaching toxins entombed in the shale beneath her.

The three of them had skipped stones here. She was never as good, never as strong. Steve told her she never would be. Michael waited until their brother was gone then told her, 'You keep practising, you'll make that arm strong.' Funny, she hasn't remembered that for a long time.

The water garden. She smiles. She'd followed a damp gully down from the creek and found a spot where a slab of granite made a shelf, moss and algae dripping below it. It had been her secret place. Brimming with pride, she'd eventually shown Michael. He was tender with it. Serious. Complimented her fine work. But Steve must have followed them, pissed off he'd been excluded, not that he'd ever let that show. The next weekend she arrived to find the stream dammed with a careful rock wall, her water garden dry. She'd yelled, kicked at it. Furious. She'd pushed her body up against it but Steve had piled it high with heavy rocks, had worked carefully, she could see, to make it sturdy. Impassable. His pool.

Michael had comforted her.

'Take it apart,' he'd said.

'I can't.'

'Yes, you can. One at a time, just dismantle it.'

It took a week. Michael did not help her, already caught up in his next thing, but every morning she went, knuckles grazed, shins bruised, lower back aching with the strain of it. Rock by rock, until it flowed again. The moss was dead, there was a slime-filled puddle beneath the slab, but in time, she knew, it would come back. It would never be the same, but it would run again.

She rubs her eyes. There is no time for this.

She pulls her phone from her pocket.

'Please call Ben,' she asks, knowing already the response she will hear.

The reception is still dodgy out here, despite all the promises, but there is enough for OMNI to tell her that her husband is uncontactable and ask her if she'd like to record a message.

She does not. She wants him here. Here. Where she can see him and hold him and ask him to fix the fucking mess he's made.

'Where the fuck are you?' Exploding out of her, loud and hoarse and ragged. A trio of ducks takes off, webbed feet paddling frantically across the surface of the dam. She drops to squat on the bank, hangs her head, picks at the small rocks in the mud.

Maybe she should call the Department. Apologise for taking off. Explain it away – the anxiety, the need for support. Ask if she can stay here until they've located Ben. She'll go see Heidi, start the work, keep the kids distracted from Ben's absence a little longer.

She stands, pulls her arm back and throws the rock into the dam, watches the concentric circles birthing from the place where it fell.

Essie is doing drills with her ball, forcing Sam to play with her. He knows the power he has, is making trades.

'Sure, I'll play for ten minutes but then *you* have to play Ninja Boy versus the World with me.'

'Sure,' Essie lies easily. 'Line up, goalie.'

Mim shakes her head at Sam's gullibility. He must figure it's worth taking a punt every time.

Behind the house paddock is the eucalypt-rimmed pasture. The smell is grass rot and fertiliser and, from somewhere up the road, the pungent smoke of one of the neighbours burning off. It is achingly familiar. If she were to attempt to create the chemical equation for this smell, she would have no hope of getting it right; it is so singular. It must come down to its parts.

She sips her tea. It is comforting to be made a cup of tea by her mother. She wonders, not for the first time, if things might have been different if she had chosen to live closer. Had come home to have the baby. What it might have been like in those early milk-shit-sour-sleepless days if she could have handed the baby to her mother. Mum had come down for a few days. But even after the caesarean, Dad reckoned he couldn't spare her for longer. That was the first round of the cancer and, of course, he was right – she couldn't ask, she didn't deserve the help. Millions and millions of women had done it before her. It would get easier.

Except it never did.

'I thought I might go into town and see Heidi. Get more details about this sampling work she needs me to oversee.'

'Good, good, yes. Leave the kids here.'

'You sure? I can take them.'

Her mother rolls her eyes and tsks. 'I'm their grandmother, for goodness sake.'

'And again!' Essie is waggling two index fingers in the air, running a loop around Sam who is shaking his head.

'Nine minutes and forty-nine seconds, Essie,' he says, checking his watch, 'nearly time for my game.'

Essie laughs, lines up again.

'Whatever, little bro,' she says, and kicks.

'She's very aggressive, isn't she?' Her mother holds a saucer underneath her teacup.

'She's trying out for state squad. She's really good, Mum.'

'I'm sure she is.'

Don't bite, Mim thinks.

'Your father would have loved to see them like this. He wouldn't have believed how big they've got. He would've said: "Grow 'em back down already".'

Mim sees the quiver in her mother's face. It is all still there, subterranean. She never has the right words.

'Wouldn't have taken much,' her mother says.

Mim presses her lips together, but her mother keeps going.

'To get up here more often.'

'Mum.' It's a warning tone. She cannot do this now. Doesn't have enough space in her head to try to unpick and then stitch back together these hurts, these gaps, all the broken things.

There's a ruckus building in one of the big gums just beyond the fence, hundreds of cockies flying in to land, big-winged and white in the canopy of the tree. The noise of it. She can feel the pressure thumping in her head.

'They'll be coming in for a feed. You watch, your brother'll get the rifle out in a minute.'

Mim is glad for the sideways shift. The pressure subsides.

'They that much trouble?'

'Well, your dad didn't think so.' Her mother sets down the teacup definitively. 'But then Steve's not his father.'

'No. He's not.'

Essie has finally given in and both of the kids are scaling the fence, balancing on the top, Sam directing procedures for his game.

'Is it going okay, Mum? With Steve and Jill?'

She looks over at her mother, who has one hand up to shield her eyes, her rings catching the sun.

'It's fine.'

Mim thinks she could say it now. Both of them looking out over the paddocks. She could say, *Mum, I'm in trouble*. She could say, *I don't know what to do*.

'I might head off then, to see Heidi, if you're sure it's okay.'

'Off you go,' her mother says.

～

When she gets out to open the front paddock gate, she spots the rutted tyre tracks veering off to the left of the driveway and the grief catches her in the throat. She should visit. That's what a good daughter, a better one than her, would do. She checks her watch, can't even make an excuse that she's got somewhere to be. One of the therapists had told her it would come on tenfold if she didn't try to process it.

She wonders if standing at a grave is processing, or just telling yourself you did.

She leaves the gate as is, gets back in and turns the car off the driveway and heads up the track.

Dad had already applied for the necessary permits. Of course. He reckoned these things were getting easier anyway with real estate at a premium for both the living and the dead. There were already a couple of generations buried on the hill, though he would be the first to be interred in a biodegradeable shroud and remembered with a laser-cut river rock rather than a granite headstone. She wished he'd told her those plans before he went so she could have told him she approved. It was a good spot, the family plot, on a rise dotted with a couple of old manna gums and a good view out to the east and the pink light of dawn when it came.

The day itself has been stitched back together in her mind: making tea for her mother at first light, the hard words directed like bullets at Essie when she failed to keep an eye on her four-year-old brother, Ben's silent admonishment as he put his arms around his daughter, the fact that it was Michael's name that undid her as she tried to deliver the eulogy, noticing that Steve looked away, did not come to help her.

It had been hot, breathless when they buried him, but today there is a top wind in the fingers of the eucalypts, rattling and rustling, and she would like to think he is there, telling her something, giving her some sign, but she's never really believed in such stuff.

On the afternoon of the burial, she heard Essie talking to Ben quietly, old enough to be aware of the adults around her and their strange sensitivities.

'So, his body's in the ground, and his soul is in the sky?'

She remembers thinking how apt the question was. That it was unanswerable, as were so many of the questions her daughter asked.

Where was your love for me before I was born?

How come floods always happen to other people?

Who will die first, out of you and Dad, and when will it be?

If it weren't for the anachronistic river rock, you wouldn't even know he was down there, so efficient has nature been at reclaiming the spot. If she looks closely enough she can see tiny scurries of insects in the leaf litter. She imagines them burrowing under, through the composting foliage, the topsoil, the clay, to the lacework of the shroud, the hair, the bone. Or perhaps it is quicker than that. She is more familiar with the glacial pace of the breakdown of rock than the quick and dirty decomposition of flesh.

'You'd be a little bit pleased that Ben fucked up, huh, Dad?' she says. 'Quietly smug that he was never good enough, that I would've done better to stick with the pickings round here.'

She tilts her head back and breathes in deeply – the grass scent, the warm oil of the trees, the home of it.

'I couldn't have got through without him though, Dad.' And perhaps this is what the therapist meant, the great upheaval she feels in her chest, as though her ribs are cleaving apart. 'After Essie . . .' She is almost gasping for breath. 'If it weren't for him . . .'

Breathe. Breathe. In and out. She slows and waits and visualises the bone and tissue knitting back together.

'I need him, Dad. If nothing else, I need him.'

She bends and touches the rock with two fingers, before she walks back to the car.

⌒

She takes the back road into town. Breathes deeply, realising that the sound she can hear is her own short moans as she exhales, the physical manifestation of this secret she is bearing alone. She cannot shake the feeling of being a child again. Winding down the window, she keeps her eyes on the road but turns her chin, the wind buffeting her hair back.

The farmhouses are set back, she remembers the bus stopping at the end of each driveway, picking up the straggle of kids. She notices a car behind her, approaching fast. She clearly doesn't drive at the local speed anymore. The car pulls out and races on in front of her, and she sees the silhouette of a hand go up to thank her.

Her screen rings, unidentified, a quick churn in her guts. Let it be him. She presses the button on the dash to answer.

'Hello?'

'Mrs Elliot?'

Not him.

'Yes?' Mim has her foot on the brake, sees a gravel turnout up ahead, pulls in, still too fast.

'Mrs Elliot, Karen Eton from the Department. You met my colleagues from Asset Protection at your home?'

They have found him. Say it. Just say it. 'You've found him?'

'Not yet, Mrs Elliot. But we do need to ask that you comply with the agreement you made.'

'I'm sorry?'

'We were very clear. The agreement, Mrs Elliot. That you wouldn't travel.'

She plays dumb. 'I'm at home, my mum's, my family home. Sorry – our passports – I didn't realise I couldn't go home . . .' She trails off.

'It's in the contract.'

She wants to spit at this woman: *Your people didn't let me read the fucking contract. I couldn't think.*

'The consequences for non-compliance with Department directives are quite clear, Mrs Elliot.'

Her chest starts to tighten.

'I'm sure you're aware that citizens who struggle to make good choices for themselves and their families are well looked after in our BestLife estates.'

Her breathing is rapid now. She glances in the rear-vision mirror – the empty seats where her children always are.

'Are you there, Mrs Elliot?'

'Yes,' she says, her voice suddenly very small.

'We understand this is difficult for you, Mrs Elliot, but please understand we have a job to do. There's a temporary block in place on the bank accounts in your and your husband's names.'

'But, you can't –'

The voice softens. 'We're on your side, Mrs Elliot. We're on the same side.'

She is shrill now, hates herself for it. 'Where is Ben?'

'Mrs Elliot,' a shift in the timbre of the woman's voice, soft but now self-satisfied, as though she'd been waiting to pull out her ace, 'as long as you comply with our requests, you have no need to be concerned. Look after your children now. We wouldn't want your children to be separated from both their parents.'

Gut twists. She has no words.

They know exactly where she is. Where the kids are. The lights on the dash blink. She scratches at her palm. The tiny lump there.

'We'll check in again tomorrow.'

Mim's voice is small when she replies, not her own.

'Thank you.'

She sits very still when the call finishes.

Look after your children now.

Adrenaline splices her guts and she pulls the car out in a fast arc, U-turns back on to the road, the way she came. She puts her foot down.

7

She lets the screen door slam and her mum and the kids look up when she walks into the kitchen.

'That was quick.'

'Yeah, I called Heidi to let her know I was coming. She's desperate to see the kids, thought I'd take them over now.' Mim moves towards Sam. She needs to put her hands on her children.

'Oh.' Her mother's face falls. 'We were quite looking forward to our afternoon.'

'We'll keep that for tomorrow, hey? Heidi was really keen. She thought we could have pizza for dinner.'

'Yesss,' Sam says and pumps his fist.

'You kids pack an overnight bag, yeah? I just have to check something with Steve.'

Her mother frowns. 'You're staying there?'

'Maybe.' Mim's heart races. She is making this up as she goes along, all she knows is that she can't be here when the Department come. 'Just in case I have a couple of wines.'

'Oh, no one checks that out here.'

'It's not the checking, Mum. It's being able to drive safely.'

'Of course.' She stands. 'Well then, you two go and pack your bags while your mother does her thing.'

～

Mim paces through the dust to the big house. At the front door she calls out, can hear Jill singing, the splash of the bath.

'You there, Steve?'

'Having lunch,' he calls from the dining room as she walks down the hall.

She stands in the doorway. He has a thick sandwich on a plate in front of him. She wonders if Jill made it for him. He doesn't get up. 'You right?' he says.

'Thanks for taking the kids out this morning.'

'Was nothing.'

'They had fun.'

'Good.' He looks at her, impatient.

'Network's still pretty woeful out here. Thought that was all meant to be sorted?'

He scoffs. 'Ten fucking years it's taken them. Could've done it better if I'd laid the lines my fucking self.'

'Still picks up your chips though?'

'Ha,' he laughs scornfully. 'Yeah, that never seems to be a problem. Quick to tell me if the dog's registration's due at 6 am on the day, but I can't send a bloody text message.'

'Typical.'

He picks up the sandwich, looks at her. 'That it?'

'Mum's money all sorted?'

'What kind of question is that?'

'Allowed to ask, aren't I?'

'She say something?'

'No. I just know there were some troubles, early on, after . . .'

'And they're sorted. All right?' He places the sandwich down carefully. She can see the red creeping up his neck. 'She's got all her own money, Dad's super, the transfer of the farm. She's got heaps.' He looks as though he might stand up and come at her. 'And no, I don't control it, she does. What the fuck would you know anyway? You live in a different fucking state. Are you seriously asking me this?'

She holds up both hands. 'I was only asking.'

'It's like you get off on it.'

That's not who I am, she thinks. *It's only for you I cause trouble, you and Dad.*

'All good?' Jill is at the door, Hamish wet and towel-wrapped in her arms. 'You guys okay?'

'All good,' Mim says, smiling. 'Just heading back.' She puts her hand on Hamish's cheek.

'See you later, alligator.'

'See you later,' Jill calls as Mim lets the door thwack behind her.

∽

She stuffs all her clothes in her bag. The kids' clothes, a couple of the books she'd shoved in from home, the chargers, sweeps everything – face cream, tampons – off the top of the bedside table where it has spilled from her handbag, and stuffs it back in.

Look after your children now.

They may not be back.

They may not ever be back.

She forces herself to keep moving, leaves the bedsheets tousled, the kids' dirty clothes in a pile.

'C'mon, you two – Ess, you got your ball?'

She hears the slam of it against the wall in reply.

'Come and give Grandma a kiss.'

'Why?' Sam calls. 'We'll be back tomorrow.'

'Because it's nice, that's why,' her mother says, sweeping Sam into a hug from behind and tickling him so he chokes on a laugh.

Mim feels something lurch inside her. Essie runs in and plants a kiss on her grandmother's face.

'Love you!' she calls, the excitement of pizza in her voice already.

Mim hesitates, unsure if her voice will betray her. She will be back, she tells herself, she will be back so soon, she will hear from Ben and they'll sort it all out, and she'll be back and more, she'll come back more often, and she'll sort all this shit out with Steve, she'll be a better daughter, if only she gets to be back here very soon.

'Mum, can I borrow your bank card? Just realised I've left mine at home, and the shops in town might not be chip-ready yet, yeah?'

'Of course, darling, though you might find we're nearly as good as your city down there.' She smiles and rummages in her bag, hands over the card, repeats the pin.

Mim wonders whether she underestimates her mother. 'Thanks, Mum, I'll just transfer —'

Her mother holds up her hand. She believes money talk to be grotesque.

'Love you,' Mim says, and puts her free arm around her mother's back, gripping tightly for a moment. Her mother smells of her floral perfume, of hard soap, the same as she always has.

'Go on, then,' her mother says and unhooks herself, and Mim forces herself to walk to the car, to not look back.

~

'Well, this is a surprise.' Heidi's smile is big and true when she opens the door. 'Can't get you to reply to a message, but get you on my doorstep.' Heidi hugs Mim quick and hard.

She looks the same. Dense. Brown, shoulder-length hair parted in the centre in a way that is both utilitarian and sometimes fashionable, not that she'd know or care. Jeans and work boots. Red chequered shirt over a grey t-shirt. Her skin is tanned and lined and Mim thinks her old friend probably looks both older and younger than she does.

'So,' Heidi says, sizing up Essie and Sam, who are standing quietly behind Mim, 'these are the Elliot children. You two got big!' She laughs, and the kids laugh with her and the ice is broken.

'Cuppa? Beer?' she offers in the kitchen. 'Or . . .' she pulls open the fridge door. 'Yeah, water, milk? Sorry, wasn't expecting guests.'

Essie looks at her, head inclined. Mim ushers them out the back with the soccer ball before Essie can ask.

'Sorry I didn't message,' she says to Heidi, accepting the beer her friend is holding out. 'Things have been a bit hectic.'

'You still good for the job?'

'I don't know.'

'You drove all the way up here to tell me you can't do it?'

'Something like that.'

Heidi nods. Pulls the chair out at the kitchen table.

'Go on then.'

Heidi's always been good like that. No bullshit.

'How do you track animals?'

Heidi cocks her head. 'Animals?'

'For your work. How do you track them?'

Heidi shrugs. 'GPS. Same as us.' She waggles her hand in front of her face. 'Implants.'

Mim nods. 'Like, exactly the same as ours?'

Heidi draws her brow in. 'Not exactly. Not encrypted the same way. Ours have more capacity – data, different capabilities, transactional stuff, but the GPS, yeah, the same.' She leans back. 'Why?'

'You ever take them out?'

'Have done,' she says, nodding slowly now, as though she understands that everything is going to make sense in a minute, but she's not sure if she wants it to.

'Difficult?'

'What? To take them out?'

'Yeah.'

'Depends who put them in. Where. If they've been coated with biobond.' Heidi squints one eye, takes a swig. 'What's going on?'

Mim swallows too, cold and buzzing. 'You got OMNI yet?'

Heidi shakes her head, laughs. 'Not yet. Last place on earth to get anything remotely up to date.'

Mim nods, relieved. 'Could you take them out of humans?'

Heidi's eyebrows go up, but she holds her nerve, pulls her mouth down in the same way. 'Probably,' she says.

There is quiet then for a bit. Mim isn't sure, now that she's crossed this first line, whether she is capable of crossing the next.

Heidi breaks the silence. 'You in trouble, Mim?'

'Kind of.'

'And the kids?'

'Yep.'

Heidi takes a long, even drink. 'Where's Ben?'

Mim shakes her head.

'That's your problem?'

Mim nods.

Heidi lets her breath out from between her teeth.

'I'd give you a local anaesthetic, tell you to toughen up and then I'd dig it out. They can get pretty –' she screws up her face, searching for the word, 'enmeshed, but it would be relatively easy for an adult your age.' She leans back in her chair, looks out the window to where the kids are smashing the ball against the back fence. 'Kids are different. The muscle, skin, nerves – it will all have grown around theirs. Would be tricky. A local might not cut it.'

Mim is nodding. The aftertaste of the beer is bitter on her tongue and she pushes the bottle away.

'There any other way?'

'Leaving it in there is the way most of the population deal with it.'

Mim is silent.

'I take it that's not an option?'

'I don't think so, no.'

Heidi takes a deep breath. 'The Department?'

Mim nods.

Heidi stands up suddenly and goes to the sink, her back to Mim. 'You took a fucking risk asking me.' Her voice is low now, has a fierce energy that wasn't there before. 'You know it's completely fucking illegal to remove them, right? If they find you, me, it's straight to fucking BestLife.' She shakes her head. 'Don't ask anyone else. You can't trust anyone else with this. Right?'

'I didn't know what else to do. They're coming for us in the morning.'

'Have you told the kids?'

'No.'

'About any of it?'

Mim drops her head. 'I don't know what to say to them.'

Heidi is all business now, the edges of her grown hard. 'Look, you've got to tell them. They'll have to fully cooperate for it to go smoothly.'

Mim is nodding. 'How long will it take?'

'Couple of hours. Unless something fucks up.'

'You would do this?'

Heidi looks away. A ripple of something like pain, like sadness across her face. 'I don't really have a choice, now, huh?'

A flash of resentment in Mim. 'Course you do. Just say no. It's fine. I'll find another way.'

'No!' Heidi wheels around. 'No – don't ask anyone else. It's fucking dangerous.' Her eyes are dark, face drawn. She already looks like she has aged in the minutes since they have been here. 'I'll have to get them back out to the farm,' she says to herself, turning away.

Mim shakes her head. 'Sorry?'

'The chips. I can't dump them here, can I? Eventually they'll come looking.'

Mim hasn't thought this through, a sinking feeling. 'I can't ask you. It's too much.'

'You already did,' Heidi says flatly. 'I've got my gear at the lab. There won't be anyone there. Tell the kids.'

'Thank you.' It is not enough. She wants to push her thanks into Heidi's bones, have her feel Mim's relief that she is not in charge, for this bit, that Heidi is bearing the weight of this decision, of Ben being gone. But Heidi is already grabbing the keys, heading for the door.

8

She doesn't tell the kids. She doesn't know what to say. In the car, when they ask if they are getting the pizza now, she is vague, says it's still early, following Heidi's double-cabin ute into town and round to the campus where the lab is.

She still hasn't told them as Heidi swipes them into her lab, the strange antiseptic smell of it cool as they enter.

Heidi introduces the kids to the only animals in there at the moment, a pair of little bush rats racing circles in their cage.

'Poor little fellas want to get back out there.'

'Will they though?' Sam says, all big-eyed. 'Will you put them back?'

'Sure we will – they're precious. Not many of these little guys left,' Heidi reassures him. 'We do some tests, take some notes, some DNA, implant them both with a tracker and send them back out.'

'Hah, like me,' Sam says, and holds up his palm.

Heidi looks at Mim. 'Yeah, like you, mate.'

'So, kids, this is the deal.' Mim moves over to them, while Heidi starts quietly laying out instruments on the bench. 'You know the chips in your hands?'

Essie is wary-eyed. 'Yeah,' she says.

Sam looks confused.

'And you know how you can use them for lots of different things?'

'Yeah,' says Essie again.

'Well, other people use them too. Yours, I mean.'

Heidi is angling her body away, but Mim can see the flash of the surgical instruments. She is suddenly filled with doubt.

'I can't . . .' she says softly.

Heidi moves closer. 'We use the trackers to work out where our little mate here is, right?' she says.

The kids look at her, nod.

'Well, they do the same with you.'

'I know this already,' Essie says, interrupting.

'Course you do,' says Heidi. 'You're smart. So you'll understand that right now, it's important no one knows where you are.'

'What? Mum, why?' Essie's face is panicked.

Mim reaches for her. 'Just for a little while. It's important. For Dad. It's important for Dad that we can't be found.'

'Why, Mum? I don't get it!' Essie is angry, Sam is working himself up, his little face moving between confusion and panic.

'Because Dad loves you so much, and the most important thing to him is that you are safe. That we are all safe. And the only way we can be safe now is not to be found.'

'Where's Dad? I want him. I want to talk to him!' Essie's voice is tumbling over itself.

Heidi's face clouds. Mim shushes, soothes. 'We can't right now, but we are going to find him. But we've just got to be a bit secret about it.'

'So can we turn them off?' Sam is looking at his hand, running his fingers over his palm.

She swallows. Takes a deep breath. 'No, Sam. We can't.'

'Then,' his little face is crumpling, 'then what are we going to do? How do we not get found? I want to turn it off!' He holds his hand away towards her. Eyes wild.

Essie is looking around now, taking in Heidi, the instruments laid out on the table. 'She's going to cut them out of us.'

'Mum?' Sam's voice is so small, his eyes dark and crushed.

'No.' Essie places her palms against each other, as if in a gesture of prayer. 'You can't do that.'

'Hey, hey,' Mim soothes, encircling Sam with one arm, kneeling in front of Essie, bringing them both close. 'It's okay.' She can feel them trembling under her hands. Heidi moves quietly around the lab.

'What about school? And unlocking the front door? Everything! How are we gonna do all that? How do we put them back?'

Please don't be so clever, Mim thinks. *Not now.* 'We'll sort all that out when we get home, huh? No problems.'

'When are we going home? Where's Dad?'

Mim speaks calmly. 'Let's get this done and then we can talk about it more. I'll go first, okay? And you can see, and then we can decide.'

They blink at her. Nod at her smile, her open face, the way she is fooling them, fooling herself, that everything is going to be all right.

～

'Okay, just a little sting.' Heidi holds the needle steady as the tip enters the flesh of Mim's palm. She pulls it back. 'Just apply pressure there,' she says, and Mim holds the wad of cotton down, feeling the cold of the anaesthetic already spreading through her hand.

'That look okay, you two?' Heidi smiles at Essie and Sam crowded in on either side of Mim.

'Does it hurt, Mum?' says Sam.

'Nup. All good.' She smiles at him and inclines her head. She feels sick. The stomach flip of nausea in her guts. She has over-reacted. Surely they won't take the kids away from her.

But they will.

They will.

Heidi presses her short thumbnail into the skin of Mim's palm. 'Feel that?'

'Just pressure, like pins and needles. Is that right?'

'Good. We'll give it a bit longer. Okay, kids, you're going to have to go round the other side of the table now.'

Essie pulls Sam with her, they are energised now, less scared, more curious.

Heidi takes a blue pen, running her fingers over the thumb mound on Mim's hand. 'I'm going to mark the spot. Can you guys feel it on yourself?'

Essie and Sam both begin to run their fingers over their palms.

'Yep, got it!' Sam says and holds his palm up, his index finger pressing and making an indent.

'Let's mark it right now, then,' says Heidi. Mim wonders whether it is too late for Heidi to have kids now. Whether she wants them. She'd do a good job.

The kids examine the marks on their hands, comparing, and Mim mouths *thank you* to Heidi as she comes in close, winks, the surgical blade flashing in her hand now.

'All good?' Heidi asks and Mim nods. 'If you're gonna faint, then you should look away.'

'I'm good,' she says and feels the acid burn in her throat. She swallows.

'You gonna be sick?'

She shakes her head. Breathes. Smiles at the kids. Essie's eyes are wide, watching her, and Sam's are flicking back and forward, looking from Mim to Heidi's hand, gloved now, the blade innocuous, small and sharp.

And then it is in. Mim can't look away, the disconnect of seeing the tiny silver blade slice into her skin, the dark viscous blood that wells up, the feeling of pressure.

'Mum? Does it hurt?'

'Not at all.'

'There you are.' Heidi leans in with a long pair of tweezers, poking at the incision she's made in Mim's hand. 'It's just like a big splinter, really,' she says.

Mim feels the weight of Heidi's hand but not the texture. The limb is not her own. Not connected to who she is. She thinks of the obstetrician's head between her knees, that same feeling, a disconnected rummaging in her insides – a self-protective mechanism, biological.

Mim cranes her neck to see around Heidi's elbow. She is using her thumb and forefinger to squeeze the fleshy part of Mim's hand around the incision. In the other hand she holds the long tweezers steady.

'Come on,' she says, under her breath.

Then there is a release; a tiny silver splinter, smooth and shiny, pops onto the surface of the skin.

'Oh!' Essie says, and Sam's eyebrows shoot up.

Heidi tweezers it off Mim's hand and holds it up. 'Doesn't look like much, does it?' she says with satisfaction and pings it into a small steel bowl on the table.

'Urgh. It's all bloody,' says Sam.

'It's cool,' says Essie.

'So who wants to be next?'

They both say, 'Me!', then recoil, and Mim and Heidi laugh.

'Nah, you go,' says Sam.

Essie straightens herself up. 'Yeah, fine, I want to,' she says.

'Let me clean this up for your mum first.' Heidi wipes away the blood. 'Probably could have got away with a smaller cut for you, wasn't that hard to get out. Reckon I'll just use the glue on this one.' She swabs again with a wipe, then runs the nozzle of a small tube against the cut. 'So we leave it like this for a bit, then I'll wrap it at the end. Shouldn't even be a scar eventually.'

It's always pleased her friend, Mim thinks, a job well done.

'Okay, Essie, your turn.'

'Cool,' she says, and puts her arm up on the table, but Mim can see the set in her jaw.

'Now, you reckon you might faint, Essie? Cos I could lie you down, you're not too big, and we could do it on the table.'

'Nup, I can do it like Mum,' she says, and Mim feels a collision in her chest.

'Keep your hand up,' Heidi instructs Mim, 'and sit here next to Essie, just in case.'

Just in case what? Hers all went so smoothly. Easier than she could have imagined. She wonders why more people don't just take them out.

She watches Essie settle on the chair and lean in close to the bench to give Heidi room to work on her hand, the tiny blue biro mark on her skin. The prick of the anaesthetic.

This is new territory. Essie fractured her wrist once. And they had a panicked visit to emergency after Sam bumped his head on the edge of the coffee table, but it wasn't anything major. She knows she is lucky, they are lucky. She has imagined sickness and injury often enough. Imagined it until she has made herself ill. There is a fear at the core of it, right down deep, unutterable, that on bad days she might find pleasure in their hurt. Mim hears her own blood pumping in her ears, a slight milkiness at the edge of her vision, and Heidi makes the cut into Essie's hand.

Sam gasps and Essie looks stricken at the sight of the blade in her flesh. Mim reaches and grips Essie's other shoulder. 'It's okay, it's okay,' she whispers, a nothing refrain that is comforting and meaningless at once. Heidi peers closely at the cut she has made.

'Can you see it?' Mim asks.

Heidi grunts. 'In deeper, like I thought.' She touches the blade to the wound again. 'You're doing good, Essie. You feel anything?'

'Nup,' says Essie in a small voice that is pretending to be big.

It takes longer. Heidi has to dig. It is not warm in the lab, cold really, but Mim watches sweat bead on the skin of Heidi's temple. It is hard to look, and impossible not to look, at the flap of skin Heidi has cut back on Essie's hand. The vivid red of it, the inside of skin, the messiness of it – she thinks of the soft flesh of not quite ripe mango that clings stubbornly to the underside of the skin when you try and peel it back.

'Can't pull it out. Grown over, need to cut,' Heidi says to herself, lips only moving slightly.

Essie clears her throat. 'Can I have some water, Mum?'

'You okay?' She peers at her daughter's face, pale now, her pupils fat and dark. *She is trying to be so brave*, Mim thinks, and wants to cry.

Sam is reluctant to bring the water but Mim is too worried to move away while Heidi digs in her daughter's flesh. *No one will do this again*, she thinks. *I will not let them.*

She concentrates on her daughter's face, holds the bottle to her lips so she can sip, asks her if she would like something special for dessert, she can have anything, what treat will it be? She babbles, flinches when Essie flinches.

'Can you feel something, does it hurt?'

'Not hurt, but just, I can feel it.'

'You are so brave.'

'Gotcha,' Heidi says, and Essie breaks Mim's gaze to look at her hand. Heidi flicks the tip of the blade and it emerges from the bloodied flesh with the silvered chip. Essie leans in to look and the movement catches Heidi off balance, her hand moves slightly and the chip flicks off the blade, makes an almost imperceptible clink as it hits the metal bench and then bounces away.

'Shit,' says Heidi, biting off the word.

Sam bobs down. 'Where'd it go?'

Essie's voice is panicked. 'Is it out? Sorry! Sorry!'

'It's okay, it's okay.'

Heidi is on her knees, hands spanning gently across the tiled floor. Mim moves to get down and help.

'No, stay there, don't put your feet down. Sammy, you too. Just hold for a bit.' Heidi keeps her head down.

'Should I do something to her hand? Is it okay?' asks Mim.

'It's fine.' Heidi's voice is short, flaring with frustration. 'Just wait.'

'There! Over there!' Sam yelps.

Heidi freezes.

'Where, Sam?'

'Across from your hand.'

'Which one?'

'Um, your . . .' Sam holds his hands up in front of himself, 'your left, your left!'

Mim can't see it. She glances at her own chip lying in the little bowl. It is so tiny. How can he possibly see it?

'This way?' Heidi asks, moving her hand slowly to the side, her head moving as she looks.

'It's got the light on it, I can see it!'

Essie turns to Mim. 'What happens if we can't find it?'

Mim shakes her head reassuringly.

'There!'

Heidi grunts in frustration. 'Where, Sammy, I can't —' and then she whispers, 'fuck, yes.' She presses her fingers into the line of grout between the wide grey tiles, pushes back up to her knees. 'Sam, you have bionic eyes.'

'Yesss,' Sam says and his grin is wide.

'You've got it?' Essie asks, and Heidi stands up, one hand cupped beneath the other, and deposits the chip in the bowl. They all peer at the two tiny metallic slivers nestled together.

'We'll have to be more careful with yours, Sam.'

He nods.

'How do you tell them apart?' Essie asks.

'You can't by looking at them,' Heidi says and moves her body to block Essie's view as she begins to clean the fleshy mess she's made of her hand.

Once Essie is cleaned up, Sam is eager to jump in the chair.

'I'm gonna get you to lie down on the table actually, Sam,' Heidi says, 'my back's getting a bit sore.'

'You okay?' Mim asks, concerned. 'You need water, should you take a break?'

'Let's just get this done, hey?'

'Mum?' Essie is sitting on the floor, leaning back against the wall. 'Mum, I don't feel good.'

Mim turns from Sam to watch as Essie vomits into the space between her knees. 'Mum,' she says again, holding her cut hand away from her face, and bringing up a projectile of yellow bile, heaving again so her whole body rocks forward.

'Shit.' Mim leaves Sam and goes to Essie, holds back her hair, uses the back of her cut hand to gently rub against her daughter's back.

'Oh my darling,' she croons.

'Sorry, Mum.'

'No, no, it's okay. I'll clean it up.' The smell of it catches in her own throat.

'You okay, Essie?' Sam says.

Essie coughs, nods.

'Yep, Sam,' Mim says, 'she's good. You just lie still for Heidi.'

Mim helps Essie shuffle along the floor and gets her to lie down. She finds paper towels under the bench and cleans the vomit one-handed, careful not to let anything touch her wound. The whole time she can hear Heidi talking to Sam about ninjas. She feels torn, like she should witness the cutting of her son's flesh, but she is also needed here. With Essie.

By the time Mim throws the last paper towel in the bin and kisses Essie's forehead, the flush has returned to her cheeks, Sam's implant is out and Heidi is gluing her son's hand back together.

'That was easy!' Sam crows, sitting up and looking at his hand. 'You superglued my hand back together, cool!'

Heidi smiles, pulls off her gloves. 'It is cool, huh?'

Mim puts her arm around Sam's shoulders, helps him shuffle to the edge of the table and slide down.

'Can we have pizza now?'

Heidi pulls the bowl with the chips towards herself. 'Got to look after these first,' she says. She takes a small specimen jar from the bench, unscrews the lid, and tips the bowl so the three silver implants clink into the bottom.

'A family of implants,' she says.

'Except Ben,' Mim says.

'Yeah, except Dad.'

Heidi closes her mouth, nods, screws the lid on the jar.

'How about I get these back to the farm, yeah, while you guys get the pizza? Save me some for when I get back.'

Mim frowns. 'You sure?'

'Reckon it'll be easier like this.'

Sam is talking in his sister's ear. 'Essie, what are we gonna get? Should we get Hawaiian? It's only fake ham anyway isn't it? Do you still like that one?'

'You sure?' she says again to Heidi.

'Yep. You guys go back to mine. Have a rest. Watch something. I want to check those cuts when I get back.'

⁓

The three of them eat pizza and take painkillers together when the anaesthetic starts to wear off, and Sam falls asleep in the crook of Mim's armpit. Essie is quiet, touching the bandage on her hand. She hasn't said anything yet, about Ben, about all of it. Mim is bristling in readiness, feels like she has been skinned.

She starts at the sound of the door opening, hears Heidi's voice before she can panic. 'You guys okay?'

'Yeah,' Mim replies, keeping her voice low so Sam doesn't wake.

Heidi sticks her head through the door from the kitchen. 'Coffee?'

Mim inches out from under Sam, checks if Essie wants anything, leaves the kids nestled in together.

'What took you so long?' Mim asks.

'Had to do some quick surgery.'

'What?'

'Inserted the chips into a couple of rats from the lab and liberated them on the edge of your property. Figure it's close enough if they're tracking you specifically.'

Mim shakes her head, trying to make sense of it. 'Rats?'

'Thought about doing the dogs but it was going to get complicated.' Heidi turns away from the kettle now, puts both hands on the kitchen table and eyes Mim steadily. 'There's no going back now. You get that, right?'

Mim nods, but she's not sure what Heidi is trying to say.

∽

Later, when the kids are asleep, whiskey warms the darkness, draws them in close across the kitchen table. Mim's hand throbs.

'I've been shit at being around for you.' Heidi can hold her liquor but her voice is tinged with something else now, regret perhaps, nostalgia.

'God, no, I've been shit,' Mim says, grabbing Heidi's wrist across the table. 'What happened with Yvette?'

'What always happens, I suppose.' Heidi sits back in her chair, pulling her hand away. 'A mismatch. Cross purposes. Timing not quite right.'

'You or her?' The whiskey talking now. Mim would not normally be so bold.

'Me, this time. Told her to go. She didn't want kids. I'd said it was a deal breaker. Then I had to follow through.'

Mim clenches her jaw at the grief in Heidi's face now. She was nearly forty herself when she had Sam. Time has slipped from them.

'But –' she leaves an uncertain gap, not sure how far Heidi wants to go.

'But,' says Heidi, 'it didn't work out that way for me either. Towns like this one aren't awash with eligible women in their forties who are excited about having babies.' She cracks a smile, that taut face Mim remembers from high school – *Let me laugh at myself before you laugh at me, or worse, before you pity me.*

'Heidi –'

'It's all good,' she says, standing up and moving to the sink, rinsing her glass. 'You've got to get as far as fuck away from here. Find somewhere to hide.'

The change in Heidi's tone is sudden and hard. Mim shakes her head to try and clear it, to try and understand what her friend is telling her. 'And then what?'

'They'll come looking.'

Mim cannot make the pieces come together. A small sound escapes her throat.

'Have you told your mum anything?'

'No, I mean she asked about Ben, but –'

Heidi puts her hand up. 'I don't want to know either.'

It is like tiles clinking into position. She is beginning to understand, and she doesn't want to.

'Take my car. It's old. Not networked. I'll use the work one and leave yours parked in town.'

Mim nods. Heidi knows what she is doing, what she is saying.

'You can leave here in the morning. You know you've still got problems, right? Even with these gone.' She takes Mim's hand in her own. 'Anywhere OMNI is, and the cameras, there's biometrics, data harvest, if they really want to find you they'll scan the servos, the main streets, everywhere. Leave your phone, the kids' screens. Get something cheap from a servo. You've just got to disappear.'

'The screens aren't networked.' Jesus, trying to deal with the kids minus their screens would push her right over the fucking edge. 'I can't leave the phone,' she says. 'How will Ben find me?'

Heidi shakes her head. 'Just think about you and the kids for now.'

'But he might just call tomorrow, and all this will be over, we can go back to normal.'

But Heidi keeps shaking her head, and this is the point, Mim realises, from which nothing will ever be normal again.

⌢

She wakes to a noise. Heidi beside the bed, whispering, lit only by the glow of the moonlight through the curtain. Mim's hand hurts and she pushes up on to her elbows, trying to protect it. 'What? What's wrong?'

'Time to go.'

'Shit, Heidi, what time is it?'

'It's nearly four. You should be out of town, right up the highway by daybreak.'

She sits up, rubs her face. 'Thought we could wait till morning, at least.' She feels heavy with sleep, the whiskey.

'No. Come on.'

'Okay. Okay.' She swings her legs to the edge of the bed. There is nothing else to be said.

⌒

Heidi pushes a wad of cash into her hands. 'It's not much, but it'll last a bit. You get some off your mum?'

Mim nods. She'd taken the maximum, a couple of grand at the ATM. It's unfamiliar, the flashy colour of it. Like play money when they were kids. 'Why are you doing this?'

Heidi shrugs. 'You'd do the same.'

You don't know that. I don't know that.

'Go on, off you go.' Heidi holds her shoulder, hugs her once, fierce and quick. 'Get on the road.'

⌒

And then they are going. Heidi is a figure on the driveway, still for a moment in the red lights as they pull out, Mim taking it slow in the ute, the kids amped and tired both, hands feeling out this new space in the dark.

'Where we going, Mum?'

'I'll tell you when we stop for brekkie. You have a bit more of a sleep.'

Their eyes in the rear-vision mirror, wary, but trusting her.

'We gonna see Dad?'

She smiles, quick. 'How good will that be, huh? Your screens are there, watch something if you like.'

They put their earbuds in, tune out.

For the first thirty minutes, out through the town, she drives in the quiet. No audio, just the whirr of the car, the intermittent click of her indicator as she passes someone. She concentrates on the feel of the vehicle, where it sits on the road, begins to notice a faint lightening through her window in the east. This is a nowhere space. Left but not yet arrived, where she does not have to make plans, or think, or try to make sense. Just drive. Watch those kilometres click, each one, a tiny space to breathe.

9

At morning tea she allows the kids thirty minutes for a run in a park she has pulled up near. She has already driven three hundred and fifty kilometres. The number feels big, solid enough to mark. She drinks another coffee. Three already, plus the pies for the kids. The cash isn't going to last.

You're not thinking about forever though, yet, she thinks. One day at a time. Where will we sleep tonight?

Essie is kicking her ball against a low concrete fence and Sam keeps yelling out to her to come and help him. He can't climb with his hand, he needs a push. Essie ignores him.

'Muum!' he calls.

'You can do it,' she says, nodding encouragingly.

She doesn't want to drive once it gets dark. There'll be towns, she knows, a caravan park, maybe. They'll take cash for sure. But what if they need her to swipe in? She fingers the plastic smooth of the glue across her wound.

'Let's go, you two, have a wee.'

How many kilometres are enough? Should she head for Brisbane? Hide in plain sight? There must be thousands of people hiding from someone. She hears Heidi's words, *Get as far as you can. Then stop and think.*

She pulls out of the parking spot, heads back out to the highway. Checks her rear-vision but no one is behind. She should stop and buy a tent. Imagines hiding out in the forest. Pretending they are waiting for Ben to arrive. Choosing a spot, lighting a fire, setting the camp seats up.

But it's a fantasy. The Department are not only looking for Ben now. They are looking for her, too. Her and the kids.

∽

They took Essie camping for the first time when she was six months old. It was spring, and they had travelled south to where the big old mountains rolled straight into the sea. The ground became heavy with dew overnight, but the days were sunny and cloudless. Ben said maybe she needed to get out of the house. They rented a camping cot, low to the ground, completely zipped up when Essie was inside and Mim remembers wishing she could sleep like that always, completely cocooned, where nothing could fall in on her, where she couldn't fall out.

They'd only had sex a couple of times since Essie's birth. Mim felt her body was not her own, both shamed by the heavy awkwardness of herself and consumed by Essie's need for her. She couldn't distinguish Ben's advances from Essie's hunger for her. She could not make her body respond.

But the tent, the beer, Essie zipped up in her own little bubble, the rich darkness of the space so that when Ben reached for her he was not Ben. He might have been anyone. And it was this that kicked and sparkled in her groin so that she let him reach, let him touch. She backed up against his body and covered herself with his hands. Not a child, not her husband, something other. She did not recognise the sounds she made, the sounds he made, as he pushed his hands inside of her. She bit down on his finger as he scrabbled to cup her face and bring it around to his.

They had not spoken of it in the morning. She had felt exposed. Immersed herself in mothering Essie, allowed her daughter to suckle on her far longer than she normally would, as though she were asserting the natural way of things again. Ben did not seem chastised. They had walked, traced the river, and she had relished the ache in her shoulders and her back from carrying the child strapped to her and declined Ben's offers to carry his daughter. Punishing him in ways both minuscule and powerful for his want, his need.

～

She shifts in her seat, aware of the seam of her jeans against her crotch. It is odd to have remembered this of Ben. So long ago. It is not how she thinks of him now.

She drives.

Sammy falls asleep.

Essie digs for her screen between the seats and Mim glances back to see her taking shots of the paddocks, of wind turbines, stretching out over the rounds of the hills into the distance.

'They're kind of beautiful, huh?' Mim says.

Essie makes a non-committal noise. 'I'd like to see the ones out at sea. They're more efficient, we learnt about it in Grade Two.'

Mim makes a face to the windscreen.

'You should have been using the technology earlier,' Essie goes on, well and truly on her high horse now. 'That's what they say. You had the technology and you just didn't use it.'

Essie has a way of making her feel personally responsible for the failings of the world. 'Sometimes it's hard to make people see what they have to do.'

Essie shrugs. 'Still should have done it sooner.'

She sighs. 'We were trying, sweetheart,' she says and even as she speaks, she knows it is bullshit. 'Your dad and I, the projects we worked on, before you were born, I −'

'Worked with the EPA testing groundwater. You protected the aquifers. I know, Mum. You've told me.'

Mim grinds her teeth. Doesn't respond.

'Working on a gold mine in Indonesia isn't really helping.' There is a tide of tears behind Essie's words.

Mim softens. 'He's got his reasons, you know that. He's trying to hold them to account. That's his job. To make sure they abide by the regulations. To try and make sure they do it the best way there is.'

'Where are we going, Mum? Where is he?'

Please don't ask.

She won't lie. Essie's too smart for that. But she can't afford for Essie to bear the same worries, the same nightmares that she is harbouring.

'Mum?'

'He's been held up with work, something went wrong.' She sees Essie's face freeze, hurries on. 'But it's okay. We are going to sort it out, that's what we're doing.'

'What do you mean something went wrong? Where is he, why can't we talk to him, Mum?'

She breathes. Keeps driving. Knows Essie will not jump out of the car, she's still keeping her voice low so she won't wake her brother, Mim just needs to wait until she calms.

'I need you to help me, Ess. I need you to help me look after your brother, and stay away from any Department cars, and to tell anyone, if they ask you, that we are on a holiday.'

'But –'

'Essie, I need you to do this. Dad needs you to.' A new weight in her voice.

Essie is quiet, nods.

'If you can do that, if you can help me, then I promise we will work this out, okay?'

Essie closes her eyes, leans her head against the window, nods again.

∿

Mim concentrates on the bitumen. She cannot just keep driving, she knows that, but as the landscape stretches out alongside the highway she feels something forming in her, a velocity that is pushing her forwards. She doesn't have words for it, not yet, can't articulate what it is or what it means, but she thinks, and she's not sure why, she thinks she can trust it.

Heading north. Ticking over the degrees of latitude. *At least,* she thinks, *at least if you are still there, on that island, then I am moving towards you.*

She notes each little track that heads off the highway: Stockman's Track, Little Brown Creek, Heavenly Falls, Cabbage Palm Way. Any one of them, she thinks, we could pull off there, if we had the gear, could just stop and camp. We could do that. Hide. Pull into one of the tiny towns and get supplies. No one would know us. No one would think twice. People must do it all the time.

Running from something. To something.

But that's not the answer. Up ahead a screen. The list of towns and distances flashes on the sign as she speeds towards it.

Brisbane, still hours away, but there, a name in the fat white font on blue that means a holiday spot: Eagles Nest. Fifty.

She feels it click within her. Can smell the place already, can almost hear her dad – *As good a place as any.*

She checks on the kids in the rear-view. Tests the feeling in her gut.

And when the turn comes, she takes it.

‿

It feels the same. The arc and bend of the road as they drive down from the ridge and glide into town. The water rolled out beyond.

The roofs clustered then spread out to one headland, all along the bay.

'What's this?'

Sammy's awake, blinking his eyes open to peer out the window. 'Where are we?'

'Eagles Nest,' says Essie, 'saw the sign back there.'

'We used to come here on holidays when we were kids.' Mim smiles, she can't believe how her body remembers it as they come to the main drag.

'Why are we here?' Essie asks.

'Thought you might like to see it. We can stay at the caravan park.'

'Can we have fish and chips for lunch, Mum? Can we?'

Essie crosses her arms over her chest. 'I don't get why we're here,' she says under her breath.

Mim forces brightness into her voice. 'Some pics of the beach'll be good for your project, Ess?'

~

The beach is not the same. In fact, as she turns to look at the beach road and the line of shops, she can see that all of it is different. The grassy picnic areas and car parks are all gone. There is a new seawall, higher than the last, almost at the road. She frowns, the design is all wrong. She doesn't need Ben's engineering degree to see that. Councils had tried beach nourishment for a while, moving sand from one spot to another as the hungry sea continued to devour coastlines. But unforgiving seawalls just made the waves hungrier; more elegant approaches were required.

'Kick it to me!' Sam calls out. The stretch of beach and the curl of the waves have mollified Essie, who takes her ball down and kicks it to Sam across the hard sand at the water's edge.

She's got them here. She rubs the tender part of her palm and breathes in the briny air. It's a shortcut to memory. It feels like the intervening thirty years have vanished. She remembers an uncomplicated love of the sea. Now, it is tinged with melancholy. There are no fishermen clustered on the edge of the pier, too highly regulated now. The seagulls are still here, cockroaches of the bird kingdom, but she knows that the plovers are gone, and so many more.

Down the end of the beach, in the curve of the cliff, she can see there is still a block of the old seawall. The rest must be buried under sand and the risen tide. That last year, the summer before her HSC, she sat on the old wall with Nick. It was the summer she had sex for the first time, and she felt pleased with herself. Like she was ticking off important things. It would be the last summer at Eagles Nest because the next she'd be in the city, away from her old life, the town, the farm, getting ready for uni. She didn't realise she'd never make it back. Until now.

Nick had known. And it's not like he hadn't had plans, this summer fling of hers, the local boy. He reckoned he was going to head north, see his dad up in Darwin. He was going to travel. She was too, she was, she just wanted her degree first.

She had fallen for him. In the time that it took to realise the boy she'd shied away from the last couple of summers was interesting. And sexy. She remembers the sound he had made, that first time, into her shoulder, like a giving in, something quiet and intense and secret. She'd wondered then if she'd be able to bring forth that sound from anyone else, from herself even. And she had, of course, but it wasn't ever the same as that first time.

The kids have kicked off their shoes.

'I haven't got a towel!' she yells after them. It is mild enough for swimming, always is now. She should check the water quality, but realises, suddenly, she no longer has a phone. A tugging anxiety, and also a freedom.

She wonders what happened to Nick. If his mum still lives in town. Helen. She was nice.

'Mum!' Sam calls, 'I'm hungry, can we get chips now?'

∽

The kids hang off the silver loops of bike racks out the front of the fish and chip shop, while she waits, flipping through the greasy magazines, one eye on the screen in the corner. The news never changes, the same montage of broken people, nations colliding, an exploding planet. They'd stopped some of it in time. But, like the scientists had been telling everyone for decades, the temperature would continue to rise even if they turned the carbon emissions around. And didn't everyone know what that looked like now. Aerial shots of the mosaiced remnants of the Amazon. Tidal surge refugees from the waterfront suburbs of Florida, Brisbane, Norway, who didn't look like refugees were supposed to look, too wealthy, too white, too familiar.

International relations was a moveable feast these days: American decline, the rise and rise (and rise) of China – ambassadors and their teams needed to be nimble in the creation of alliances, the signing of memos, the aiming of their SmartDrones. Who really knows what's going on out there? It's a curated news feed anyway. The Department regulate media ownership these days, or like to think they do, but perhaps it's the same as it always was. Fat cats in the pockets of power, mouthpieces spinning Department rhetoric for profit, and immunity if ever the time came. There was some backlash when the Department started censoring the internet, but even that could be spun. *Who's watching? How do you know where the information is coming from? Foreign interference. Cyber hacks.* And they purported to be fair and balanced. They even let through some of the articles on the international outrage when a BestLife asylum seeker made it to New Zealand in a kayak. But it was all for show, a chance to place the propaganda right back at them. Glossy stories, made-up mothers talking about finally having time to get back into the workforce, grateful for their kids being housed and cared for, before and after shots of homeless men, addicts (Mim looked for pictures of Michael) who'd been given a second chance at life.

And then they stopped bothering with the propaganda. No one else got out. And the Department had long arms, and fists that squeezed, that knew no borders at all. Besides, words and diplomacy never meant much before, and they meant even less now.

At the end of the news feed, the Department logo flashes up, and the screen fills with ID photos. Wanted for fraud, for assault, all the anti-social behaviours, a category that has particularly nebulous definitions. The contact numbers for those who want to dob someone in the old-fashioned way.

'Number 20?'

Mim realises the man is talking to her, repeating the number, and holding the wrapped package across the counter.

'Sorry!' she says.

'You're right,' he says, nodding towards the screen. 'I always keep my eyes peeled for those ones myself. Dodgy bastards. Like to see how many they've caught.'

She stares at him, reaches for the package. 'Yeah, right, thanks,' she says.

'You done yourself some damage there, love?' he says, nodding to her hand.

She smiles quickly, takes the hot paper bundle. 'Ta.' She lifts the package in acknowledgement, walks out through the coloured streamers.

Behind her, he calls out, 'Look after yourself!'

The streamers tangle on her shins, catch her there, but she kicks out and they break apart.

'Let's go,' she says. The kids continue to flip and hang. 'You two, now!'

'Geez! We're coming.'

But she's strung tight now, can feel eyes on her, the cars slowing as they pass, the man from the chip shop boring holes in her back with his stare.

'Well, come quicker!' She waits until they are in step with her and then strides towards the car.

～

There are still prayer flags on the porch. The same probably, by the looks of them. She let the kids eat their chips at the end of the back beach and then drove the long way back into town, towards the caravan park. She tells herself she just wants to see if it's still there.

'Is this a hippy house?' Sam whispers and Essie snorts.

'Who lives here?'

She idles the car. She only ever came here a couple of times. They preferred the anonymity of the beach, as far away as they could get from both of their families. Still, it strikes something in her, like the cells of her body are remembering themselves.

If I look in the mirror now, I will be young again, she thinks.

'A lady named Helen. I used to know her.'

'Doesn't that mean you still do?'

A bit tattered, needs a paint job, but the roses, the roses she remembers. The heady perfume of them. Peeling a petal and placing the soft velvet of it on her lip. Heat and kicking the cracked pink paint of her big toenail in the dust while she waited for Nick to run back inside and grab a towel.

'You can't *used* to know someone,' Sam is saying. 'If you know someone, you always know them.'

'But maybe you haven't seen them for ages, dumb-brain.'

She sighs. 'Don't call him that, Essie. Come on.'

'What?'

'We're going in.'

'Why?'

'You said we were going to the caravan park! With the pool!'

'I want to say hello.' And because, right now, this is the safest place she knows.

The kids stand behind her as she gathers herself, knocks on the door. She turns around to smile, reassure them, or herself, while she waits.

The door swings open, a short woman with shaggy dyed blonde hair and an oversized pale blue shirt over black leggings steps forward onto the portico as Mim steps back.

'Hello there.' She is all crinkly eyes and curious smile.

'Hi, hi.' Mim laughs nervously. 'It's Helen, isn't it?'

'Yes,' she draws out the word in surprise.

Mim ploughs on. 'I don't know if you remember me, Mim Franklin I used to be, I mean, I'm Mim Elliot, I'm someone else now – we used to holiday . . .' She trails off.

Helen's eyes widen. 'Mim! Goodness me, what a blast from the past. The Franklins.' She places both hands on Mim's shoulders and pulls her in. 'Come here and let me look at you!'

She hears Sam giggle. Helen even smells the same, a floral perfume, an undertone of cigarettes, or perhaps that is just the memory trying to assert itself.

Helen pulls back, clicks her tongue. 'Goodness,' she says again and flicks her eyes sideways. 'These aren't, they can't be – look at you, so slim and two big kids!'

Mim laughs, gestures to the kids. 'Essie and Sammy.'

'Sam,' he corrects her.

'Sorry, Essie and Sam – this is Helen.'

'Well,' Helen says and crosses her hands on her chest. 'Come in, come in! You got time for a cuppa?' She holds the door open, still talking, expecting them to follow and Mim shepherds the kids ahead of her.

The house smells of tea rose and lemon dishwashing liquid and, faintly, of musk. Along the narrow hallway there are framed photographs and a hall table filled with shells and trophies of some sort. The kids are quiet as they follow Helen. Mim tries not to look for photos of Nick.

'Now, what'll it be? Juice for you two? I've got apple? Ribena? Keep it on hand for the littlies.'

'You've got grandkids?' Mim asks.

'Three,' Helen says and smiles indulgently. 'Georgie's little ones. A handful, delightful, but a handful. You'll have to have a play – how long you in town?'

Mim sidesteps the question. 'Gosh, Georgie – she was only – what, ten? Last time I was here, I can't even . . .'

'You wait, my love,' Helen says, shaking her head, 'yours'll do it to you, too. Now,' she claps her hands, 'for you, what'll it be, tea? Coffee? Wine?' She opens a cupboard and pulls down two glasses. 'It's past two, isn't it?'

'Thanks,' Mim says, accepting the glass.

'Sit! Make yourself at home. Don't get so many visitors these days.'

Mim pulls out the chairs for the kids and they sit at the green and white laminex table.

'No, Nick's given me none so far. He's in town, though, at the moment. Divides his time between here and Darwin – checks in on his dad up there still. Doing up his dream boat. He tells me it's a sounder investment to have a boat than a quarter acre these days, s'pose he's right! I'll give him a buzz, he'd be so chuffed to see you. How long are you staying? Where've you set up?'

Mim feels a rocketing in her stomach. 'Well, we haven't yet . . . it was spur of the moment really, we've only just –'

Helen jumps in. 'Stay here!'

Her face. Mim wonders how often she gets to see those grand-kids. How much loneliness is settled in those lines.

'No, Helen, oh no, that wasn't my intention.' But maybe it was. A little.

'Be a pleasure to have you. I've got a kids' room for you two there, bunk beds, you don't mind sharing do you, love?' Helen cups her hand around the back of Essie's head as she asks her, a gesture Mim knows is too intimate for her daughter to handle usually, and yet, she does.

Mim raises her glass. 'Well, let's have this drink, shall we, and see if you still want to insist once we've been here for an hour.'

It would mean no dealing with ID. No using the cash. And it feels good in this house, cluttered with the stuff of family, homely in every way her own family home no longer feels to her. This place does not make her think of Ben. It is before. Her body isn't cracking with the memory of him, the fear of what's ahead.

～

Over their glass of sweet white they lay down the major dates of the last twenty-five years as though they are playing cards. Helen, then she, choosing the next for its connection to the last – marriages, births, deaths. Sam tugs at her jeans.

'Yes,' she says, 'you can go outside.'

'Can I grab my ball from the car, Mum?'

Helen laughs. 'Oh, I have every ball you could want out there, honey!'

Mim passes Essie the keys. 'Ess is rather particular about her soccer ball.'

'Are you just?' Helen raises her eyebrows. 'But what have you done there, love?' Helen gestures and Essie seems to freeze, her bandaged hand in mid-air. Shit. She hasn't worked it out yet, hasn't concocted a story. Lying is so fucking complicated.

'Oh, that,' Mim says and Helen looks at her. Notices her hand too.

'You too! What have you done to yourselves?' She swivels now to see Sam's hand too, just as he tries to shift it behind his back, his face wobbly with six-year-old guilt. Helen's forehead creases in worry and she looks at Mim, waiting for her to explain.

'We had some trouble with our implants. With the network upgrade back home. They had to adjust them.'

'Goodness!' Helen says, shaking her head. 'Thought they just did all that with their little keyboards, thought you never had to feel a thing.' She reaches out to Sam. 'Is it sore, love? Do you need some Panadol?'

Sam looks at Mim, eyes unsure.

'Oh, he's fine, aren't you, Sam?'

He pouts a little but nods.

'Well, they'd better not go digging for mine, when they finally make it up here with the upgrade. Was bad enough when they put it in!'

Mim scrabbles wildly in her mind to change the subject.

Helen goes on. 'Nick, he wasn't having a bar of it. Refused one! Still does. Bit shifty that boy, like his old man, didn't like the idea of it.'

Things are shifting inside Mim in a way she can't make sense of.

She laughs and it sounds forced in her mind. 'Ha, how'd he get away with that?'

'Always finds ways and means that boy. I've found it's better not to ask!' And then Helen moves the subject away of her own accord, just when Mim could have lingered.

'Now, you two going to show me your football skills, or what?'

⌢

They sit in white plastic chairs on the patio and watch the kids boot the ball back and forth. Mim lets Helen's words roll over her. The late afternoon sun is warm where they are, sheltered from the wind, and she feels she could be someone else. Some previous version of herself. The urgency of the past few days flickers at the edges of her brain, but she leaves it there. Tomorrow, she thinks. For now, we are here, safe. No one knows where we are.

Helen is talking about Nick. 'Restless feet, that boy. Always grand plans for adventures, and he does some of them, mind, takes off to places I can't even find on a map. Comes down to visit me. Keeps an eye on his dad. He's on dialysis now, in a home up there. Yes, my boy, always known his sea legs to be more steady than his ones on land, that's for sure.'

'You said he's doing up a boat?'

'Mmm.' Helen takes another gulp. 'Got his dad's old one in Darwin. He's put it on the market, needs some cash to do up this dream boat down here. He's got his adventures all planned out. Now,' she leans in, lowering her voice, 'I was being polite not to ask before.'

Mim looks at her expectantly, the flick, churn of her gut.

'Your bloke not being with you, on this little family holiday, everything okay there?'

Yes, you're right, she thinks, *normally you wouldn't ask*. Mim thinks about how she should play this. She feels so comfortable here, so at home, but she knows it's dangerous. Thinks about Heidi's words. *You can't trust anyone else.*

'You haven't left him?'

'God, no. No, Ben travels, for work. He's in Indonesia right now.' She stands up and stretches, turns her back on the kids.

'He's been held up. All a bit stressful, really. Kids are pretty sensitive about it.'

Helen frowns in concentration.

'We just needed to get out of town for a bit.'

Helen nods slowly. 'When'll he be back?'

'I don't know.'

'You're not thinking of going over there?'

She brushes the comment off. 'God, no. Just can't be at home. For a bit.' She laughs dryly. 'Couldn't get to Indonesia even if I wanted to – they've taken my passport, our passports.'

Helen frowns. 'Department?'

Mim shrugs, non-committal.

Helen nods once, firm. 'I'll keep my nose out of it.'

Mim smiles gratefully and Helen waves her hand, calling out, 'Now, kids, what do you fancy for tea? I'll nip down the shops.'

∽

She hears the door, and comes out of the bathroom to greet Helen. Except it's not her. It's him. Nick.

'Hi.'

'Hi.'

It is shocking, the way the memory and the now fit together. He is in work boots and blue jeans crusted at the bottom with mud, the denim at the knee almost white with wear. Grey t-shirt under blue and white flannel. He's got a ponytail now. Close beard and his face, maybe that's where he is holding the years, coastal with lines.

She is aware now of him looking at her. Of what he is seeing.

'Did your mum tell you we were here?'

'Yeah, she called.'

Mim hasn't washed her clothes yet. No makeup. She realises she is holding her stomach in, feels stupid, breathes out, then holds it in again. It is written on her body, the years and the kids. Not so him.

They both go to speak at the same time.

'We didn't mean to –' she starts, feeling the need to explain her presence here. He lets her go on. 'It's really good to see your mum.'

'She said you hadn't changed a bit.'

Mim laughs, a quick squawk, which she swallows back. 'She was lying.'

'I see what she means, though.'

She walks to the window to check on the kids, just to be away from the moment.

'You travelling?'

'Something like that.'

'Where you headed?'

Where am I headed?

'North,' she says, 'chasing the sun, same as everyone else.'

'Must be strange coming back?'

She thinks of the seawall. Sneaking out from the pub, Nick laughing beside her. The sea in the air and ears ringing in the quiet. The way she stepped out in front and he laughed and said, 'What, you the local now?' And she said, 'I want to show you something.' Stepping out, braver, turning and laughing. 'What, doncha trust me?' Feeling wild. Like she could be anyone.

And the seawall, she had run her hands along it so many times, the rough catch of it on the pads of her fingers. Pebble dash, her dad said, made up of all these different little stones – black, grey, white, red, brown, some shiny, some dull, glittery quartz. Some time in the future she will be able to name them all. 'Feel this,' she says, and puts both her hands on the wall. She can hardly see him, just his eyes, his gleaming pale skin. He hesitates and she says, 'C'mon, do it,' and so he does, his pale hands next to hers, close but not touching, yet. And then she leans into the wall so her face is up close against it, and she giggles a bit, unsure now, but come too far. And she says, 'Smell it,' and takes a deep breath. He says, 'What?' She's so close to him, she can smell him, feel the heat off him, turns to see him breathing in the smell of cold rock, salt, and then she says, 'Lick it'. And just the words, she feels them go right through her, the vibration of him next to her, and he doesn't make a sound, but moves his face back, waiting for her to do it first, and she does. In the faint light, her mouth open, tongue out, the tip of it just touching the rock and then, slowly, she licks the stones, the pebble dash, and then she closes her eyes, her mouth, tucks her lips, looks at him and says, 'Your turn'. And she knows that in his head, he is saying, *You crazy fuck, don't lick the fucking wall, is this a joke?* But she knows too, the way he has looked at her, that he will do anything now. The promise of what's to come. He turns his head and closes his eyes and his tongue is quick, touching the rock and then drawing back in. She is shocked, pleased, and she puts her hand on the back of his neck and turns him around to face her. With one hand, she is flicking her hair back, exposing the skin at her neck and she's guiding him down, right to the spot her collarbone juts out and she says, 'Now here'. He puts his tongue out and he licks her skin there, and it is –

And she says, 'See?' and he makes a sound and then stops. He is embarrassed. But she knows what he tastes, everything the other was not, warm and alive and soft, but she also knows what is the same, the same faint mineral taste, sweat and pheromones and something older, ancient – and she pulls his face up, just his eyes glowing in the dark, and there is no going back from there.

∿

She swallows now. 'Yeah. It is a bit strange,' she says. 'You think a place will have changed, you know, with so much time, but . . .'

'It's not that different.'

'Yeah.' She holds his gaze. 'Not so much.'

'Hellooo!' Helen comes through the doorway laden with shopping bags.

'Ah, thought you'd be here.' She dumps the bags and goes to kiss Nick. 'You're staying, love, aren't you.'

It's not a question, Mim can hear it in her voice, and Nick raises his eyes to Mim, to check, maybe.

'Wasn't going to, Mum, actually . . .'

'Don't be silly, of course you are. You can go and do whatever else afterwards. It's curry!' She begins unpacking the bags. 'Besides. There's thirty years for you two to catch up on.'

They both make a sound, a nervous laugh, like they're not really sure if that's such a good idea.

〜

It is odd that dinner feels so normal. There is a lot of passing – rice, and the curry, and yoghurt and naan bread that Helen's pulled from a paper packet and heated on the stove and it is good. It's all really good. And the round table, the smallness of it, so they are all, *Sorry* and *Here you go* and *Let's get that out of your way*. And it feels full. There's no gaping hole for Mim and the kids to comprehend because Ben couldn't fit a chair at this table anyway.

'Have you ever seen a tsunami?' Sam looks at Nick.

'Nah, mate, I haven't.'

Mim laughs and is shocked by the sound of it. 'Sam is into that kind of stuff.'

Sam frowns at her tone. 'You would've if you lived in Japan. It's not a silly question.'

Essie leans into the table. 'Sam's a bit obsessed, if you hadn't already figured.'

'Got it,' says Nick, and Essie flushes.

A pain in Mim's chest. Ben is not here. And she wants him to see his kids, being all funny and show-offy to this guy they've never met. And she wants to catch his eye across the table at the details, at Helen, who is like a caricature of herself, and she wants him to incline his head and raise his eyebrows at Nick, because he knows, he knows that this is the guy, her first, and he would find it funny and not intimidating and they would giggle about it in bed maybe, later, and have quiet sex, quiet staying over in someone else's house sex. And she cannot. Is this it? Is this the moment when denial isn't possible anymore? Inside her mouth the rice has turned to concrete and she can't swallow at all, and she pushes back from the table, puts her hand up to say sorry, points to her throat.

'Mum, you okay?'

She nods, points to the bathroom. Her eyes are beginning to water.

Helen is saying, 'Just got something caught, I think.'

She makes it to the bathroom, flips up the lid of the toilet. Spits, coughs, gets it all up and it's out. She knows it's out but she still can't breathe and she can almost feel him, feel Ben's hand on her back saying, *Easy, easy now, you're okay*. She can hear him, he's right here, and god, she lets go of the clench in her chest and then she breathes in and she thinks, *I'm handing it all back to you, you just tell us how it's going to be, just pack us up and take us home and then we'll feel normal, feel home, and we'll wonder what this was.*

But then she is breathing, and there's rice floating in an oily slick in the toilet bowl and Sam saying, 'You right, Mum?'

She nods.

'So, you be round for a few more days?' Nick says, grabbing his keys off the table as he heads off.

'Don't know.'

'Mum said you were having some trouble. Your chips, or something?'

She senses that he is digging, and she likes that he is.

'Your mum said you managed to get away without one?'

'Yeah, never in one place long enough for them to get a hold of me.'

'I didn't really have a choice.' *Maybe that's not true*, she thinks.

'Figured I'd use the conscientious objector line if I ever got pulled up.'

She smiles. 'That work?'

'Always worth a try,' he says and returns the smile.

Her stomach fizzes.

Mim looks at his face. Remembers how she trusted him once. She decides to take the gamble. 'Anyway, I sorted it,' she says.

'Yeah?'

She rubs her finger along the line of glue. She won't be able to feel it in a couple of days. 'Yeah,' she says.

He looks away. 'Good for you,' he says softly.

⌣

Later, kids in bed, she sits on the couch on the back patio having swiped one of Helen's cigarettes. God, it's been so long. They must be black market, there's no way Helen could afford them now.

In the glow of the lights from town, she watches the seagulls circling the oval down the road, underlit with orange. Mim can hear the sea, faint, and the smell of it, unmistakable, even through the cigarette smoke. God, it's good. To suck it in and hold it like that, to feel her brain buzz, the familiar almost-weight of it between her fingers.

It's like the seaside town of her childhood never grew up, never got weighed down by adulthood – even now, in the off season, there are loud backpacker vans, travellers whooping through the night streets – as though this is a place where you might forget what it was you came to do.

10

In the morning, Mim and the kids take the path to the headland. It's windy and there are new signs. *Welcome to the lands of the traditional owners.* She wonders how welcome they are, really. This would have been a good place. The sheltered curve of the bay, the rocks at the base of the headland thick with shellfish, the freshwater creek curving back inland. But what would she know? If she can feel this tug in her guts at being here, a place where she knows the smell of the air, the quality of the light while the sea mist is still sitting low, if she feels this after a childhood of summers, what might it feel like to have been here forever? The imprint of it in her DNA?

She calls the kids back from the edge of the cliff. There's a fence there, but she's wary. Always more so when Ben's not there. Quick to pull them back. Scared they might fall. Or worse, that she might fail to catch them.

'Let's go down and check out that park.'

The kids run down the path ahead of her.

～

Essie loops her legs over the edge of the monkey bars and hangs upside down, her bandaged hand pressing her skirt against her legs at the front, her other hand at the back.

'Here, I'll help.' Mim tucks the edge of her daughter's skirt into her undies. 'There, try now.'

Essie drops her arms and places her hands on the tan bark, tentative with her bandaged one. Her hair a drift of dark as she neatly shifts her weight and scissors her legs down to dismount. Sam is at the top of the playground, in a little cubbyhole. He pokes a stick through a hole in the shape of a star.

'Pow! Got you, Mum!'

'No guns, Sam.'

'It's not a gun! It's a numchucka.'

'Then it should make a different noise.'

'Wooosh, wooosh!' he cries as she walks to the picnic table on the crest between the park and the seawall. She opens the box and pulls out the new phone. More of the cash gone, but she needs to call her mum. She inserts the new SIM and the screen lights up in her hand. It's the only number she knows from memory, thank god. She takes a deep breath as she hears it begin to ring. The click of an answer.

'Mum?'

'Mim? God. Where –'

A series of muffled sounds, her mother's voice in the background now.

'Mim, what the fuck?'

'Steve?'

'What have you done? Do you have any idea the fucking trouble you've caused here?'

'Is Mum okay?'

'The place has been crawling with the Department. What fucking game are you playing? They threatened to take the farm. The whole fucking farm.'

She imagines her brother's face, red and spitting, can hear her mum in the background, her low voice trying to placate her son.

'I'm just trying to look after my kids.'

His voice explodes. 'What about the rest of us? Huh? How about my fucking kids, my whole fucking life? They've threatened to take Mum in. To an estate, Mim. Are you fucking hearing me?'

Mim is frozen. She hears her mother in the background, 'Let me speak, let me speak,' but Steve doesn't hand over the phone.

'Unless you're calling to come back here and sort this fucking mess out, we are done with being dragged into your shit.'

'Wait! Did they know where I was?'

But he ignores her. 'Do *not* fucking call here again.'

The line cuts out.

Her breath is shallow. How long before the Department work it out? What if someone makes the connection to Eagles Nest? They'll be trawling the network for Heidi's car. *Shit, shit, shit.*

∽

Helen is more than happy to give her Nick's number. 'Be lovely for you two to have a chance to catch up. Why don't you head down the pub for lunch? Kids'll be fine here with me.'

Mim wonders if Helen, too, is wedded to some other version of the past.

'How's it going?' he answers. His voice. She barrels backwards through time, an image of her curled around the landline, wedged behind a door at the farm, ignoring Steve's catcalls and blocking her ear so she could hear the boy her whole body is missing now that summer is gone.

'Yeah, good. You around today?'

'Yeah, what do you need?'

'A hand with something.'

'I can come round now.'

'Meet me at the pub?'

'Sounds better. When?'

'In halfa?'

'New one or old?'

'The one on the foreshore.'

'See you there.'

It's too easy. She wonders what else she will get away with.

～

The big glass doors open on to a deck overlooking the sea. She suspects he wouldn't drink here usually. It's all tourists now. She tries to remember how it used to be, where the doors opened out on to the beer garden, the string of lights, but it's changed too much. She's dressed more like a local than a tourist. She hasn't cared for the past few days but now, just a little, she does.

She can't see him and she hesitates for a moment, trying to decide whether to grab a drink first or sit down.

And then he's there, next to her.

'Hi.'

Her fingers go to tuck her hair back and she stops them. *Get a grip*, she thinks.

'Drink?' she asks, head nodding towards the bar.

'Thanks, schooner of ale.'

'Right.'

'I'll get us a spot.'

She finds him at a high table in the corner of the deck, closest to the sea.

'Thanks.'

It is his ease that unnerves her. She shifts the beer mat in her fingers, one side and then the other. The idea now seems preposterous.

'All good at Mum's place then?'

'Good, yeah, great.'

'She'd like having the kids. Georgie's are great, but she doesn't get to see them so much.'

Mim runs her finger through the little puddle left by the beer glass on the coaster. 'You never had any?' Immediately she feels exposed by the question, wishes it back.

He doesn't smile, takes a long drink. 'You said you needed a hand with something?'

Mim slowly nods her head. She won't try that again. 'Can you sail a boat to Indonesia?' She says it quick, looks at him, releases her breath.

He takes a sip of beer. 'Sure.'

'Is it hard?'

'Depends.'

'On what?'

'The boat, the weather, experience. Indo's a big place, thousands of islands –'

'Yeah I get that.' She stops, hasn't meant to jump in.

'But no, not really, it's not hard.'

'You done it?'

'Yeah.' He nods, half smiles. 'Yeah, I have.'

'How long does it take?'

'From Darwin? Depends on the wind and where you're headed, three to six days, maybe longer.' He takes a long swig. 'From here, well, you've got to get all the way round the coast, the cape, before you head up across the Timor Sea, a couple of weeks, give or take.'

She looks over to the park, thinks she needn't have left the kids with Helen, could've brought them here, watched them from here. It is like an itch, being without them, she wants to get back.

'You thinking of going sailing?'

'Hah.' She shifts in the chair. 'Something like that.'

'You done it before?'

'Nup. Not really. Couple of times here when we were little.'

'You got a boat in mind?'

She looks at him directly now, remembers the feeling that night at the seawall. *I could ask anything.*

'Yes,' she says.

His face breaks into a real smile now, and he shakes his head. 'Easier ways to get to Indo, if you need to get there in a hurry.'

'Yeah,' she says, 'but I've got no passport.'

He nods slowly. 'I mean, technically, you need one if you do it by boat, too.'

'Technically?'

'Well, yeah. I mean, there's a lot of stuff that comes in and goes out unofficially.'

'People?'

'Out, yes. Not in, anymore. They put a fucking stop to that. There are border drones, guards on the docks. It's risky, sure, but not impossible.'

'The kids.' She looks back to the park. 'They've never been on a boat.'

'Kids are pretty adaptable.'

A waitress pauses at their table, brunette with two braids, glossy pink lips, low-cut black singlet. She asks them if they'll be eating, holds out the menu. Mim shakes her head but Nick takes one, and the waitress smiles at him, a megawatt smile and looks back over her shoulder as she walks away.

Nick is looking at her. 'You not going to eat?'

'Nah, I should get back.'

He nods, scanning the menu, then without looking up, says, 'So, I'm not sure exactly what you're asking?'

'Would you sail us?'

He looks up from the menu.

'To Indo?'

She keeps her gaze steady.

He laughs, pushes his hands against the table, straightening his arms and stretching back as if to move away from her request.

'You're serious?'

She nods, but she feels far less serious than she did a moment ago.

He shakes his head. 'Mate, if you're looking for a fresh start, or, I don't know, somewhere to get away, there's better places than there.'

She shrugs, defensive now. 'That's where I need to go.'

He nods, looks out to sea. 'You looking for something?' he says, after a moment.

She could play it, she knows that, has felt the invisible crackle in the air between them that is memory and possibility both. But she knows this manoeuvre requires trust, and she can't start it with a lie.

'Someone,' she says. 'My husband's there. He's missing.'

He nods slowly, turning to face her. 'Shit, eh? That's why you got rid of your chips, the passports?'

She nods.

He drops his head. 'I'd like to help, I really would, but I've kept off the radar so far, risky avoiding getting chipped, I'm not keen on getting a flag on me now.'

'They don't know where I am yet.'

'You reckon?' he says and she realises she hadn't bargained on his saying no.

'I can pay you, I've got cash –'

He holds up his hands. 'Yeah, nah, I just . . . I can't help you. I'm sorry.'

She can't speak.

The girl with the braids is back with her smile. 'You ready to order then?'

'Nah, I'm good actually,' he says.

'Anything for you?' the girl says, dropping the smile for Mim.

She shakes her head and the girl whisks the menu up, her bum swinging as she walks away. Nick watches for a moment then looks back at Mim.

'Beer?'

She stands up, shaking her head, needs to leave now before she bursts into tears. Humiliation slow burns in her guts.

'Should get back to the kids. Thanks, anyway.'

He puts a hand out. 'I'm sorry, Mim, I just –'

She puts her hand up to cut him off. 'All good,' she says, and walks away.

Essie moves in the bunk bed above and the mattress springs creak.

'Did you try Dad again?'

Mim strokes Sam's head next to her. 'Yeah, honey, no luck.' She does not want to say that she has no way to contact Ben. That they are offline, untethered. She hears Essie roll and wriggle above.

Essie's voice comes again – blunt now. 'Are you splitting up?'

A breath of disbelief. 'What?'

'Are you getting a divorce?'

Mim looks at Sam, his eyes unsure, questioning. Has Essie already said this to him? Have they talked about this?

'No!' she says and rolls off the bed. She stands next to the bunks where she can see both of them. 'No! Ess, is that what you think is happening?'

Essie won't look at her, is staring at the ceiling. 'That's why he hasn't come back from his trip. Why we've left. You're having a big fight. This is what happened with Stacey's mum and dad. You can't just hide it from us.'

'Essie – no.' It is a relief, partly, that her daughter is so wrong. If this is the fear, if this is the worst, then maybe it won't be so hard to tell the truth. 'No, we are not splitting up. Dad's just . . .' she trails off. Their faces, both looking at her expectantly now. 'He can't come home yet.'

The sound of the doorbell chimes through the house.

'Why?' Essie persists.

Mim can hear the low murmur of voices and realises she is listening intently for Nick.

'Why can't he come home, Mum?'

She sighs in frustration. 'I don't know, Essie.'

Essie humphs and rolls away and Mim puts out her hand to rest near her daughter's back. Not touching, but close enough that she can feel the warmth.

'I don't know, but I'm going to find out. Okay?'

Essie doesn't respond and Mim whispers goodnight as she pulls the door shut behind her.

Helen is in the hallway.

'Visitors?' Mim asks, smiling.

Helen frowns a little, then seems to shake the look. 'No, yes, just the neighbours.'

'Everything okay?'

Helen flaps her hands and urges Mim back down the hall to the kitchen as she speaks. 'Yes, yes, nosy buggers, the lot of them. Apparently someone's got their knickers in a knot about the unknown vehicle in the street.'

Mim turns back quickly.

'Don't worry, love, I let them know it was nothing to worry about.'

But nothing feels like nothing, anymore.

∽

She spends too long in the pounding heat of the shower. At home, OMNI would have turned it off on her already. There are benefits to being outdated.

People are asking questions. They have to leave, she knows it's only a matter of time before the Department connect all the dots and find her here.

The water scours her, her breasts pinked by it. She lets it run over her face, her hair, turns so the pummel of it hits her shoulders. She wants to wash away the embarrassment of the gamble she took today, asking Nick. His face, the shake of his head.

Fuck him. She doesn't need him. Fuck him and the Department and the whole fucking lot of them.

She turns the water off, and stands for a moment, dripping in the steam.

Time's up in Eagles Nest. They will leave in the morning. Before anyone else starts asking questions. If Nick won't help them, she'll find someone else who will. And she will push down the regret that is blooming quietly within her, that she is leaving the town, and everything it holds, so soon.

∽

It is late when the phone beeps, but it is as though she is tuned for it, scrambles her hand to pull it in, hold it close in the dark.

Let it be Ben.

But it is not.

Thought about it more.
When do you want to go?
Nick.

She sits up. Rubs her face to try and wake up, think.

Tomorrow?

She holds her breath until she sees the icon that tells her he is replying.

Right! Can it wait another day?

She half-smiles at the exclamation mark.

Not really.

The icon blinks for far longer than it takes him to reply. This makes her smile, too.

Taking your car? Cost a bit.

I'll pay for everything

She waits a moment before adding.

There's more if you take us all the way.

Take a bit to get it all ready.

I've got 7k.

Another long wait.

She prompts.

Is that enough?

Should do it.

She scrolls back through the messages to check she hasn't misunderstood.

Tomorrow, then? Early?

Holds her breath again while she waits.

Be there by 6.

She does not sleep, but lies back in the dark, adrenaline coursing through her. Her plan, blurry and nebulous, has surfaced from her mind and become something solid, something real.

I am coming, she whispers into the dark, to Ben, to herself.

11

She's been up for an hour already, quietly packing things, before she knows she has to wake them and tell them.

'I don't understand,' says Essie, annoyed at being woken, belligerent and slow to move.

But Sam is thrilled. 'You mean it's like a secret mission?'

'Yes!' Mim says, helping him into his t-shirt. 'Yes, Sammy, a secret mission, because we can't tell anyone about it.'

'But we can't drive *all* the way to Dad.'

'Idiot,' Essie mutters under her breath and Mim ignores her, at least she's sitting up now.

'That's the exciting bit,' Mim says, keeping her voice buoyant for Sam, 'we're going to sail there.'

'On a boat?' Essie looks unconvinced.

'Uhuh.'

'Whose boat?'

'Nick's.'

'Nick from dinner?'

'Yep.'

Essie's face is still sceptical.

Sam jumps in. 'What kind of boat?'

'We'll find out when we get to Darwin.'

'Seriously?' Essie's arched eyebrows, her tone – will she question everything?

'Yep.' Mim is nodding, convincing herself now. 'Yep, we'll drive up there and it'll take us a few days, and then we'll get on Nick's boat and we'll go to Dad's island and we'll see him and everything will go back to normal.'

Just like that.

'Cool,' says Sam. 'Do you think Helen will make us jam on toast before we go?'

∽

Helen does make toast. She also plies them with packages of sandwiches and tubs of cut fruit and packets of chips until Nick puts his foot down and says there isn't any more room.

'You take care,' Helen says into Mim's ear as she hugs her. 'Of you, them, *and* my boy,' she adds and Mim understands how it pains her to watch her son take off again.

He wants to drive first and he doesn't even look back as they pull out and up the street. Mim thinks she sees a curtain twitch in the house on the corner.

It is a relief when they pull out on to the highway, watching the turn-off recede in the rear-vision mirror.

It's just shy of four thousand kilometres to Darwin. That's what Nick says. They can each take a turn driving, stop for a few hours, sleep overnight in the car if they have to, take a proper break in Isa, maybe further, if they can make it. They drive for thirteen hours on that first day. Crossing the border, feeling the land change beneath them. She agrees they will swap every four hours, but the third time she opens her window, Nick says, 'My turn, pull over,' and she gladly takes the passenger seat. Stepping out of the car, the heat hits her like a furnace. It beats down from the cloudless sky and radiates up from the sticky bitumen so that she is engulfed by it. She makes Sam piss in the shade of the tyre and Essie refuses, says she'll hold on. The heat shimmers on the plains on either side of the road. *You could die out here*, she thinks, *so quick, you wouldn't even know it was happening*. She turns the air conditioning up when she gets back in, her face feels fried from just a few minutes out there, but Nick turns it down again.

'Uses too much fuel,' he says. 'Your cash'll be gone.'

She wishes they could have brought her car, the one Heidi took. Thinks of the comfort. The cool. Still, the Department would've picked them up immediately. Plus, she wonders if there's anywhere to charge out here. They drive on.

She wants to text Heidi, *We've left the state*. But she doesn't. She will call from Darwin. Wants to be ready to leave, to jump off the map, when she risks it again. Nick lasts the full four hours, makes it five. It is endless road. The kids watch movie after movie and she diligently swaps leads to charge, not caring how their eyes are going red, how they don't look out, even when she calls, 'Look at that!' A hawk hovering above the long ditch grasses, a rocky outcrop breaking the flat expanse, a sign in bad font – *The end is nigh!* – fluorescent and strange at the edge of a paddock. Every now and then she sees movement on the road ahead, leans forward and recognises, only as they take flight, the thick bodies and black eyes of eagles, frightened off from where they have been beak-deep in the bloody innards of roadkill. When she drops her head to watch them in the side mirror, she can see them wheel around and alight again to feast.

Nick drives until dinnertime, where they have the choice between three types of burgers and sweating chips at a roadhouse and she says yes to all of it because, god, she wants it too, the sugar salt fizz of it all. To keep her awake. To keep on driving.

'You right to keep going?' he asks and she says yes, and makes the kids get into pyjamas and brush their teeth in the toilets before they do the next stint. Because she can keep some little bit of normal, she can do that.

'Are we gonna drive all night?' Sam asks as they walk into the hot night air.

'Maybe, maybe we will, it's our secret mission, remember?' And he tucks his hand into hers.

∿

Headlights on bitumen, the white lines. The ragged vibration when she lets the car slip too far to the edge. Because night is hard. The weight of her eyelids. Her neck jerks and she wasn't asleep, she'd never, but she knows that this is the kind of tired that won't be fixed by another bit of chewy, by opening her eyes wider. It was always Ben who did the night driving, the long stints of it. Ben to keep them safe. Ben to get them there, get them home.

She pulls into a truck stop to piss and wakes Nick.

'I can't go any further. Can we stop?'

He blinks, stretches. 'Nah, I'm good.'

∽

She tucks her jumper in under her neck, rests her forehead against the cool glass, adjusts the seat, back then up again, remembering Sam's little legs behind her.

'You good?' she asks, checking his profile in the low lights of the dash.

'Mmh hmm,' he murmurs. 'Mind if I have music?'

She shakes her head, closes her eyes. She can't place the song, guitar, a woman's voice, but it's nice.

'You gonna tell me any more?' Nick asks.

She waits, keeps her head against the window.

'About what you're doing.'

'It's complicated.'

'Yeah. I get that.'

The slumbering darkness outside, the stars. She wonders what they look like from up there. A tiny cocoon of light, barrelling along in the dark. The boy from the beach, from her past, she would tell him everything. Wants to feel the lightness of passing it on. But something tugs at her. Heidi's voice, maybe. The danger of nostalgia. The world has changed. We have changed. You can't go back.

'You're gonna at least have to tell me which island we're headed to, and what the story's gonna be if you have no ID on you.'

She stays quiet.

'I don't care what your deal is, but I do care about my boat, and I'm not really into the idea of an Indo prison.' He shakes his head.

'Yeah. Nah. Neither am I.'

He nods. 'Your husband. He's there?'

'Working on the Golden Arc project.'

'He in trouble?'

'Something like that.'

'And you reckon you turning up there . . . that's gonna be, what? Useful?'

Will it be useful? The same pit of doubt swims and simmers inside her. Maybe he's right – what good is she going to do, turning up there with the kids?

'Well, I can't stay here.' An edge of defensiveness in her voice. 'And he's there – or he was – and so it makes sense.' She looks away. 'It did make sense.'

'Just want to make sure we're on the same page.'

'Okay.' She looks at him. 'So are we on the same page now?'

'Yep.' He nods, briefly returning the look. 'Yep, I reckon we are.'

They drive on.

∽

The ache in her neck wakes her. They are stopped. She looks around. Still dark. Nick has the driver's seat all the way back, his head turned from her, snoring quietly. She twists around, kids both asleep, blankets tucked around them, they've got pillows at least to prop against. A patch of white, dried dribble on Essie's chin. She'll hate that when she wakes up.

She stretches her neck back, to the side. She has to move.

Outside, it's cooler than she'd expected. A half moon and scats of blue cloud moving quick, swathes of stars revealed in between. They're in a truck stop. The big bodies of road trains lined up. She can see a toilet lit up a hundred metres away. She looks back at the kids sleeping in the car. Squats down where she is, pulls down her jeans and pisses next to the tyre. It's loud in the quiet but she can't stop now.

She tries to close the door quietly when she gets back in, but she hears Nick shift.

'You okay?' he says.

'Yep. You?'

'Just needed a break.'

'Where are we?'

'Outside Winton. What time is it?' He clicks the ignition and the dash lights up. Four ten.

'I can drive,' she says.

～

She has never watched the sunrise from the driver's seat before. They are all still asleep. In the night they have travelled so far and she feels as though morning is breaking in a dreamscape. The sky is underbellied with cloud and the sun blushes deep red against the dark far off in the east. Slowly it begins to glow, pink then amber then a fiery golden light that surely cannot be real. This new jewelled light of dawn reveals a space so big she cannot comprehend it. God, the sky, the sky! She resists the urge to touch Nick's shoulder, to whisper in awe, *Look at that!*

The warm orange of the earth begins to glow. She shakes her head at the colours. She hasn't been up here, in this part of the country, but she knows what it is. They are crossing the northern arc of the Tasman line. Or someone's delineation of it anyway, one of the great many lines in her profession that are unclear. Beneath her feet, the tyres, the bitumen and down further, ancient earth meets less ancient earth, a continent built from west to east, each block and plate abutting the next, fusing, subducting, mountain-making. The deep, deep time of it had always been comforting to her. The element, perhaps, that attracted her to geology in the first place: something old, slow. Trying to get her head around the rate of continental drift – both infinitesimal and monumental. It had calmed her anxiety to speak in epochs. There was something quietly immovable about those in earth sciences, their dry fingers loosening over rocks, the steady accumulation of data, cautious findings, bedrock beliefs.

∽

She remembers picking up the stone and handing it to the professor on one of her first field trips at uni. 'Like this?'

'Ah,' says the wild-haired woman, 'close, close, but this is not a tektonite. So rare, it would be incredibly lucky to find one.'

Mim returns the black stone to the dry riverbed, hears the clunking reverberations of the other first years as they wander, search, sketch.

The gorge is deep. In the middle of the day, it is flooded with sunlight, but within an hour or two it will grow cold in the shadow, the damp of the stone rising up, the subterranean smell of it.

The professor puts her old hand against the rock, identifying each layer: limestone, basalt, karst, sediment upon sediment, a timeline in rock.

'See here,' she implores them, 'the water, and here, the wind, tree, charcoal, shell, crustacean – the history of the earth writ upon itself. It makes sense now?'

The past is a timeline compressed neatly in order. Mim feels the shudder of understanding move through her as her teacher asks them to imagine what this rock might have witnessed over the millennia it has been forming, the calving of continents, the retreat of oceans, the creatures that may have passed it by. It calms Mim, makes the unknown that trembles and undulates in her solid.

What she won't remember is that he was also there. When they realise they will laugh about it. Ben will make out he noticed her, she will enjoy the fact that she was more taken by the rocks than by him.

But she will think about it often. A girl on that same field trip eleven years later will find a tektonite. Mim will remember back to that day in the gorge and the unfolding of time within her, the feeling that she could lay herself down and become part of the rock. The deep quiet that settled. At the same time as a crack had appeared, fine and granular, the beginning of something; the two planes of herself, past and future, ready to collide.

〜

She had thought herself immovable. She and Ben both, before Essie. The naivety of it stings now, but they had spoken of a shared workload, both working, both in projects they were passionate about, both taking time off to parent.

But then.

The cataclysmic arrival that had begun moderately enough, but finally left Mim a fragmented version of herself. She couldn't even remember all the pieces to gather back up to remake herself. There was Before Essie. And After.

And now this.

She concentrates on the colours. The astonishing expanse of sky striped with apricot, mauve and pale blue. The red earth on either side of the black strap of highway. Behind her the kids murmur and, ever so slightly, she accelerates into the north.

〜

The fields of black solar panels begin a couple of hours before they arrive in Isa. A town with a boom and bust past. Got big with extraction, and nearly died as the government, finally and against all odds, decommissioned mines right across the country. Isa would have had its final death throes, except for a mad Queenslander with pockets as deep as his chest was wide, who decided to make it the hub of the solar industry and sink his dollars and political clout into ironing out the legislative issues, the synching, all the problems people threw at it to make the solution so much harder than it needed to be. There is something reverent in it. The way the acres of black panels turn to face the sun in worship. The glare. The way, out here, you can see the sunlight streaming in, turning itself into capital.

It is late afternoon when they arrive. She feels her body cramping into the seat. Nick is still asleep, head lolled to one side, shirt wedged under his chin. Essie, awake in the back, notices the turn.

'Are we stopping?'

'You want to?'

'Can we go to a caravan park?'

She glances at the rear-vision mirror. Essie tucks her chin into her neck and smiles. Maybe they don't need to go further today.

They choose the one with the pool. And pay for the privilege. But it's worth it. The water is the blue of childhood. The clap of skin hitting water, puddles of sun on the surface, the pleasant stink of chlorine. Sam runs at it, ignoring her calls to slow down.

'Can he swim?' Nick asks, coming up next to her.

She dumps the towels from the cabin on the end of the wooden bench. 'Yep. He's good.'

Mim fiddles with the straps of her singlet. Black undies and top will have to do.

'Coming, Mum?' Sam calls.

She pulls off her shorts. Feels flabby, too many days on the road, shit food, her legs all white. God, how badly does she need a shave? She hurries to follow Essie up to the deep end, trying to stand up straight, her hands behind her, covering the black cotton of her undies.

Essie drops her towel, scurries towards the edge and dives straight in, clean and long. Under the surface her daughter's body distorts, grows longer again. Mim is struck by the thought that her daughter will one day be taller than her. She clamps her toes around the chipped blue tiles of the edge. Before she dives, she looks ahead, sees Nick watching her, and she concentrates a little harder, lengthening her body as she arcs into the water.

'Stupid,' she mouths to herself underwater before she surfaces, shaking the image of his face turned towards her. She kicks out hard towards the edge.

12

The main drag is wide and bisected by stunted trees in the strange peachy light of dusk. Cameras hang bulbous like oddly uniform fruit bats from the streetlights. She dips her chin. She'd considered trying to find some fresh food. Her mouth feels coated with salt and fat from roadhouse bain-maries. But the cash will last longer if she resists the lure of expensive apples and the green crunch of lettuce. There is the flashing sign of a Krave Burger up ahead and she is already feeling the billowing absence on either side of her where the kids would be if she hadn't told them to wait in the cabin and watch the screens.

She feels herself stretching now that she is out of the car, as if the water today has unspooled something in her that has been twisting and tightening since they left the farm. Since before that. She feels purposeful. That she is going towards something, towards Ben. Not just reacting, hiding, running.

A boy with a singlet and a beanie overtakes her with his skateboard and she flinches at the sound. There are a few cars cruising down the main street, headlights beginning to glow in the darkening evening. Families pulling in, kids in the back, faces lit by screens while a parent jumps out to pick up something for tea. She wonders when they will be this again. When she will be back to those hours post school, never enough and always too long, when the kids begin to fight and whinge and the bags bulge with all the homework and the special family activities and the requests to volunteer and the bullshit, the endless bullshit of it. Because right now, despite the finger press of fear around her guts, despite the fact that she has left things broken and dangerous for people that she loves, and despite everything unknown that stands before her, she is okay with being here. In the heated dark of this town, striding out towards the next thing – to feed the kids, to get to the next place, and the next.

Across the road, a police car slows as it trawls the lit part of the street. Without moving her head she watches as it passes opposite her, slowing to turn. They are not the Department, but they might as well be. Not as corrupt anymore, sure, but also just pawns of the state. At least their methods still seem old school, their standover tactics more Keystone cop and less Stasi. She ducks through the greasy plastic strips of the shop and feels a tightening in her back as she hides from view.

When she steps back out onto the street ten minutes later, paper bags of chips and faux burgers in her hands, she sees the cop car hasn't moved on, but is idling right outside the shop. A female officer is leaning up against the passenger door, and the other bloke, an older guy, bald and solid with his thumbs resting low on his hips, pelvis pitched forward, stands with his legs spread, blocking the path.

'Feeding the family?' the male cop says, nodding at the bags in Mim's hand. The woman's face is pleasant, but the man's is blank.

Mim smiles quickly, nods, keeps moving.

'In town for long?' he says, a little louder this time.

She slows, looks back over her shoulder, smiles again. 'Just overnight.' She lifts the bags. 'I'd better get this . . .'

'Back to the kids?'

The woman pushes herself slowly away from where she leans against the car and angles her body towards Mim. The man continues to stand side-on, arms folded, a throwaway line, perhaps, just keeping his eyes on his town. Or something else.

Mim nods. 'Hungry little buggers,' she says and waves her hand, tries to leave.

'How many you got?'

She feels sweat beading behind her knees, under her breasts. She stops and turns around to face them directly.

'Two,' she says and drops the smile now.

The woman speaks next. 'You travelling alone with them?'

A ute revs as it goes past, music blaring. The cops don't turn around. The back of Mim's neck ripples with tension.

'No. With my bloke,' she says and tries the pleasant face again. 'Sorry, I should . . .'

'Course.' The man pulls his cheeks back in an attempt at a smile. 'Can't keep them waiting. Where you staying?'

'Just the . . .' Mim waves towards the end of the street. 'The caravan park around the corner there, not sure of the . . .'

'That'll be the Golden Inn,' the woman says.

'Think so, yeah.'

Mim turns to go. She sees the man pull a device from his belt. 'Before you go – just conducting spot ID checks. Won't take a minute.'

Her spine locks. Sweat begins to thread down her calves.

'Sorry?'

He fingers something on the screen, doesn't raise his eyes. 'Week-long blitz across the whole state. You'd be surprised at how many people are attempting to evade fines, responsibilities.'

Mim clamps her hand around the cardboard handles of the bag, lets her nails dig into her palm, the raised scar tissue there. 'I'm not chipped,' she says.

The man lifts his head from the screen.

'And why's that?'

'Medical.'

'You got your card?'

She laughs, knows the sound is strangled. 'Not on me, with the travel, you know, everything's a bit of a mess.'

The woman's voice is curt. 'Offence to travel without a card if you're unchipped. Automatic data log to the Department.'

'Oh, it's back at the room. With all the stuff, just didn't think . . .'

The man holds her eyes. A colony of bats squeal above them as they come in to land on an old palm.

'Why don't we give you a lift back, then? We'll make sure everything's in order.'

'If it's not too much trouble.' She smiles. Sweats.

The radio on the woman's belt crackles. She pulls it out, turns away and speaks into it. Mim cannot hear what she is saying. The man's eyes slide away from Mim's. She stands straighter, drops her free hand to the back pocket of her jeans, feels for the phone there. What message could she send to Nick? It's getting darker. Could she run? She feels her pulse quicken at the thought. How quick could she go? To where? Through someone's garden? Jump a fence. They're coppers, they'd outrun her for sure. But what happens if they take her back to the cabin? When the kids open the door. When they realise there is no card.

'Dave. DV in Aspen Street. Got to go.' The woman flicks her head, moves around to the front of the car.

The man's face is part grimace, part smile. His eyes are dark shadows in the pissy glow from the streetlight.

'Looks like we can't give you that lift.'

'Thanks anyway.'

'Might drop by later to see that card. Golden Inn, you said?'

'That's it. Heading off early, you'll excuse us if the lights are out.' She tries for a laugh.

'Best make sure you don't head off before we see that card.' He holds the device out. 'Name?'

Quick snort of breath through her nose.

'Leah.'

He scrawls, cocks his head.

'Leah . . . ?'

'Mason. Leah Mason.'

The sound of the car starting.

'We'll see you, Leah.'

Mim nods, raises her hand as he steps back and turns to get into the passenger seat. She walks quickly. Turns the corner, gulps for air. Runs.

～

She locks the door behind her. Nick is sitting in the armchair next to the bed, the kids sprawled out there. They look up from the screen.

'Took long enough!' Sam says. 'We're starving!'

It takes her a moment to speak. 'We have to leave.'

Essie sits up. 'What?'

'Now.' And she finds the propulsion she needs. Dropping the bags of food, moving towards the packs spilling clothes and tooth-brushes on the small desk.

'What's happening?' Tension in Nick's voice.

'Mum?'

'We need to leave. We need to go now.' She stuffs the packs. Turns when she realises no one else is moving. 'NOW! The cops are coming to check our IDs.'

Sam's voice, almost squeaking with panic, 'But where will we go?'

'It's okay, Sam, we'll just keep going tonight.'

Essie stands up. 'I'm over the car!'

'Not now, Essie. Get your stuff!'

'Hang on, can you calm down, you sure you're not overreacting?' Nick has risen from the chair but isn't moving yet.

She pulls her wallet from the bag, grabs cash. Puts it on the desk and sticks the remote on top. 'Yes, I'm fucking sure,' she hisses. 'Kids, move.'

Sam's face is changing colour. 'I'm not going. I'm not. I'm not!' Teeth gritted. Arms crossed. His little face fierce, unmoving.

'Mum,' Essie's tone a warning note. She knows what happens when he goes. There'll be no coming back from it. Full meltdown.

'Get the stuff in the car,' she says, hoping one of Nick or Essie will take the cue. She kneels with Sam.

'I won't,' he is saying, screwing his eyes shut. 'I'm not getting back in the car. I have a sore tummy.' He is starting to cry, jagged breaths.

Mim puts her hands on his shoulders, gentle, gentle like she might a horse who has spooked. It can go either way. 'Sammy, Sammy, hey, hey,' crooning, song-like. 'It's okay, Sammy, not for too much longer, my darling, you've done so well, hey, hey.'

It doesn't work.

He shakes his head. Yells louder now to block out the sound of his mother calming him. 'NONONONONONONONO!'

'What the fuck?' she hears Nick say as he comes back through the open door.

Now Mim must hold her son. She lunges forward, hugs him tight around his torso, folding his arms in so they can't flail and hit.

'Nick, get the car going.'

'Where are the keys?' Nick flounders. 'Can't you shut him up!'

'Don't say that to him!' Essie says, quick and loud.

Calm this down, Mim thinks. *Get him out, now*. 'It's okay, Ess, he doesn't get it.'

'What the fuck don't I get?'

Essie pales at the sudden fury in him.

Mim holds Sam, rocking him, running her hand over his face, partly to calm him, partly to mute his cries. 'Just get in the car, please. Please. They could be here any second.'

Nick shakes his head hard, glares at her.

'Sammy, Sam, mate, I'm gonna put you in the car now, okay, we gotta go, Sam, we gotta see Dad.' She starts to lift him and he arches his back, the back of his head knocking hard against her chin.

'Fuck!' She squeezes her eyes shut. Tears pool. She stops herself pressing her hands into his flesh in retaliation.

Essie's voice. 'Sammy, look what I've gotcha.' Mim opens her eyes. Essie is holding the red ninja mask. 'You gotta be Ninja Boy to get us out of here, the baddies are coming.'

Sam is quiet, Mim feels him still.

A little voice. 'Ninja Boy isn't even real.'

Essie grins. 'He is tonight. And I'm your sidekick. And Mum. And him.' She juts her chin to the side and Mim sees Nick hanging back in the doorway. Essie holds out her hand. 'Come on. You gotta show us which way to go.'

And Sam puts his hand up and takes his sister's.

Mim closes her eyes again in relief. Holds her chin. Slams the door shut behind them all.

⌒

Not until the lights of the town are out of sight in the rear-view mirror does she roll her shoulders back, let her breath hit the floor of her lungs.

Nick is restless in the passenger seat. Pissed to be back in the car. Something about the way he is holding his shoulders reminds her of the boy she used to know.

'That was pretty full on,' he says quietly.

She bites. 'Be careful what you say around my kids.'

He is taken aback. Rolls his eyes a bit. The teenager again.

'Sorry,' he says in a voice that says he is not. That she is over-reacting. That this is her shit, not his.

'I want Dad.' Essie's voice is blunt.

Headlights, straight white line. All she can do is nod to her daughter to show she hears her, to show her she understands.

13

It is another eighteen hours before they will hit the outskirts of Darwin. The adrenaline keeps her awake but does not quell her temper. They are all tired. Shitty. Nick makes them turn the air con off overnight and by the time they stop for breakfast and fuel they are sweating and restless and foul. She makes them wait in the shade of a lone tree near the edge of the car park. Hands over a ridiculous amount of her stash for the fuel. Averts her eyes from the panel of screens behind the attendant.

'How long to go?' asks Sammy, and she will not answer. She does not want to know.

Nick eases, softens. Angles the air-conditioning vents in her direction. Perhaps this is his apology. Why the fuck are words so hard for men?

∽

The road. The road. The endless fucking road.

Nick sits on one thirty. It had seemed hellishly fast when she first got behind the wheel and he urged her to give the accelerator a nudge. Now it feels sluggish. She likes it when he overtakes, though she hasn't attempted a couple of road trains in a row, which he does with ease. Up here, when they pass oncoming traffic, he lifts his forefinger from the wheel in acknowledgement. The gesture is so nonchalant, so at ease, she finds it incredibly sexy. Her neck burns and she turns away, closes her eyes, pretends to doze.

～

Lush green regrowth on the squat burnt trees that line the highway. They've seen fire along the way, great brown smudges of smoke in the sky, the Parks utes lined up, the flicker of orange flame. The kids even take their eyes off the screens.

'What are they doing that for?' Sam asks.

'Make it grow,' says Nick. 'Manage it.'

'What, by burning it down?'

Essie pipes up. 'Mosaic burning. It's how it's been done for thousands of years.'

Nick and Mim exchange a glance. A smile. It's the first time Essie's spoken in hours. Essie sees them.

'We learnt about it at school,' she says defensively.

'S'good you're learning about that stuff,' Nick says. 'I never did till I was a grown-up.'

Essie hmmphs and mutters under her breath. 'Maybe your generation should've asked more questions.'

'What was that, Ess?' Mim asks in amusement, but Essie has already disappeared into her screen, and she lets it go.

～

'Nearly there now,' Nick says, under his breath as plains of estates appear on the horizon.

'That BestLife?' she asks quietly.

He nods. 'Yeah, some of it. Camps too. The dongas are for the climate refugees.'

'Yeah, right,' she says as they get closer. 'God, I didn't realise how many.' She can spot movement, clusters of people grouped under shade sails punctuating the sea of beige rectangles.

'Just the offshore ones. The ones displaced from the flooded suburbs of Darwin, the locals, they've shifted them out on the east side. Nicer there.'

'Us and them,' she says, shaking her head.

'Always.' There is a jut to his chin and she is wary of what it means.

She shrugs, lets the potential disagreement slide away. 'I was thinking the kids and I'll stay at a caravan park for a couple of nights. You know a good one?'

'Nah,' he says, 'just stay at mine.'

'Just thought you might want a break.' She glances at the kids in the rear-vision mirror, says quieter, 'From the kids, and everything.'

He shrugs. 'Easier at mine.'

'I'll give you the cash when we get there.'

He nods. 'That'd be good.'

She wonders what kind of transaction this is. What hidden costs there might be ahead.

⁓

She is surprised by the pink flush of bougainvillea tumbling down the drainpipe on his porch. It seems showy against the heavy brick square of the house. The fence is wire at the front, tall tin to block out the neighbours at the side. It doesn't feel like the kind of street that would have a Christmas party. A pile of rubbish – old fan, couch spewing its fluffy insides, a smashed screen – is heaped on the nature strip next door.

She stretches, unfurling, bones cracking, muscles remembering the act of standing. 'Grab your backpacks and your pillows at least,' she stops the kids as they try to race each other to the front door.

She ferries bags over the pebble path, stuccoed with weeds, to the concrete porch. The kids follow Nick inside, but she hovers, busying herself, uncertain about entering a space that is so his. She tries to imagine what Ben would do. Awkward, polite but blustery, he can't pick up on other people's stuff. A man of science, not intuition.

Nick and the kids don't re-emerge. She loops bags over her wrists and heads inside. It's darker, stuffy with hot damp, a hint of mould.

'On!' she hears. 'Turn on, you fucking prick.' She hears the kids giggling, then Nick's voice again. 'Air con on!'

It kicks in, the whirr of it. The hall opens out to the kitchen, all white tiles, Formica, a shitty print of a beach at sunset on the wall.

'Network not working?' she says to Nick.

'Never fucking has, up here. Thank Christ. Still on the old system.'

There's a whoop as Sam calls out from the back, 'Mum! Can we go in?'

A pool glitters, an unreal blue. They're still allowed them up here, treated sea water. Special legislation for anyone above 25 degrees of latitude. Extreme heat policy. The kids will be in heaven.

She slides the door, dumps their gear in the spare room that Nick points to. Everything else will wait till tomorrow.

∽

Before bed, she changes the dressings on their hands. They look good. Skin puckering, clean.

'Leave the bandages off tonight, huh,' she says, running her finger along the scars on both their hands. 'Let them breathe.'

'This is a good bed,' says Sam, closing his eyes, smiling.

'You sleep well, my loves, I'll be in soon,' she says and closes the door. Pulls it tight, so that it is four walls and a roof and a floor and a closed door, and her right outside. She wonders if there will be a time soon when she will feel she can let them be away from her. If she ever will again.

Nick is sliding open the patio door as she comes back into the kitchen.

He pulls out a joint, pre-rolled. 'You want?'

Him and Helen, both, cheeky little black marketeers. 'Nah. I'm good. You go.'

He nods and slips out through the sliding door. She sits there for a moment, feeling stupid, then she grabs a glass of water and slides the door across.

He looks back over his shoulder. 'Change your mind?'

'Kind of.'

He holds the joint back to her.

Skirting the table, she sits with him on the bench. The patio is thrown with an orange glow from the streetlight round the side. The air here swims with moisture, so it's warm and damp and the orange feels like it's part of it, some strange tropical atmospheric condition.

She takes the joint from him and for a second she wonders if she should. Remembers the swirling panic that used to engulf her, the terrible gap she would feel widening in her chest like she had just fallen outside of herself.

But she also remembers not thinking.

She takes a puff, draws it into her and feels fifteen again. The smoke scratches at her throat but she's determined not to cough. Holds it in, hands it back. Slight fumble as their fingers work out who's got it.

She exhales, the smoke orange-tinged against the night. Imagining the cells in her body buzzing, realigning, remembering her other self, her younger self, the bolshy brave of her.

'Did you like school?' he asks. A question that slips out of the night and doesn't feel out of place.

'Yeah, nah. Just like everyone, I s'pose.'

He offers her the joint again, but she shakes her head. One puff is all she needs, and it's given her permission to sit here, with him, in the night.

'What about you?' she asks.

'Sorry?'

'School?'

'Yeah, same. Just school.' He takes another drag. 'Probably enjoyed what I did out of school more.'

She nods, the particles of the air glowing brightly now.

'Being on the water, with Dad, before he left. You know.' He dips his head and grins. 'Summer was pretty good, hey?'

She smiles too. 'Yeah. Pretty good.'

'We gonna talk about it?'

'What? No!' She shakes her head, half smiles. 'We were kids.'

He nods, puts the joint out.

Later, in bed, she wonders what might have happened if she'd said yes.

~

The next day all she wants to do is leave the house. To get this thing moving, to career down the aisles of the supermarket loading supplies into the trolley, to be done, to be gone. But Nick reckons they should lie low. And he's right. After the scare in Isa. Her chest freezes in fear when she thinks what might have happened.

Nick heads to the shops alone, says they will go down to check the boat after lunch. Tells her, as if she needs reminding, probably best to stay there, to make herself at home.

The coffee pushes her past buzz to anxiety. She tells the kids to get out of the pool, to come inside and help her organise what to take on the boat, because she feels compelled to do something.

To get moving, to feel less like a sitting duck and more like she is actually making something happen.

'We'll do it later,' Essie says and dives under the water as Mim tries to argue.

'Sammy!' she calls, but he sticks his fingers in his ears and tucks his legs into his chest, bombs into the water from the brick edge.

Mim yanks the gate, slams it shut behind her so that the clank of the metal reverberates through the bones of her wrist. Hurts. She stands right at the edge of the pool.

'You two,' she yells, as their heads bob up, 'out NOW!'

Essie laughs and it gives Sam confidence. They dive under again.

She wants to jump in there and grab them hard and pull them out. See them dripping and sorry and compliant on the edge of the pool. Why can't they just *listen* to her? Don't they *understand* what she is dealing with?

'I'm counting down,' she yells quickly as they come up again. 'Five, four . . .' But they are gone, laughing and diving under again, so that she is all froth and indignation at the rippling surface of the pool, the bodies of her children made alien under the light and the water.

She nearly breaks the safety catch as she wrenches the gate open, storms across the crackling grass and inside, slamming the door behind her. She shouldn't leave them out there on their own, but see if *she fucking cares*. Little shits, not listening, making fun. She upends their bags on the bed, she'll treat them like children all right, she throws t-shirts and undies across the bed. Serves them right.

'Mum!' A shriek from outside and her legs don't even hesitate, already making deals with fate, *sorrysorrysorry* stuck in her throat as she races out, through the gate, sees them both out of the water and a long trickle of watery blood down Sam's shin, a small rupture of flesh at his knee.

'He got caught on the brick climbing out,' Essie says, glaring at her. 'You shouldn't have left us.'

Mim holds Sam's wet head against her chest. 'It's okay, it's okay, you're all right,' she says and it doesn't even hurt, her daughter's admonishment, because it is just the way it is, she will never get it right.

14

The sound of the marina is all clacking, tinkling, whistling. A background noise like a flock of birds used to make. She looks up at the plantation of masts and sails and ropes that stretch out into the bay.

'Don't know what condition she'll be in,' Nick says. 'Might have to give her a bit of a clean-up first.'

'Which one's yours?' Sam yells, swivelling back and forth on the spot as they wait for the gate to open.

Nick grins. 'Down the end, mate. You see if you can find her, called *Sandfly*.'

'He can't read yet.'

'Ess,' Mim warns, and Essie rolls her eyes.

'Starts with an S!' yells Sam. 'Like me! Why's it called *Sandfly*?'

'Boat was my dad's. He used to say it was like the mosquito quote – is it Gandhi's?'

'What's it got to do with a sandfly?' Sam asks.

'Something about not underestimating a mosquito – when he's in your room he'll keep you awake all night.'

Sam's face is screwed up in confusion.

'It's about small things still being powerful,' Mim says.

'Like the mouse and the lion,' Essie chimes in, smug.

Nick nods. 'Exactly. Can't even see a sandfly, little pricks, they're that small. Sure as hell know when you've been bitten though.'

'What's that?' Essie says, pointing down into the green water, the faint sheen of oil reflecting on the surface and making it hard to see the shadowy shapes beneath.

'Old yacht club.' Nick laughs ruefully.

Mim peers over, and yes, she can see now, a roof, the tops of poles, it makes no sense to read it like this, a bird's eye view underwater.

'The tides have always been massive up here,' Nick says. 'So the rise and the surges really caused some shit.'

'But how come they left it there?'

He shrugs, keeps walking down the pier. 'Why bother trying to take it out? Easier with the floating marinas, the lock system – just float the whole thing higher every year.'

It chills her a little, this nonchalant adaptation. The stereotypes are true, the northerners' sneering disregard for the southern city-dwellers with their big ideology and limited experience.

'Hi!' A small smiling face appears over the edge of the yacht to the left of them.

Sam waves. 'Hi!' he calls, then turns to Mim. 'Look, Mum! Another kid!'

Mim resists the urge to pull him back as he skips towards the edge where he can see the other kid up close.

'Is that your boat?' Sam calls up.

'Yep!' says the child, standing taller now. Maybe the same age as Sam, perhaps a little older, wild hair and the pulled neck of a faded t-shirt that has been well-loved.

'Where are you going?' Sam asks.

'We live here!' the child replies.

'In Darwin?'

Laughter. 'On the boat.'

Sam's voice is awestruck. 'You *live* on a boat?'

'Yep.' The child's face is round and wide with pride. 'Where do *you* live?'

Mim rushes forward, interrupting Sam's answer and apologising that they have to go. 'Say goodbye, Sam,' she says and steers him away down the jetty.

'But, Mum, I wanted to see the boat.'

'I found it!' Essie yells and turns back to them, waving.

Sam races ahead to look and they have got away with their clumsy evasion, again.

The kids are both standing reverently in front of a yacht when she catches up. The old-fashioned blue font of the name on the side of the boat is a little scratched. Thick ropes stretch from the upright rails to heavy fasteners bolted to the dock.

Nick is light as he moves past them, and jumps over the thin wire railing onto the deck.

She hears him murmur under his breath, as his hand goes out to touch ropes, the yellowing fibreglass of the cabin.

'Come on,' he says.

'How?' she calls back, an edge of panic in her voice.

Essie is shuffling forward along the edge of the dock. There's still at least half a metre of space above the water. They'll have to leap over to get on. She grabs Sam's shoulder as he rushes past her. 'Careful,' she warns.

'Oww, you're hurting.'

She doesn't let go.

Nick leans over and reaches out an arm to Essie.

'Shoes off first. No shoes on deck.'

'Isn't it slippery?' Essie asks.

'Your bare feet are the best way to hang on.'

They all take off their shoes, line them up along the jetty.

'Get yourself up on the outside,' he says to Essie, 'then put your leg over and in.'

Mim watches her daughter frown in concentration, stretch her skinny leg up, grip Nick's wrist as he pulls backwards, her weight shifting from the dock to the boat.

'I'll pass you up,' she says to Sam.

'I want to do it like Essie!'

'Your legs aren't long enough, you won't be able to reach.'

'I can!'

She feels her jaw start to tighten. It's all the water, making her feel on edge. She's not sure if she's going to be able to do this.

She keeps her grip on Sam as they move to the spot where Essie went up.

'Let your mum give you a hand, mate, once I've got you on the edge you can do it the same.'

Sam wriggles as she grips him under the arms.

'You ready?' she asks, the panic again betraying her.

'All good,' Nick says, arms out.

She lifts Sam, not looking at the water, just at the hands reaching out for him, and it's done in a second, over and in, Sam already taking off, racing around and exploring the deck as she tries to clamber on, taking Nick's hand when she realises she can't manage the manoeuvre on her own.

'Should the kids have life jackets on?'

She sees him trying to swallow a laugh.

'Reckon they're all right while we're berthed, they can swim, eh?'

'Can you go over the rules with them then?' She bites off her words at the end.

He squints at her, nodding his head slowly. 'Yep, yep, I can, if that's what you'd like.'

'Kids! Come here and sit.'

'Tour first, eh? Down the hatch.'

'Down the hatch, that's funny,' says Sam as they follow Nick through the opening, and Mim watches their heads disappear.

'So, this is the galley,' he's saying as she squishes in behind them. 'Cooking, sleeping, eating – and here,' he reaches past Essie and swings open a narrow door, 'this is the head.'

She cranes her neck to look inside at the tiny toilet. The space is smaller than an aeroplane bathroom.

'Why's it called a head?'

'No idea,' says Nick. 'So, you have to hold on for a crap till we're outside the marina.'

'Why? Wait,' Essie's voice drops in astonishment, 'does it just go straight into the water?'

'Where else would it go?'

'Gross,' says Essie.

'Awesome,' says Sam.

Mim wonders if she can delay shitting for a week.

〜

The setting sun throbs orange along the horizon by the time Nick is done and he starts to lock things up.

'I want to go now, why can't we go now?' Sam is whinging to Nick.

'Just got to wait till this spare starter arrives, mate. Another day or two and we'll be right.'

Essie sees the Border Force guards first, notices the dogs, calls back 'Mum' in a voice that is unsure.

It is two men in black uniform, weapons at their sides, two dogs in harnesses, coming towards them.

'Nick,' she says quietly down the stairs. 'Border police.'

He sticks his head up, a crease between his eyebrows.

'Evening,' calls one of the officers as the dogs both obediently sit at the edge of the pontoon.

'I've got this,' Nick says quietly to Mim as he steps forward to greet the men. 'How you going?'

'Not bad. You heading off somewhere?'

'Just cleaning her up for a daytrip.'

'Been a while since you've been out?'

'Yeah.' Nick keeps his body relaxed but Mim notes the tension in his neck.

'Increased activity's been noted.'

Nick laughs once. 'Yeah, we keep an eye out for each other down here.'

Mim looks at the other boats, wonders how many eyes have been watching them all day.

'You're not in the system.'

'Nah!' Nick laughs. 'Still old school. My dad's boat. Haven't made the switch yet.'

'You got the papers there?'

Nick nods slowly. 'No worries, give us a tic and I'll get them.' As he turns he looks at Mim, smiles quickly, touches one finger to her wrist as he goes past.

'You kids like sailing?'

Essie sweeps her eyes to Mim, Sam goes to the edge of the boat. 'It's our first time,' he says.

'Is that so?' says one of the officers, glancing at his partner.

Mim moves forward. 'We're just visiting. Nick was determined to get us out on the water.' Her mouth is dry. She wills the kids to keep their bandaged hands turned down.

'Welcome to Darwin. Where you from?'

'Southerners,' Nick says, coming up from behind her and jumping on to the rail before he steps down to the pontoon. 'Been telling them to head north to visit for years. I've told 'em lots come and never leave!' He laughs and hands a plastic folder of papers to the officers.

'So where're you off to then?' asks the officer holding the dogs.

Nick crosses his arms. 'Got a few plans, harbour cruise for sunset, maybe out round the point in the morning for a fish, haven't decided yet.'

The officer nods. 'You know you still got to log your trips, yes? Might want to think about getting the network on board sooner rather than later.'

'Even local trips?'

'All of them.'

'Righto. When did that come in? Like you said, it's been a while.'

'Since July. Simple check-in with the harbourmaster portal, should be able to do it via your nav. Be easier with OMNI, though. We can start that set-up for you now, if you'd like.'

Nick puts his hand out for the papers. 'Nah, all good, I'll sort it out. Makes sense, good to know who's where, I suppose.'

'We've been monitoring a number of boats doing some unregistered island hopping, doing pick-ups. You ever seen any of that while you've been out?'

'Nah, mate, keep well away from that.'

'Well, keep your eyes out. Reward system in place for those who help out. When you get online you can log any unusual activity. Worth your while.'

'Eagle-eyed kids on board, we'll keep a lookout,' Nick says. 'If we're sorted,' he raises a hand apologetically, 'need to get these kids back home for dinner.'

'Of course,' says the officer, 'have a good day out on the water tomorrow. Keep your eyes peeled.'

Nick leaps back on board as the officers head back up the pontoon, the dogs slightly ahead, sniffing the ground, eerily obedient.

~

Later, when the kids are asleep, she asks him for another joint. She needs to slow down her thoughts, the panic of the Border Force guards and their questions.

'Wish we could just go now. Those guards spooked me.'

'They get off on doing that. We'll be out of here in a couple of days.'

She thinks about what that means. What leaving means.

'Can I use your phone?'

He squints at her in the dim light.

'There's this website. A journalist. It's not traceable. I just want to leave a message.'

He shakes his head. 'It's always traceable.'

'Not this. Encrypted. For whistleblowers.'

'You reckon that shit works?'

She laughs, shakes her head, the dope has made her sweet and reckless. 'What are you? A conspiracy theorist?'

He shrugs. 'If you trust it,' he says, and hands over the device.

She finds the site quickly, before she can think about it too much. Selects Raquel's name from a dropdown list. Hesitates, then moves her fingers fast.

Going to find him. Will be in touch. She presses the green button. Done.

The relief in telling someone else. She hands his phone back, pulls her own from her pocket.

'What you doing now?' he asks.

'Got to call Mum.'

'Nah. Leave it, yeah?' He shakes his head. 'Wait till we're out of here. Not worth the risk.'

Fuck you, she thinks. *You and my arsehole brother.* 'I need to check.'

He looks at her. Seems to be on the edge of saying something, his lip twitches. 'Be quick,' he says and goes inside.

In the strange orange darkness she calls.

'It's me,' she says as soon as she hears it pick up.

'Oh! Mim!'

'I've got to be quick –'

Her mother's voice is shrill as she cuts in. 'Your friend.' Then there is silence.

'There was a fire.'

Mim cannot breathe. The light is pulsing around her, in her eyes, her mouth, it is stealing the oxygen. 'What fire? Where?'

'Heidi's house.'

'Is she okay?'

There is a gulf of silence. 'No, Mim, no, she's not okay. Burns to eighty per cent of her body. They've put her in a coma.'

The phone is ripped from her ear. Nick. 'Too long,' he says as he hangs up, 'they'll fucking track that. Hey, you okay?'

She looks at him, tries to focus.

'Mim? What is it?'

'There was a fire.'

'A fire? Where?' He puts his arm out to steady her. The pulse, the pulse in her brain, she can't think.

'Hey, Mim.' He shakes her arm. 'What happened?'

'Heidi. She's in a coma.'

'What? Who?' His face is close, wrinkled with concern. The night, the words, her mum's voice – why can't she make it fit together, make it make sense?

'She did this,' she says, holding up her hand. 'She cut our chips out of us.'

Nick's face is confused. 'But, what happened?'

'A house fire.' And now she is clear, sharp as a tack. 'They must have done it.'

His arm on her, gentle against her sudden rage.

She pulls away from him. 'FUCK!' She yells it, the sound ripping up into the trees above them. A dog barks next door.

'Keep it down,' Nick says quickly. 'Come inside.'

He leads her through the door, sits her on the couch. He sits beside her but seems so far away. And he is not Ben. She needs Ben. What the fuck has happened? What has she done? What have they done to Heidi?

She feels it gurgling and frothing up from her guts, tries to move then vomits on to the floor next to Nick.

'Jesus,' he says, jumping back.

She is racked by it. Again and again she brings up the weak yellow bile, until she rests her head on her knees. Can only lift her hand to wipe her mouth, taste the acrid sour of it. Then a noise comes from somewhere inside her. A howl.

She is aware of Nick moving, cleaning near her feet.

'This is my fault.'

Nick looks up to meet her eyes.

'It's not.'

'Yes.' She stands up. 'Yes, it is. If I hadn't asked her, they would never have . . .'

He stands up, blocks her pacing. 'Hey.' He puts his hands up to absorb the impact of her walking into him. 'You don't know that's what happened. If it's the Department, they would have taken her in, right? She'd be in an estate, worst case. Maybe it was an accident.' He tries to pat her arm and she shakes him free.

'No, you're wrong.' It's all so obvious. 'This is exactly what they do. This is sending me a message.' She paces again. 'Can't you see? Can't you see how they do it?'

He holds her. Tight. Hugs her close and slows his breathing until hers slows too. 'You've had a shock,' he says quietly. 'You need to sleep. We'll work it out in the morning, huh?' She allows herself to be led. To take the half valium he gives her. To be put to bed next to the kids. She allows it, but she knows that come the morning she must find a way to get back to Heidi, to fix what she has done.

⌒

She wakes later, snagged in a knot of sheets. Drenched in sweat. Her hands stretch out to feel the kids, pat around until she touches flesh, slows her heartbeat until she can hear their quiet breathing in the bed next to her. She dreamed she was under a boat. Floating in the cabin – water, cups, pots and life jackets suspended in the green murkiness around her. And she could see where she needed to swim to get herself out. Knew, in that deep knowing of dreams, that if she just swam forward, pushed through and kicked up she would break the surface, there would be air, she would survive.

Except, except. Somewhere, just beyond her vision, down there in all the little rooms, bunkered cupboards, doors flown open, water now in every place, filling up every space, there are the children.

She opens her eyes wide against the dark of the room, breathes in tandem with her sleeping children, here with her. On land, breathing air, not water. Safe.

This dark press on her heart, on the inside of her, a growl that is building in the back of her throat. She is mad for taking them out to sea. Mad to stay. She pushes herself up and out of bed. Remembers Heidi coming to her in the dark. *You have to go*, she had said, *you have to go now.*

Nick's room is dark, fuggy with the smell of him when she opens the door.

'We have to go,' she says.

He rolls in the bed, brings his arm up to cover his face where the light from the hallway is crossing him. The dark thatch of hair in his armpit.

'We have to go in the morning.'

He groans softly. 'Can't yet.'

'We have to.'

'Gotta wait for the spare.'

'Nick.' She moves further into the room. 'It wasn't an accident. We need to go.'

'Can we talk about it in the morning?'

'No.' She straightens up, anger splits in her now. 'It wasn't Heidi they're after, it's me, the kids, Ben.' She raises her voice. 'She's lying in some fucking hospital bed and she might die, she might fucking *die*, Nick, but it's me they're after. I'm paying you, Nick,' she is hissing now, 'I'm paying you to get me out of here. I don't really give a fuck if we are just floating out there, I want to be away from here. Do you understand? I need to get the fuck out of here.' A tiny fleck of spit flies out of her mouth and lands on the doona.

They are both quiet.

'We go tomorrow,' she insists.

Nick blinks long. 'All right. Your call.'

15

The sun pinks the sky as they motor out of the marina, Nick slowly manoeuvring them into the tight space of the lock. She watches the way the light falls on the trees at the marina edge and wonders when she will next have her feet on this land.

She just wants to be away. For a moment when she woke this morning she didn't remember. Her mouth dry and ashy, pain like a pin above her right eye. Then it came like a wave. Heidi. *What did they do to you?* There is no comforting image she can lock on to in her mind, it keeps scudding away so that she sees flames bright and consuming, Heidi's body blistered and blackened.

She took Nick's phone again. Found the link on *The Advocate* site.

Heidi Fulton. House fire.

She doesn't know if Raquel will look, or follow up, or find anything at all. But she has to do something. Has to try.

The children cannot know. She repeated this, low and urgent, to Nick as they packed the last things, as he asked her for just one more day and she said, 'No. No, we have to go now.'

~

There's a man standing high above them on the edge of the lock, a cigarette balanced on his lip. He would reek of salt and fish if she got close.

'Hold her there,' the man calls down.

Nick has the wide wheel of the helm in his hand, and uses his other to pull back the black lever next to him.

'What do you need me to do?' she asks.

'Grab that sheet there, in the middle. Throw it up to him.'

She looks to where he is pointing.

'The red one,' he says.

'The rope?'

'Yeah, you call it a sheet.'

She clambers over the back of the seat in the cockpit.

He motions to Essie. 'Come hold this steady, yeah?'

Essie rushes to hold the helm and Nick, sure-footed, leaps across the seat behind Mim, up on to the front.

'Let's go, careful there,' calls the lockmaster, 'throw it up, love.'

The rope is coiled perfectly and she's not sure how to pick it up off the deck.

'C'mon, love!'

'Here you go!' Nick calls, and the lockmaster quickly moves forward along the edge of the wall. Mim sees the white mooring rope that Nick throws from the front, looping up before the lockmaster grabs it out of the air.

Mim collects herself, steadies her breathing, picks the top loops of the coil and throws. It goes wide, but the man stretches out to grab a handful of it.

'That'll do it,' he says, and she feels a momentary surge of pride.

Nick is back at the helm.

Sammy yells and points. 'The gate's closing!'

'Hold this,' Nick says to Mim, and she holds the helm steady, as Nick leaps around again, tightening ropes, leaning out over the edge and adjusting the fenders. It's close enough to push against the wall as the water begins to gush in around them, lifting them higher. Then there is quiet as the water stops pouring in and they are still.

'Here we go, then,' yells the lockmaster, sticking his head out from the little box at the edge of the wall, and the gate in front of them begins to open and, suddenly, there is the harbour, all stretched out before them. Ripples of wind across the morning light in the water, boats bobbing, picturesque. There's a pain in Mim's chest, just looking at it.

'You all good, Essie?' Nick says.

'Like this?' Essie says, her hands steady at the helm.

'You got it. Just keep the bow –'

'The point?'

'That's it – the point at the end – you keep that aimed right at that marker out there.'

'With the black arrow?'

'That's the one.'

Essie holds her arms straight. Eyes not moving.

'Relax a bit. You're okay. It's not like a road, yeah? You can't fall off the edge!'

'Mum! Look at Essie! Can I? I want to!'

Nick leaps across the surface of the boat. 'Where are you going?' she calls urgently.

'Gotta do these ropes. She's got it!'

She frowns after him, shitty at his nonchalance. 'You okay, Ess? You feel okay with it?'

'I've got it, Mum. It's easy.'

She hovers, moving a little closer to Essie. 'Where are those life jackets?' she calls out but there is no reply. 'Nick!' she repeats.

'Mum! Don't worry about it, we'll be careful!' Essie seems completely in control as she laughs off Mim's nerves.

'Humour me, huh?' she says, steadying herself on the handholds and lifting the seats to look for the life jackets. Eventually she finds them, dragging out the fluoro orange puff of them. They are enormous. All of them adult-sized.

Nick is not perturbed when she holds them up.

'They'll do the job if we need them,' he says, moving quickly away to his next task.

She makes a noise in exasperation. 'They won't do their job if they don't fit properly!'

'Hey, Mum,' Essie says, 'come watch me do this.'

Mim clutches the useless life jacket in her hand as she sits next to Essie, slowly calming her breathing.

'You can have a go next, Mum, okay?' Essie laughs and keeps her eye steady.

∽

Nick is all action, barefooted, skipping from one end of the boat to the next, knotting and pulling and hoisting. Mim feels useless. He calls instructions to her – *Hold this, Pull here, Through there, No, there*. She cannot imagine ever knowing how to do this. He says it will take them four days, seven at most, perhaps she will not know herself by the end. Around the boat the sea is a green she could not have imagined. There are other boats, lots of them, at least this makes them kind of inconspicuous. He hasn't logged the trip. He shrugged when she questioned him, told her that an omission would be easier than a downright lie. She figures it doesn't matter in the end. As long as they don't get caught.

'Gotta get this sail up,' Nick says.

'Can I help?' Sam is buzzing with it all, fingers flittering near his sides.

'Is it safe?' she says.

Nick shrugs. 'Long as he does what I say.'

'He's six.'

Nick points to where a silver handle is resting in a slot on the smooth edge next to the bench seat. 'Grab that out, mate.'

Sam reaches over and pulls it out. The handle is longer than his own arm, and awkward for him to manoeuvre over the top. Nick doesn't try to help.

'Good one,' Nick says as Sam manages to get it into position, 'now slot it in there.' He points to a spot on the top of a rounded winch. There's a red rope already wound a couple of times around the base. She follows the trail of it with her eyes as Nick explains how it works.

'So, I'm gonna be up the front winding this up, right?' He points to the configuration of ropes and tackle above their heads. He's enjoying it. His total control of the boat, his knowledge. The way they are in his thrall. 'What I need you to do is, when I say, you got to wind this up, all the way, and then you got to lock it off.' He touches Mim's arm, pulling her in slightly so she can watch how he does it, sliding the end of the rope into a notch, removing the winch handle.

'Now, Sam, you got to watch us get this right. First time, I reckon your mum should do it, next time you get to.' He ducks under the canopy and heads to the foredeck.

'Wait,' she calls, 'I'm not sure –'

'You'll be fine,' he calls back.

Essie and Sam watch her. She can feel panic building in her gut. This is bullshit. She doesn't know what she's supposed to do, he hasn't told her properly. They're on a fucking boat on the fucking ocean and if she stuffs things up there will be real consequences, for the boat, for her kids.

'I don't know what to do!'

'Mum,' Essie cuts in when Nick doesn't reply, 'you're okay. You can do it.'

Sam adds, 'Take a deep breath, Mum.'

'Okay,' Nick calls, 'start winding.'

Above them, the whisper and whoosh of fabric, the clank of metal as the sail begins to unfurl.

'Come on, let's go!' he calls.

She grabs the winch handle and begins to turn. The rope immediately goes slack, curling back from the base.

'Shit,' she murmurs, tries again. 'It's not working!'

Nick's voice comes back. 'Unwind the sheet!'

'What?' The panic vibrato in her throat now.

His voice carries under the rigging, she cranes her neck to try and see his face, to understand.

'The rope,' he calls. 'It might be wound on the wrong way. Unwind and put it back the other way.'

'This bit, Mum,' says Essie, leaning over and pointing to the end of the red rope.

She can't do this. She'll stuff it up.

Essie starts to unwind the rope, and Mim grabs her hand.

'Careful, I'll do it.' She unwraps the three loops, switches hands, hesitates for a moment as she tries to work out what the other way is.

'How you going?' Nick calls.

She loops it back on, winds it around, once, twice, three times, then takes the crank in her hand again. She feels it grab, then starts to wind. Heavy. It's heavy. There's no way the kids could do this.

'That's it, keep going, let's go.' Nick's voice is far away, and she can hear his breath in it – this is hard work, even for him.

'Go, Mum! It's going up!'

The sound of the wind in the sail is eerie, flapping and whistling. Her arms burn, she has both hands on it now, doesn't know if it is helping or hindering, the muscles on her left arm are no match for the right.

'Nearly there, let's go!'

She grits her teeth, it's slowing now. So much pressure on the rope.

'Okay. Hold it there. Lock it off. I'll come in a sec.'

She slots the next loop of rope into the jaws of the catch, feels it lock. Breathes. Shakes her arms, feeling the ache in them.

'Good job, Mum!' Sam is grinning.

Essie has her chin tilted right back, looking up at the sail. 'Wow,' she breathes.

And it is like that. This first look. The wind catching it. The arc of it so big. It is at once so strange and so familiar, a thousand paintings and pictures and movies and books where she has seen this white shape and yet has never known the way it sounds, the way it moves, how alive it is above them.

She remembers the first time she got a fire going on her own out in the back paddock. Seeing the smoke, then that first tiny flame licking up the twig. Later, seeing the huge fire, all the stuff they heaped upon it, and knowing that she'd made it happen. The power of that.

This feels a bit the same.

She is smiling when Nick arrives beside her, nods his chin in acknowledgement and grins back. 'See.'

⌒

'Muum! Where are my earbuds?' Essie's voice is on the edge of whinge and Mim feels it prickle up her spine.

'Stop it, stop it, they're mine! Mum!'

Mim pulls her head out of the cupboard.

'Stop it, you two!'

They are both at the table, Sam is clutching a pair of earbuds and Essie is levering his fingers to get them out.

'These are mine!' Essie uses her other hand to push him away.

'Hey! Stop!'

'But these are mine, Mum. I know they're mine, I left them on the table, and look, here,' Sam opens his hand to reveal the buds, 'there's red texta on this one and I know it's mine, it's been there for ages.'

'They're mine.'

'They're not!'

'Just stop.' She raises her voice, holds up both hands. Breathes. 'Come on, you've been doing so good. Essie, come on, you're too old for this.'

Essie grits her teeth and pushes Sam's hands away from her. Hard. His clenched hands fly back into his face and he howls in rage and pain.

'Essie!'

She rounds on Mim. 'I hate you!' she yells, her face twisted. She clambers out of the bench seat, muttering in frustration at how tight the space is. Mim can almost see her looking for a room to hide in, a door to slam, but there is nothing. Essie stomps up the steps of the companionway. Mim hopes Nick keeps his mouth shut this time.

She goes to Sam.

'There's blood!' he says, holding his hand out from his lip in astonishment at the blood smeared on it.

'It's okay, Sammy, lips bleed. It'll be fine.' She hugs him to her.

He mumbles into her shoulder. 'They *are* mine, Mum, I promise.'

She goes to the drawers and pulls each one out until she finds paper towel. Wets a corner at the tap, takes it to him to hold on his lip.

'Has it stopped bleeding?' he asks.

'It's all good.' She kisses his head. Leaves him with his screen.

∽

She sticks her head up through the hatch, squinting in the glare.

'Ess?'

She is lying belly down on the bench in the cockpit. Nick is at the helm and he catches her eye. 'I gotta duck under for a bit.'

'You want me to take that?' she asks.

'Nah, autopilot, all good. Just keep an eye out.'

Mim touches his arm in thanks as he passes her, and he smiles quickly with his eyes averted. She sits on the bench beside Essie, takes the sunscreen and begins to rub it into her own arms.

She begins, 'Hun, that wasn't –'

Essie's voice is muffled, her head resting on her arms, as she cuts Mim off. 'I know. You don't have to say it.'

Her daughter is all limbs. It feels as though Mim hasn't been paying attention. There is a long scratch, red-rimmed, from the back of Essie's thigh into the divot behind her knee, finishing on the back of her shin. Mim leans in and places her finger to it, Essie flinches her leg away, but not enough to break the touch.

'What happened here?'

'Huh?' Essie turns her head over her shoulder to see, runs her own hand down. 'Dunno.'

'Does it hurt?'

'Nup.'

'Want me to put something on it? Got to be careful of infection out here.'

'Whatever.'

Mim fossicks amongst the gear on the little table, finds the red tube of balm, squeezes the goo on to her index finger and rubs it gently along the ridge of the scratch. She checks Essie's hand while she's at it. The wound's closed over now and she's let them both take the bandages off. But she's got to watch them. Wouldn't take much for that puckering line of skin to split, to suck in whatever strange bugs this new seascape holds. She traces the scar with the balm, layers it on thick.

'Mum?'

'Hmm?'

'I'm not going to get to do the tryouts, am I?'

'Sorry?'

'The tryouts. For the state team. I'm going to miss them.'

She rubs the rest of the balm over the back of her daughter's hand, feeling it melt into the skin.

'Yep.'

'That's okay.'

'Come here.'

Essie gets on her hands and knees and then curls her head and shoulders round and into Mim's lap. Mim rocks her ever so slightly, as if Essie were her baby again. The rhythm's never left her. It's deep, deep down in her bones.

∿

It takes ages to leave the land behind. As they move steadily away from the other boats in the harbour, she keeps her eyes on the squat head of Darwin, the strange shapes of the buildings. From here, it's easy to see why so much of it was swamped in the surges, and then the gradual, unrelenting rise of the sea. There is water all around them. Nothing is still. It is all wind and the whipping noise of the sail, the hum of the rigging, and then the tilt of the horizon, the dip and rise of the water, the white arc of the wake behind them. The sun is fierce, but there is the shade cloth, the cool of the wind.

Nick emerges from the companionway.

'All good?'

'I didn't realise . . .' She stops because she does not have any words. Does not even know what she is trying to express, except that it is entirely new and foreign, this perspective on the world. It is opening something that she did not know was closed. That she did not know existed.

'Makes you feel small, huh?'

'Something like that.'

'Never gets old, that feeling.'

'You still get it?'

'Kind of like coming home. Dad was gonna take us round the world, he reckoned.'

'He didn't?'

'Never got round to it. Bit shifty, my old man. Mum got fed up and kicked him out.' He runs his hand across the wheel and she is surprised at how gentle it seems.

A dark shape appears in the air, an electrical whirring, getting closer. They all look.

'Is that a drone?' Essie says.

'Under!' Nick barks. 'Now, quick!'

They scramble. Mim pushes Essie ahead of her. Sam's head pops up, and she yells, frantic, 'Get out of the way, Sam, get under!'

as the three of them tumble through the hatch, cower on the couch, listening to the whirr above them.

They make no sound. They wait.

She feels the gallop of their heartbeats in tandem with her own as she squashes them to her. It would be too fucking unfair, after everything, to only get this far. She's risked it all for this. Other people, too. *Heidi* – the name sears in her brain and her chest and she swallows down the choking terror she feels rising. She can't go back. She understands now. Finally, Nick's head appears above them in the hatch.

'You're good,' he says. 'Come up if you want.'

But they stay under. For a while, anyway. Spooked that the sky is watching them too.

⌣

Later, she tries to make sense of the cupboards in the galley, stacking things in under the sink. Every surface serves a purpose: books and papers tucked into shelves with high edges, long padded bench seats that fold down into beds, heavy wooden boards that cover the stovetop and the sink to create a kitchen surface. Sam thinks it is a cubby. Especially the narrow passageway through which Nick stoops to get into his tiny cabin at the end. A slab of bed stretches back into the corner so that surely only his feet could be comfortable there. When he showed them, back in berth, he jumped up on the bed and stuck his head through the hatch above him so that they might all fit in to see. Even then, Sam had to climb in her lap and Essie on the bed behind her, ducking their heads down when Nick instructed her to pull down the chart table so they could see all his maps. She had been transfixed for a moment by the intricate markings, so like the maps she was familiar with. The reefs and deep trenches and shorelines all visible as if there were no water here at all, as if you were sailing over a mountain range. Something about it is just slightly beyond her grasp, the combination of the boat, the current and wind. She feels like she could understand the technicalities and, yet, there is something else that Nick has – an instinct for it.

～

By dinnertime, they have left Australian waters, and Mim feels more comfortable letting them eat up on deck, bowls of steaming pasta in their laps. The kids glow with the light of the sunset and she realises she must look the same. The colours – pink and orange in the high straits of cloud – are reflected in the water's surface, which is the gunmetal polish of oil. It's like they are sailing through sky and she has to remind herself to eat, slack-jawed with the beauty of it.

'Pretty special, huh?' he says.

She nods. 'What do you reckon, kids? Not a bad view?'

The kids shovel in spaghetti. They are not old enough yet, she thinks, to realise that this is a kind of magnificence they won't see often.

16

She can hear him now on the deck above her as she dries the tin plates, quietly stacks them in their little cupboard. The children breathe steadily, tucked into their narrow beds.

She wipes her hands on the tea towel. Needs a drink. She shouldn't, but god, now that she has allowed the thought, it consumes her. She can taste it. Can feel the warm ease that will rise from her stomach, that will fog her brain a little. She will welcome the fog, gladly, as she always has. *Take the edge off it*, the kinder mums used to laugh, giving each other permission to blank out the tedious evenings ahead. She needs more than fog now; she needs erasure. Visions of Heidi lying cocooned in bandages, hearing her scream in her mind.

'Should we have a beer?' she calls up through the hatch, stopping her brain.

'Wouldn't say no.'

She grabs two bottles, flips the tops, carries them up on to the deck.

'Kids asleep?'

'Yep. Exhausted.' She hands him one of the bottles. 'How do you stay awake?'

'Stop at one beer.'

She nods. Looks out at the surface of the ocean ribboned with the light of the moon. The space around them is so big. So vast. There seems to be no end to it. They have sailed into a watery world and she wonders how long they could stay, suspended between places, out of time. The hushed sizzle of the wash as the boat slices through the waves. The blow of the sail.

'I can usually go twenty-four hours,' Nick says, 'then I'll have a snooze. We can switch on to autopilot once we've cleared these islands.'

It is easy to forget. What they are doing. Where they are going. He must sense her holding her breath, because he shifts, starts something new.

'Best night I ever had sailing, I was crewing for this bloke. English guy. He'd come into Darwin with his wife and I joined them there. It was so still, this night, in the middle of the Banda Sea. Full moon. Never seen anything like it. When it rose, the sea turned white. Milky. No horizon, nothing. A complete whiteout and us in the middle of it.'

Mim watches him, how far away he is when he tells her this, back in that moment. He swallows and she watches the movement in his throat.

'Never seen anything like it again. We asked a few people when we were in the islands, apparently only ever happens in the Banda Sea, maybe phosphorescence.'

'How long did it last?'

'Minutes, I think.' They fall quiet. The breeze plays the rigging, a whispering.

'Sometimes I wonder if it really happened. Or if it's just a story I've told so many times I've made it real.' He looks at her. 'It's like it got inside me. That night.'

'Sounds amazing.'

Keep talking, she wants to say. *While you talk, I can't think, and not thinking is what I want.*

'You did that. A bit,' he says. Soft.

'What?'

'Got under my skin.' He taps the bottom of his bottle against the steering wheel. The boat creaks and she's aware of the lull, the movement.

'Yeah?'

'Yeah.' He takes a swig. 'Back when we were kids.'

Not this. Not now. That's back there, and I can't think about back there. Here is all.

He breaks the silence. 'Did you end up travelling? I remember your brother, he went away for years, didn't he? You follow him?'

She shakes her head. Not sure of what will come out of her mouth if she begins.

'Hard to come back when you go for that long, they reckon. He still over there?'

The stars spatter the dark and flicker on the surface of the waves. Wind, gentle but persistent, moving into the hollows of her ears and out again. Perhaps she can say it here and the weight of it will be taken from her, carried away by this westerly, borne up and dispersed.

'Michael died.'

She feels his gaze shift to her in shock.

'Fuck, sorry, I didn't –'

'He was an addict for years. Ice. He was taken into BestLife for those synth clinical trials, when they were doing the "radical change" to drugs policy.'

He is breathing quietly, his eyes still on her. He is giving her space, he is listening and it is intoxicating. There are so many words to be said. They itch her tongue. She goes on. 'I only visited him there once. It was bizarre, unreal. Something deeply, fundamentally wrong about the place. Spooked me, even though Michael seemed totally fine. Too fine.'

The wind picks up for a moment and above them the tell-tales flutter and snap. They both look up and Nick moves his hands on the wheel, changing direction ever so slightly. The sound eases.

'How long was he in there?' Nick says softly, prompting her.

'Only another three weeks after that. They said it was an overdose. His tolerance was down after the detox and someone must have smuggled some in. Who knows?' She cannot look at him.

'I should have got angrier. Should have made them explain. Should have been in there every day holding them to account, making them speak to my broken mum, my bitter dad. But I didn't.

'And later, god, years later, just after Sam was born, I got an email. Encrypted shit. Ben was terrified, reckoned he could lose his job just for the fact of it in our house.'

'What was it?'

'Michael's file. Or that's what it looked like. The names were all redacted. There were dates and medical files, and then copies of pages and pages of Michael's handwriting, scrawled, but still his.' She spits out the words, they feel as though they are burning her tongue.

Nick waits, his quiet is gentle and open and she feels like she might say anything, everything.

'A lot of it was mad. Images, ranting, it looked exactly like the ramblings of a drug addict. I pored over it. Trying to find him in there. And I did. Kind of. In the middle of one page I saw my name. It was like a letter to me. Said he was sorry. Said he loved me. All of us. He said something like "it wasn't what I thought after all". Described himself as a rat in a cage. The last pages, they were just the same word, again and again and again, written so hard in places he had ripped the paper.'

'What was the word?'

'Resist.' She throws her head back, lets out an enormous gush of breath. 'I never showed Mum, figured she had enough on her plate. And Ben was stressed out about it. When I said that maybe we should try and get it to someone, a journalist in New Zealand, there was obviously some sort of underground that had got it to me in the first place, he just flat out said no. We couldn't risk it. Couldn't risk coming to the attention of the Department.' She scoffs, looks at Nick in the half-light. 'Blown that, haven't I?'

'I suppose you have, yeah.' She hears a smile in his voice.

'Anyway, that's it.' She wipes her mouth, as if she has just vomited. 'Essie loved that, today, driving, steering, whatever you call it.'

He pauses, thrown by the suddenness of the shift, but he goes with it. A new tenderness in his voice. 'She did great. You didn't get a turn, though.'

'Happy to leave it till I get my sea legs.'

'Come take it now.' His face in the shadows, the strange colours from the deck lights, the moon. The way his gaze strikes at her throat in a way that she doesn't want. She doesn't. She doesn't.

And yet.

'Nah. I'm good.'

'Come on. Do you good. Anyway, I need a break.'

She is annoyed to be patronised, pleased to be pushed. She feels like he thinks he knows something about her that she doesn't know herself. She balances against the force of the lull, stands up and steps around to behind the wheel. It's big. Her hands out straight from her shoulders when she places them at the top, ten and two, like she would a car.

'See this?' Nick points to the little screen behind the wheel, crisscrossed with coloured lines, a flashing dot which must be them.

'All you got to do is keep this,' he indicates the dot, 'lined up with this,' he shows her the green line that is their course. 'All good?'

'I'm pretty good with maps,' she says.

It's as if she's doing nothing at all, but when she tests, dropping her left hand just a fraction, after a moment she can see the dot move ever so slightly away from the line. 'So, what? You set this up first and then all I have to do is follow the line?'

'Basically.'

'I can do that.'

'Course you can.' He hasn't moved away and she can feel the heat off him all down her right side. Only a couple of centimetres between them. She hopes he moves away. And she hopes he stays.

'Unless a boat turns up.' He laughs quietly. 'Or the weather changes.'

'Then I hand over to you.'

He leans back. 'You'll be captain in no time.'

They are quiet for a time. But the heat of him, the closeness.

She cracks the quiet. 'There's just so much water.'

'Once you've been out for a few days, not seen land, not seen another boat, it feels even bigger then. Start to wonder if you imagined it, land, the rest of the world. If it's not just you and the water. Odd feeling. Can't explain it very well.'

'I can see how that would happen.'

'I'm sorry about your friend.'

Her breath catches. 'Don't.'

'Sorry, but this is the first time I've had a chance.'

He is looking at her, she can tell, feels the focus ziplining up and down her body.

'I can't think about it.'

'Okay.'

'I just. I have to just concentrate on the kids, on getting there. Please don't –'

'Okay.' He nods. 'You finished?'

'Thanks,' she says, reaching across to pass the empty bottle to him. He closes his hand around her fingers.

He doesn't move and she doesn't take her hand away. She's got her eyes on the green line, one hand on the wheel. She feels him move closer to her, the weight of his leg, his hip, his elbow now, against her. This isn't happening, she thinks. This is not me. She turns her head to look at him. His face open like that night at the seawall. A stirring at the core of herself. She drops her head forward, enough, enough, like she has granted permission, and then they are face to face, foreheads first. She can still back away. This is the line, if she crosses it, she doesn't know how she will get back. The smell of him, up close like this, it's complicated. Skin heat and sunscreen, sweat, diesel. It is not the same as it was, back then, not exactly, but there is something in it that unhooks her, takes her over.

She kisses him.

It's not right, at first, noses squash, teeth clink, her shoulder wedged between them, but then he moves closer, something urgent now and there is more touching. He takes the bottle from her, bending a little, but won't take his face from her face, mouth from her mouth, so he drops it and it clatters, rolls. She hopes it won't roll off the edge but she's not stopping now. Christ, she can smell the heat of them both, the panicked quick of it, the starbright, moonlit tide of what comes at her now, something remembered, something known rising up to wash her away.

~

After, she blinks in the dark of the cabin. Her body is electric. She imagines him up there, adrift, still caught in it, but she has pulled away, a clear voice in her head, something out of a dream, *Stop now. Stop.* So she has. She did.

He is up there awake, in the dark, in the middle of a sea, the kids asleep and there is no one who can say, no one who would blame, it is entirely conceivable, regrettable but understandable. She grips the edge of the narrow bed. Holds tight. Feels the waves, the current beneath them, taking them forward, pushing them on.

17

She wakes to the tinny beep of her alarm going off. For a second she is unsure of where she is, and then there it is, the rock of the boat, the thrill-dread of remembering they are in the middle of the ocean. A moment later, the full body remembering of the kiss.

Her hand goes to her face, touching the skin there, her cheek, the crevasse between her nose and lip. A sudden urge to vomit, shame or adrenaline or desire, all three. She swallows, holds it. Breathes. *Ben*, she thinks, and she conjures an image in her head. Thinks about his hand on the small of her back, how sometimes, if he wakes before her, he'll touch his forehead to hers, let her sleep, strangely intimate. Ben. She tries to hold him steady in her head, wishes she were a lover from a past time with his black and white portrait in a tiny gold locket at her throat. Maybe then such things wouldn't happen.

The kids stir as she gets up off the bunk and pulls on a shirt. It's her turn for the watch. She brushes her teeth, eyeing herself in the tiny scrap of mirror above the toilet. She only realises how hard she has brushed when she spits pink blood in the white mess of toothpaste. She wants a shower. To scrub herself hard. Thinks of medieval monks slicing their own backs as they flagellate themselves. She wonders the weight of transgressions at sea. This is why captains don't like women on board.

The light of sunrise is so kind, pale pinks and blue compared to the golden orange knowing of the end of a day. Nothing done yet to mark it.

Nick is looking out to where the sun is rising up out of the sea. His eyes red-rimmed with fatigue.

'Hey.'

He turns at her voice and there is no start, no sudden awkward, shifting eyes.

'My turn,' she says.

She takes the wheel, avoids touching his hand. He says they are on autopilot now, she just needs to watch. He tells her it'll be smooth sailing. But if anything changes – the wind, something on the horizon, a boat on the nav – to wake him. He'll leave the hatch up so she can just yell down and he'll be there.

'All good,' she says.

'You sleep okay?'

She looks towards the sun, balanced now, the bottom of it skimming the surface of the horizon, light spilling over the water, over the two of them.

'Not really.'

He crosses back and leans towards her, sudden. She hears him breathe, like he is sucking her in.

'First night,' he says, pulling back. 'It'll be better tonight.'

⌣

For an hour or so it is just her. Eye on the navigator, on the mainsail, then out on the water. The sun is warm but not too hot yet, the sparkly throw of light where it catches the waves. Suddenly, beside the boat, something cleaving the water, dark. She starts, stands upright, heart pounding. Again. Dolphins! Two of them, three, god, six; more! Cutting the waves, leaping next to the boat.

'Kids! Ess! Sam!'

'You okay?' she hears from Nick's hatch.

'Dolphins,' she calls and she hears a quiet murmur, a half laugh.

'Get up here, you two! Dolphins!'

In a moment, the kids are at the top of the steps, crusty eyes blinking in the sun. 'Where, Mum?'

'Here, come here,' she beckons with both hands, 'look, see!'

The kids kneel on the seats, leaning forward, wanting to clamber up on to the edge.

'Careful!'

'There's so many!'

The pod leap and dive. The sun glistens on the surface of the water so it is impossible to see where they will rise, leap, one after another. A break for a moment, a lull, and then there they are again, the kids calling, 'Look! There! Mum!'

'I need a picture! I can't believe this! Aren't they nearly gone? Mum! My screen!' Essie yells, 'Can you get it?'

Sam puts out his hand to his sister. 'It's okay, Ess, just watch them.'

Essie humphs, but turns back to the sea. Mim calls to them to be careful.

But they don't listen, or if they hear they choose not to respond. Essie holds on to the rail with one hand, stretches the other out over the waves, and the next time a great grey body cuts up out of the sea the water flicks up and sprays her hand and she laughs. Sam yells in delight. And he puts his arm out too, leaning further for he is littler and his arm can't stretch like hers, and Mim is calling, 'Careful, careful, hold on!' but they are just laughing, dolphin-sprayed, sun-lit.

∼

Afterwards Essie brings breakfast up on to deck for the three of them, balances the bowls and hands them to Sam at the top of the steps.

'I'm not sure about the kettle, Mum.'

'That's okay. I'll do it soon. Thank you, for doing this, this is really nice.'

Essie tries to hide her smile. 'You think they'll come back, Mum?'

'Maybe. It's special, to have seen them. They're pretty rare now. Maybe they're coming back. Maybe it's a good sign.'

The muesli is good. She is hungrier than she realised. They all crunch and chew and watch the waves.

'Did you wake up, last night?' she asks, fleeting anxiety at the thought of what they might have heard. 'You feel okay in your beds?'

'It was kind of like being in a hammock,' Essie says.

'Yeah, or like one of those things that Aunty Jill put the baby in. That hangy cradle thing.'

'Like a baby?' Essie laughs.

'Yeah.' Sam sticks his chin out.

'I felt like that too.' Mim smiles at Sam. 'When you two were babies,' she says, 'me or Dad carried you on us all the time, you liked the feel of us rocking. It was the only way you would sleep.'

'What? All the time?'

'Most of the time!'

'What about when you had to go to the toilet?'

'Sometimes.'

'Yuk!'

'But if we put you down, on the big bed or in your cot, you would just cry and cry and cry.'

'I remember you doing that, Sammy.' Essie nudges her brother. 'You were so loud!'

'You did it too, Ess!' Mim says, laughing. 'You were worse. Sometimes we'd lay you down and then we'd slowly, slowly, drop to the floor and we'd crawl back out the door and we'd think that we'd made it, we'd look at each other and be ready to high five, quietly, so quietly, and then there'd be this noise, the start of your cry. You just knew we were leaving you and you wanted us all there together, in one space. So we'd bring you back out, wrap you up, sit on the couch with all the lights off and you'd fall asleep.'

She remembers the bone-heavy exhaustion of it. The way she would hold Essie's tiny body, and then Ben would prop her against his shoulder, his chin on the top of her head, so they would stay upright, so they wouldn't smother their daughter in their sleep.

'But how did you go to sleep?' Essie says.

'Sitting up. On the couch. Like that.'

'That sucks.'

'Yep. It did.'

'Did you wish we were like other babies?'

Yes, yes, yes, yes, yes. All babies cry, she thinks to herself, *but not like you cried, Essie, my darling, my love.* 'I didn't know any better,' she says. 'We didn't know any better. We were new at it, we were just learning.'

'You should have had your L plates!' Sam says.

'Yes,' she says and laughs. She wonders whether Nick will have heard them talking. Kind of hopes he did. Kind of hopes he's heard her talk about Ben. Her husband. Ben who she loves. Ben who is missing.

She stands quickly and stretches, a great yawn escaping as she does. 'We all need a shower.'

'I don't want to go in that stinky little shower.'

'Why do we need one?'

'What about we do it up here, on deck? Didn't Nick say he sometimes did that?'

'Do you know how to do it?'

'Yeah. I reckon. You can help. Go and get your bathers on, if you want. Or don't. It's not like anyone is going to see.'

Essie pulls a face. 'Gross, Mum. You have to put yours on.'

'Why?'

'Cos Nick might see!'

'He's asleep.'

'No, Mum.' Her daughter's face. Aghast at the thought.

'Okay, okay.' She laughs. 'Here, Sammy,' she passes him her bowl, 'can you take these down for me?'

She thinks about the breakfast scene played out at home. Always a rush. The coaxing and cajoling and grumpiness. The soundtrack to each morning – 'I forgot', 'I need a red t-shirt for sports day', 'I don't want cheese' when cheese was good enough for yesterday, no socks, shoelace busted, forgotten reader. And then racing to not be late, in the car. *God, I should make them walk, they'll get fat and unhealthy. I'm a terrible mother. Tomorrow, tomorrow we are going to walk.* And they never do. And then home, after the inane conversations with ten other mothers she pretends to not be like, *I am not like them,* but she is, they are, they are all one and the same, and all of them breaking away to their cars, 'So much to do', 'Doesn't stop, does it?', 'Oh well, now the madness begins', 'See you at pick-up', desperate for their days to be weighty with task and significance. Busy, so busy. I know, right? And the muesli-crusted dishes in the sink, the quiet of it that she has so yearned for that now feels stale and full of all the things that did not used to be important, and now, for some reason, are.

And the ticking minutes until Ben leaves, when he's home. The way time is heavy with her inexplicable rage that he should go and she should stay.

She hears the kids down below getting towels, and she looks out at the sea, feels the boat beneath her. She is steering a yacht. In the sea. On her own.

⌒

They fill the bucket with the desal water from the shower. Chuck in a kettle full of hot so that it's warmish. She's not sure about soap on the deck, the slip of it, so she gets Sam to bring up another towel. They each soap themselves with the little bottle of bodywash she's got in her bag, and then dip a corner of the towel in the bucket, sponge it off. She sluices the kids, once each with a pour from the bucket when she thinks they're de-soaped enough.

The kids towel off, lie on the deck for a moment, blissfully sun-screen free for the two minutes she'll let them.

She slips her old bra off. Soaps under her arms. Sticks her hand down and washes herself. Keeps her knickers on, the kids will have a heart attack if they see. Grabs the bucket. Tips and pours.

'Mum!'

'What?' She picks up the towel and holds it across her front. The sea damp of it, not crackly dry the way she likes.

Essie is sitting up, her eyes wide with mortification. Mim turns to see Nick, shoulders and head up out of his hatch, leaning forward, grinning.

'What's the racket?'

Ah, she's so aware of herself. Towel crossed over her chest, too narrow to hide the mum-cut of her undies, the bristle of hair at her bikini line. God, how bad is it? The solid pale of her thighs in the glare.

'Sorry. Shit, did we wake you? Sorry.' She tries to wrap the towel around more of herself.

'S'okay. I was awake. Need to check the position. Coffee?'

'Yes, okay. Want me to do it?'

'Nah, that's okay.' He looks at her intently now, still grinning. 'You should probably get dressed.'

Sam starts to giggle and then Essie can't help herself and Nick shakes his head and smiles as he goes back under.

'Don't move,' Essie says and disappears down the companion-way, reappearing a moment later with her screen. She points it at Mim, who is finishing pulling her t-shirt over her head.

'No!' laughs Mim. 'God, what do I even look like?'

Essie takes a shot. 'I haven't got one of you yet.' She takes another as Mim acquiesces, makes silly faces, a model pout then squished-up ugly face. 'Anyway, you don't care about that stuff.'

Mim laughs. 'Don't know if I should take that as an insult or a compliment!'

Sam is laughing too. Mim pulls him close and Essie takes them both. Then squishes in, flicks the screen, squeezes them all into the frame.

'You look happy,' she says to Mim as she swipes through the images. She stops on the one of the three of them, sun bright on the waves behind, their three faces caught in glorious laughter.

'Just Dad missing,' says Sam, and the moment is gone.

～

Later, as the afternoon burnishes, he looks at her. Smiles. Tells her she should sleep. 'You're going to need to do watch tonight.'

'I'll be all right.'

She feels loose. Dangerous. She feels seen again.

'You need to sleep,' he says. 'You'll have our lives in your hands, right? You can't afford to be tired.'

He's smiling when he says it, but she understands she's being told.

'Kids, you need to do what Nick says, huh? Maybe come down into the cabin with me. You can watch –'

'They don't need screens.'

A flicker of annoyance at his confidence.

'Yeah, we're okay,' Essie says.

'You gotta do exactly what Nick says. Okay?'

Maybe she will just lie there and pretend to sleep so she can make sure. He's clueless, really, around the kids.

'You can come down any time, Ess, watch a movie or whatever. Okay?'

They are transfixed by the fish they have caught, swimming in the bucket.

'You two! Okay?'

In bored unison they call back, and she heads down into the cabin. 'Wake me in like two hours or something, I probably won't be able to sleep anyway.'

'Just try, have a rest. Close your eyes. And use my bed, then if the kids come down they won't disturb you.'

She cocks her head. 'Thought your bed was off limits.'

He shrugs.

'Yeah right, thanks.' She has to move immediately before he sees her blush.

She ducks into his cabin. It is bright there, with the light through the hatch, but if she crawls up on the oddly shaped bed, she can tuck her head into the corner, in the shade. The hatch is propped open so she can hear the kids above, but the schlock of the underwater against the hull, too. She thinks about all the water beneath them and what makes them float. How deep is it, all that water? How easy would it be to sink? For the watery depths beneath them to open up and swallow the boat whole, not even ripples left on the surface.

She rolls over, squints her eyes shut, pushes her face into the pillow, but it is all him. The pillow, the sheet. She rolls on to her back, takes a deep breath, but it's like she's caught the scent now, it's everywhere.

It is not the same as Ben.

The smell of Ben is comfort and deodorant that is probably too young for him, but he doesn't know these things, doesn't take notice of them. Ben is onion sometimes, cut grass, the glass of red that he has after dinner. Sweat, but not sweat on skin, no longer such sexy sweat. His sweat is on clothes she has to wash and towels damp and pooled on the bathroom floor – that grim smell – damp soap and skin cells. Ben is the after stink of a shit even when he turns on the fan. She feels her lip curl.

She knows it is chemical. That the scent of Ben used to do the same thing to her body, her brain, as the smell of Nick's pillow, his sheet is doing to her now. She gets that. But it doesn't undo it. Chemical reaction, the basic principle of consequence, of rules.

She is wet. She keeps her eyes closed, tries not to imagine him crawling into the space beside her because right now, this moment, she would not do a thing to stop him.

These thoughts are not useful. She conjures Ben. The way it was to sit with him, rubbing her feet on the couch. Knowing the spot that makes her groan with pain, but releases something deep in her tendons.

She brings her body back from its feverishness. Dozes. Half in. Half out.

～

When she comes back up after an hour or so, Essie is rolling her foot over and around her soccer ball.

'That a good idea, Ess?'

She's in the main deck, bounded on three sides by the flexiglass seats, and she knows what she's doing, but still, it's making Mim's skin crawl.

'It's good for me, Mum. Sharpens my skill.' She starts to kick the ball into the seat. 'Hey, how would Nick sleep if we weren't here?'

She looks at her daughter, squints at the question.

'Like, how long can he stay awake for?'

'I don't know. A long time? It's not good for you, though. They have those signs, on the highway, you know, where they have the picture of what the road looks like through the eyes of a drunk person, and then what it looks like through the eyes of a tired person and it's the same.' She's distracted by the thumping ball. 'Can you stop?'

Essie keeps kicking. 'Like, can you just drift in the middle of the ocean?'

'I'm not sure.'

'How long until we get there?'

'To the island?'

'Yeah.'

'I don't know, I think Nick said we might be five or six days.'

'And then we'll see Dad.'

'Not straight away, no.'

'But soon.'

'Yes, yes, I hope soon.'

～

They play Uno. Nick shakes his head and laughs when they ask if he wants to join in, but he makes his coffee slowly, she notices,

staying down under with their banter. Sam has a mitt full of wild-cards, and can't contain his glee. Essie is exasperated that he can't keep poker-faced.

'You've got to be able to hide it, Sam.'

'Hide what?'

'I know you've got good cards cos of your face!'

'You don't know!'

'I know exactly.' Essie raises her eyebrows and smirks.

'Hey,' Mim warns, but she is smiling.

'It's stupid, Mum, he'll never learn.'

Mim can't follow suit, picks up a card, sighs. 'It takes a while to learn to be poker-faced, some adults can't do it. Your dad's not very good at it.'

The air between them sharpens at the mention of who is missing.

'Are you?' Sam asks.

'Yeah,' says Essie. 'Mum's good at it.'

Sam turns around to face Nick who is still leaning against the galley bench. 'Sure you don't want to play?'

'Maybe next time, huh?'

But Sam is losing interest now. He stays twisted around to Nick, the sailor holding more potential thrill than the game.

'Are you good at fishing?'

Nick's face shows surprise at the question that seems to have come from nowhere. 'Not bad, I s'pose.'

'Sam! Are we playing or what?' Essie says, frustrated.

Mim puts her hand on Essie's. 'Yeah, c'mon, Sam.'

'Wait, wait.' He scrambles up from the seat and over to the narrow shelf on the wall at the end of the couch. There is a stack of books, some photographs, a dish of odds and ends. Sam holds up a brass medallion, the size of his palm, etched with the crude shape of fish. 'What's this?'

Essie throws down her cards and picks up her book and earbuds. Rolls over on the bench seat to face away from them. God, the space is so small.

'Sam,' Mim says, gentle admonishment.

'I can tell you later, mate, if you want to play?' Nick is awkward in his negotiations with the kids. Doesn't own that he is the adult.

'Tell me now, Essie doesn't want to play anyway.' Sam thrusts the medallion forward.

Nick looks at Mim, checking to see if he should go on. She sighs and nods.

'Well, what does it say? Is there writing on it?' he says to Sam.

Haltingly, Sam sounds out some letters, but stops, shakes his head.

'Won it with my dad, fishing competition. When I was about ten, I reckon. Caught the biggest flathead on the day.'

'Cool,' says Sam, grinning. 'Are there more?' He scrambles up and over to the shelf again. 'Is this your dad?' He holds up a frame.

Nick nods. 'Yeah, that's him.'

Mim is struck by how much she wants to hold him.

'What about this?' Sam says and holds up another frame.

'Sam,' Mim says in warning.

Nick laughs and moves over to Sam. 'Nah, it's all good. That's my sister and her kids. My nieces,' he says.

'What are their names?'

'Jasmine and Elly.'

'How old are they?'

'Umm,' he says and looks at Mim sheepishly.

She laughs and shakes her head.

'About your age, I reckon,' says Nick.

'This?' Sam holds up an embroidered piece of fabric, a bookmark perhaps, garish colours, tasselled fringe.

'Ha!' Nick takes it from Sam and runs his thumb across it. 'I got that off a little kid on an island. South-east of here. They don't get many visitors. I stayed for two weeks, helped build a new room at the school. This was a thank you gift.'

'Cool,' says Sam. 'Could we go there?'

Nick looks at Mim. 'Maybe. One day, huh? Not this time though, got to get you somewhere this time.'

Sam nods, eyes and fingers roaming the shelf. 'What about this?' He holds up a stone, a shell perhaps, deep green, as long as his fingers. 'It's so smooth!'

'Sea glass,' Nick says and this time he doesn't look at her, and then she knows.

'Is that –' She leans across the table, taps Sam's hands and takes the green glass from him. The weight of it, the smooth rounds of the edges, the clarity when she holds it up to the light. 'You kept it?'

Nick takes a long drink of his coffee, avoiding her eyes. Then he can't anymore. 'I really like green glass,' he says and laughs.

～

She's tucked away from the wind behind the rocks at the base of the headland. Low tide, pool of sun, tucking her hair behind her ears, shading her eyes, the cracked red nail polish of her big toe as she flips shells on the tideline. Knowing he is watching her. How alive and at home she feels in her body. Grains of sand sticking to flesh, skin that he's touched, speechless, adoring. He turns back to look, crouching in the sand. *This one?* he asks, holding up the purpled insides of a pipi shell, mock sad when she shakes her head seriously. All afternoon he brings her treasures: the sunshine yellow of a small scallop shell, the milky butterflied wings of a clam, oiled pearlescence of a broken abalone, half a sea urchin ribbed with tiny holes. Each one she takes and holds and lays out in a line, before she kisses him her thankyou. When he bounds away to bring her more, she adds her own. Smooth charcoal pebble. Perfect whorl of a white trapdoor. Electric pink seaweed frond. And then the sea glass, green and smooth and weighted just so, nestling in the deep part of her palm. She holds it out to him as he holds his final gift to her. They unfurl their fingers at the same time; in his palm, a triangle of blue

glass, in hers the rounded smooth of green. They laugh and kiss and kiss and kiss. On their knees in the sand then, for it has weight, this serendipity, means something bigger than them, fillets their hearts a little, for the sun is getting low in the sky now, this summer is nearly done. Solemnly, they exchange the pieces of old glass. Safe into pockets, stroked under fingers, tucked into hearts.

⌒

'I can't believe you still have it,' she says.

Nick runs his thumb across the glass in his palm, hands it back to Sam. 'Your mum found this. She gave it to me.'

Sam's eyebrows shoot up. 'Really! When?'

'Oh, ages ago, when we were kids.'

'At Eagles Nest?'

'Yeah.'

'Why'd you keep it?'

Nick smiles, screws up his face. 'S'pose it reminded me of something good. A good memory.' He looks at Mim and she can't meet his eye.

Sam's face lights up with suspicion. 'Orrrrr,' he says loudly, with delight, 'were you boyfriend and girlfriend?'

Nick laughs as Mim says, 'Sam!'

Essie stands up and puts her book down hard. 'I'm going up on deck.'

Nick puts the sea glass back in the dish. 'Good idea, I'll come up.' Glances at Mim as he goes past, eyes bright.

Sam shakes his head as Mim cleans up the cards, pushes the table back to make the bed. 'You were never a kid, Mum. That's too weird.'

She billows the sheet over his head and reaches under to tickle him. 'I was so!' she says and laughs, and wonders at the thrum of that old self, awakening under her skin.

18

Lights glow on the deck. Red, green, white against the black of everything else out there. They do different things, he's told her, but there is so much new information and she's got nothing to hook it on to. He instructs her how to tie the line off. They are keeping the sail down. He's happy for them to stay this way for a bit. Still need to watch though, no getting off the cycle of watching this vast dark water, even though, so far, she has felt like they are the only ones out here.

'You sleep all right, this afternoon?' she asks to fill the silence.

'My bed smelled of you.'

She hears the words in her knees.

She knows now that it is inevitable. Or maybe she knew that from the very beginning.

Out past the deck lights she can see something. A glow rising up out of the sea. 'What's that?' she asks and points.

'Rig. Oil, gas maybe.'

'Will we go past it?'

'Closer, not too close.'

She is captivated by the otherworldliness of it, the eerie lit quiet.

He goes on. 'It's big, an optical illusion. It'll take us all night to get past it.'

'They really do go anywhere to find the stuff, huh?'

'They? Thought that was your gig, too?'

A warmth, that he has listened, even if he hasn't understood.

'Not oil and gas. Always tried to steer clear.'

'Your husband must be doing it, if he's with that China project.'

'That's gold. Other minerals too.'

Nick nods, tinkers for a moment with a switch. Mim watches the rig in the distance.

'All the same though, really, isn't it? Taking stuff out of the ground?'

She laughs once. 'It's a bit more complex than that.'

'Yeah, maybe.' He smooths the heel of his hand round the rim of the wheel. 'Reckon people say things are complex sometimes, when they're kind of really simple.'

'Oh yeah?' She's had these arguments before. Always after the bristle when people realise she's come through geology. *So, mining?* they'll say. And she'll have to say, *Sometimes, that's part of it.* For the most part, she'll hold herself back from attacking the smug satisfaction in their faces. She won't argue that it's essential services really. For everyone. For them. That without the industry they

wouldn't be able to move around their adored cities, wearing their curated outfits stinking of oil somewhere down the line, even if it's as ethically sustainable as it purports to be. That the screens they religiously upgrade are powered by the very stuff the evil industry extracts from the earth.

People find it hard to acknowledge such duplicitousness. Hard to acknowledge, but not hard to do.

He must take her silence for hurt. 'Suppose I'm saying the simple part of it is needs and wants. As long as there's a market, there's a reason to dig it up.'

'Exactly,' she says. 'We all compromise on stuff, right? Principles. Ethics. What we want.'

He nods.

'You ever wanted it all?' she asks, after a moment.

'All what?'

'Kids, love, all of it.'

'Haven't found anything to keep me in one spot yet.'

'No?'

He touches her wrist.

She's not even sure how the space between is breached, it is so quick. And there's a rope, so many ropes, and there's the edge, *Shit, hang on, careful don't fall in*, quick laugh, not now, not now that we're here, and so backwards, into the pit, into the fire, him down on the seat, and she straddles him, her legs across. Who is she? What is this? How so soon, so quick, so right? And his hands are under and rough and damp and she knows that when she takes

them in her mouth, because she will, they will be salt, but now, now is for mouths and hands in hair and tongues on necks and the sound and the moon behind and his beard where it scratches, and fingers now, ducking his head and mouth on her nipple so she drops her head back and gasps and they are gone, they are done, they are so far in. *Like this? Here. Now.* Fingers down now, wet. *Like that? God, yes.* And his hands, a moment of strangeness, of feeling too intimate. He is hard and so hot on her belly and *fuck, fuck this is good.*

He speaks, low, into her mouth, 'I wanted, from when I saw – at the house, I thought, how is she here?'

And his want, it is something else. He wants her.

'You got something?' she says, quick, coming back to herself.

'Yep.'

'Pretty sure of yourself.' Grabbing. Helping.

'You knew too.'

'No. I didn't.'

'Yes. You did.'

And then tearing and *Get it on, fuck, there? Okay, yes, god,* and kiss now again, lips, mouth, tongue, bite, *Ahh, sorry, no, god, good, again, please,* and *now,* and hand on him, taking him, wanting him, pulling him, so that she guides him in, and then

Jesus

fuck

All starlight and wave upon wave on the boat up against and hard and then soft and *please god more keep going I'm not* breath mouth

you this is just you're so hard wet good come now please god not yet can't we all night just forever again and again and again and she sees a planet she is sure that it must be so tiny so bright like it's searing inside her it's seeing inside her she has never been open like this in her life it is everything, everything, just noise now, and sound that they make which is tender, star song and breath, and breathe and slow and still skin heat wet heartbeat slows.

The quiet, then.

The quiet of after.

∽

She is cold. Awkward, a little, and she needs the darkness of the cabin, sleep. Can't bear to see his face, all stripped back and open. The flutter in her gut threatens to make her vomit. She pulls on shorts, untwists her long-sleeved top. No words now. Like the night will shatter if they speak. In the dark ahead of them, the rig glows, beautiful and monstrous, rising up out of the dark sea.

Down the companionway, feeling with her feet, her hands, she doesn't want to turn on another light. Allows her eyes to adjust to the blue glow from the nav desk.

Then she yelps.

In the half-dark, Essie is sitting up. Sheet loose around her middle, hands resting in her lap, whites of her eyes glowing, looking directly at Mim.

'God! Ess! You okay?'

'Yes.'

'You gave me a fright.'

'Sorry.' Her voice is clipped.

Like a wave, fear comes to Mim. What has she heard?

'You been awake long? Can't sleep?'

Breathe, breathe, take the edge off your voice.

'Yeah. Awhile. It's hard to sleep. It's noisy.'

'The water? Autopilot?'

'Must be.'

'You want me to get you a drink? Lie with you? You want a head torch to read for a bit?' Mim knows she is babbling, but her daughter, serene and still in the darkness there, *God, what has she heard, she must have heard.*

'I'm okay.'

'Sure?'

'Shouldn't you be asleep? Isn't your watch in the morning?'

She reaches for explanations. 'The ropes,' she says, 'wind change, Nick needed a hand.' She feels the blush begin in her neck. *Oh, you lie.* She makes her voice tired. 'I'm going back to bed. If you're sure you're okay.'

'I'm okay.'

'Night, my darling.' She doesn't go to her, feels she can't, she can smell him on her.

'Night.'

Mim waits until Essie lies back down, and then she crawls across to her own slim bed. The rocking is gentle now, moonlight on the droplets of water on the small windows above her. She is wired, painfully aware of every point the sheet touches her skin, of how he just touched her, of how he breathed her name, the catch in his voice, the feeling that surged in her.

She is turned on, again, and ashamed.

She thinks of how loud her own breathing was in her ears, the feeling of all that space, the water, the sky, no one else out here, the gasping pleasure of it.

She must have heard. She must have heard.

∽

In the morning, she takes the breakfast bowl from Sam, passes it back.

'Finish it off, there's another two spoons there.'

'I can't. Full.'

'Well, you'll have to take it up and throw the rest over. Essie, can you go with him?'

Essie's voice is level. 'He can do it.'

Mim stays facing the little sink, looking through that little rectangular window, the tilt and lilt of the horizon.

'I can do it by myself, anyway,' says Sam.

'Fine. Up you go.'

She wipes her hands on the tea towel. They don't dry, nothing is dry, and turns to watch Sam climb the ladder, one hand gripping the bowl. She's not controlling, it's not that, it's that she can see the inevitable disaster and she wants to prevent it.

She looks at her daughter, all puffed up with her indignation.

Does she know? She thinks she should say something, warn Nick, but then to say it would be to make it real and it is still just a star-tinged moment, a way of rationalising, of swallowing the guilt.

⁓

Up in the cockpit, Essie drills the ball into the fibreglass, again and again, so it comes back perfect and hard. Her face is set. Hair pulled back so she looks fierce, determined.

There is a breeze this morning, the sail is up, they are moving, and all she can think now is *Don't go so fast, wind. Give me something, give me an extra day.* This is a betrayal. To think like this. They must get to Ben. To Ben. To Ben.

'Muuum. Booored.' Sam holds the rope above his head and swings his body forward so it takes the weight.

'Don't do that.'

Sam snaps his head at Nick's voice.

'On the rope, you can't pull on it like that.'

Sam drops his head and Mim glances at Nick. Her look must say it all.

'Sorry, but –' he begins.

'Yep. It's fine. He got it.' She looks at Sam, puts her arms out to him. 'What can we do, huh? You want to play Uno? We could do it up here.'

Sam shakes his head, wounded.

'C'mon,' she says, cocking her head to Nick and Essie, 'these two seem like they need some alone time anyway.'

Essie is quick. Devilish. 'It's a pretty small boat,' she says.

Mim tries not to react. Goes down below with Sam, plays two hands.

⌣

And then Essie is yelling.

Mim is up the steps so quick and she's yelling at the same time. 'What? What happened, are you okay?'

And she can see her, thank god, she is there, and Nick too, at the edge.

'Get it!' Essie screams.

'What, what?' Mim is behind her.

Sammy is yelling from behind her, 'What's going on?'

Nick says, 'We can't.'

'Can't what?' Mim yells. 'Fuck! What?'

'Her ball. Her ball went over.'

'Shit. Ess. I told –'

Nick says, 'Don't,' warns with his eyes.

Fuck you, she thinks, *you are not her parent.*

But then Essie is standing on the edge. 'Just turn the boat around to get me,' she says and moves to propel herself forward.

'No, Essie!'

Nick has grabbed her and is holding her against the rail and then Essie begins to scream, to really scream and to wriggle and squirm and Mim goes forward, watching in horror, as Essie smacks her head back into Nick's mouth.

'Fuck!' he yells, lets go, grabs his face and Essie wobbles, grabs the rail, goes to get one leg over but Mim is there.

'No, Essie, no!' she yells.

Mim tries to be careful of Essie's legs but not really because all she knows is that she has to haul her back in, haul her back over the rail and fall backwards onto the deck so that she has her in both her arms, and Essie is yelling, crazy, trying to bite her arm, but she holds, like iron, she holds her arms across her and she is crooning, 'It's okay, it's okay,' and across Essie's head, out to sea, she can see it, the ball, already so far. It's crazy how quick and how far already and then there's the chop of a wave, small. And then it's gone.

~

Essie quietens. Slowly. Until it's just shuddery breaths, her face hidden by her hair.

Mim won't let go. She says her name, pulls back. 'I'm sorry,' she says.

But this is not the end, she can see when Essie's red face snaps up, the bite in her voice when she speaks through gritted teeth.

'It doesn't matter anyway!'

'Hey,' Mim says quietly.

But Essie is up now, roaring.

'I'll never make the team,' she yells. 'This was my chance. And we're here, on this stupid *bloody* boat in the middle of the ocean and I hate this, I hate this. I hate that we are here, and that Dad isn't here, and that we're not at home where I can just go with Jo's mum and do the tryout and make the team and have something else which is all mine which I am really, *really* good at, which you and Dad will come together to watch, and we can all go and have pizza afterwards like Meg's family do, because they are a normal family, and I just want to be as good as her, I want to be better. I want to be the best. But I've missed my chance. And I don't care the ball is gone. It's good it's gone. I'm glad it is, anyway.'

Mim tries to reach out for Essie, but she ducks away from her hands, goes down under.

Mim looks at Nick, there is blood on his hand, and he is sitting a few feet away, watching them, the shock of it writ on his face. Like he suddenly knows who they are.

'There'll be other balls,' says Sam.

If Ben were here this is the moment where he would temper Mim, tell her to wait, *I'll go in a minute*, and everything of Mim that was prickle and bluster and hurt and try would be relieved that Ben could approach sideways, no agenda, no *Can we talk about this*, just Dad. And she might go in an hour later and find them reading together, or lying back on the bed talking, staring at the ceiling, side to side, that careful considered approach, not head-on like her own.

Mim pushes the heels of her hands into her eye sockets, hard, so that the darkness bursts red-veined, and she thinks she might make them pop, if she pushed hard enough. Because in this dark behind her eyes there is Ben. Ben. Even the fact of this absence, this unknown, is so extraordinary to her because she has never, not in all their years together, gone this long without talking to him.

19

Another day at sea. The early shift, then the midnight, the tell-tales flip-flipping against the sail. Counting knots, counting hours, the kids with their cards. Cups of tea, pots of coffee, the kids into the lollies, bored. And the sea, the sea, the endless swell. The way the light shifts, bounces sometimes off the planes of the waves, the deep roll of the current moving one way underneath, the quick flick of the wind pushing white caps the other way. Nick tells them they've now crossed the Timor Sea, and Sam traces the lines on the nav. States, a country, now an entire sea. They are so far from where they began. She wonders how much a kilometre weighs. She can feel them inside, the distance from what she has left behind. Heidi, Heidi. She cannot speak her name. The ever-shrinking distance between her and Ben.

Time, distance – they are both held in suspense out here, liquefied.

'Mum!' Essie's voice is frantic, pitched high over the engine and wind. Mim's stomach cinches, body moves before her brain.

Down the companionway, her hips jolting against all the surfaces as her panicked body forgets to move with the sway.

'Essie! What! Is it Sam?'

But he is lying on his bunk, book in hands, eyes peering over the top, concerned at the pitch in his sister's voice.

'She's in there,' he says softly and inclines his head towards the tiny bathroom.

Mim puts both hands against the door, pushes gently, but it's locked. 'Ess? You okay? You sick?'

Her daughter's voice is quiet. 'No.'

'Let me in?'

'You won't fit.'

She almost smiles. 'Come out then?'

'Is Nick there?'

Mim feels the cinch in her throat this time. 'He's up on deck.' The lock rattles and the door pulls back. Essie's face all blotchy, her hand clenched around a bundle.

'Ess?'

'I think I've got my period.'

'Oh, Essie.' She wants to laugh and cry and hold her all at once. She wants to run from the change in her. Wants to grow her back down already, back through time, limbs growing shorter, flesh plumper and softer, words falling backwards to sound, take her back to the breast, back to her inside. Keep her there. *Stop*, she thinks, *please stop*. 'Oh my darling,' her voice cracks.

She puts her arms out and Essie caves into her, sobs, crunches the bundle to her, which Mim realises now is covered with her daughter's blood.

'Have you got something?' Mim says. 'Do you need a pad? A tampon?'

Essie speaks into Mim's shoulder, 'I used toilet paper.'

'Here.' Mim gentles her back, takes the scrunched ball of undies from her daughter's hand. 'Let's get sorted.'

Sam is sitting upright now. 'What is it?'

'Nothing!' Essie explodes. Then softer, 'Mum, make him go away.'

Her rawness. It hurts. 'Sammy, upstairs to help Nick for a bit, yeah?'

'But he doesn't need help.'

'Sam!'

He grumbles, but goes. He wants in on this secret whispering between mother and daughter. Mim wishes he could be part of it too, but Essie is crackling with emotion. The unfairness of it. What I have to bear that my brothers do not.

Mim finds a pad in a side zip of her bag. There are five there, and tampons. Essie might have to learn from necessity. She is stupid for not packing more. Yes, she was ready for this, and no, she was not. Would never be.

'Does it hurt?' Mim asks, boiling the kettle. She'll try and soak the rust brown stain of her daughter's blood from the blue-spotted underpants. She is going to cry. 'I can get you some Panadol?'

Essie nods and Mim doesn't know whether it is pain and shock or some other older, primal thing which has cowed her daughter's shoulders a little. She wants to tell Ben. Needs to tell Ben. Needs to say all the things that she can't to Essie. *I'm scared, and sad. What if this means she is gone from me? She is not a child anymore. Where has my child gone?* She feels her daughter cleaving from her, and is grateful then that they are tight up against each other here, that Essie has nowhere to run and hide from her.

∽

Mim sits with Essie, legs dangling over the edge of the boat. Sun on their shoulders, fingers laced in the wire. They have both grown brave out here.

'What's that?' Essie points out to the water, one hand shielding her eyes. 'Something floating?'

'Where?' Mim stands to get a better view of where her daughter is pointing. The sun flashes on the water, mirrored spangling. She tries to make out a shape. 'What colour? How far out?'

Essie points, voice frustrated, 'There! A round thing. Looks like a ball!'

It's a fair way out, but now Mim can see it. Sitting high on the water, big and white, bobbing with the waves but holding its position. She wonders, heart cracking for a moment, if Essie thought it was her ball. 'It's a buoy.'

'All the way out here?' Essie looks at her, incredulous. 'Why?'

Mim sits down again, lets the sun soak her, wants to extend

the moment with Essie. 'Could be sensors, they use them to detect tsunamis.'

Essie calls out, 'Sam! Tsunami buoy!', pointing out to where it is receding in the waves behind them. 'Sam will lose his mind,' she says and sounds incredibly grown up. 'Do they work?'

Mim smiles and sighs. 'They should. But they haven't always. Sometimes fishing boats use them to moor on, or no one checks them. Funding is a problem. These places out here, they don't have as much money as us.'

'But if they are working, then . . .' Essie looks at her.

'Yeah.' Mim nods. 'In theory, they're placed strategically to detect seismic activity, then to issue an early warning so that people can evacuate to higher ground.'

'So have they ever used them?'

'When they're working, sure. This whole area is tectonically complex.'

'Explain.'

Mim laughs at her daughter's tone. 'Well, right now, we're sailing over the edge of the Australian plate. There's a collision zone with the Pacific plate to the west of us, a collision with the Eurasian plate to the east and then, right here, it's subducting beneath Indonesia along these trenches. Right here, underneath us. Australia moves seven centimetres further north each year. Eventually they'll meet.'

'What does that mean?'

'It's an earthquake belt. Volcano, earthquake, tsunami, it could happen at any time.'

'Don't say that!' Essie pushes her with her shoulder. 'Sam might be into it. But I don't wanna hear if we're about to get sucked under a huge wave. I'd prefer not to know.'

Mim nods. Runs her fingers lightly down the knobbles of her daughter's spine. 'Yeah, I get that too.'

'But you like it. It's weird.'

'What do you mean, weird?'

Essie puts her head on one side, traces a finger along the horizon, squinting, as if she's trying to measure it. The late afternoon sun turns the waves a deep gold. 'That you think about that stuff.'

'It's kind of part of my job.'

'Do you ever wish you had a job like Dad? Where you could go away?'

She pushes her sunglasses against her face, surprised by the sudden hot burst behind them. You can't lie to an eleven-year-old. Not really.

'Sometimes.'

Essie nods, puts her hand on her mother's. 'We'll see him soon, Mum. We've just gotta hold on a bit longer.'

No stopping the tears now. She turns and presses her lips hard against her daughter's head. Lets her tears drip into her hair.

'We should make dinner,' Essie says, but Mim holds her there, just a little longer.

~

In the night, a tugging low at the bridge of her hipbones. She moves to the tiny bathroom in the dim light of the navigation desk. Pisses.

Wipes herself and sees, of course, her body momentarily tuned to her daughter rather than herself. In the middle of the sea, she is bleeding too.

When she opens the door, Nick is at the galley, filling the kettle.

'I can do that for you,' she says. 'Sorry, is it my turn? Here, let me.'

He looks at her with tired eyes, nods, thanks her, tells her to bring it up, brushes his body against her as he moves back up the steps.

The tired, quiet need of him. It turns her off.

She makes the coffee strong. Makes herself one too. Thinks she will sit with him. Try and convince him to go and have a sleep while she does a couple of hours. She is up now, awake enough, and she can see a small and reckless mean rising in him the longer he stays awake.

'Thanks,' he says, taking the hot cup from her, loosing his fingers across hers, pausing there.

She pulls away.

He shifts sideways. 'Right,' he says. 'That how it is?'

'It's like nothing,' she says. 'I just – I'll sit with you.'

He tries again, turns to her. 'I don't want to just sit with you.'

She inhales, wraps her fingers more tightly around the cup. 'I can't. I want to and I can't. I have to stop.'

He jerks his head back. Laughs low, cruel almost.

'What changed?'

'Nothing, it's not . . .' She turns so he can't see her face. *Don't cry, do not cry*. 'I didn't mean for this to happen.'

'You sure about that?'

She reels back. 'What the fuck?'

'You found me.'

She stands up. 'You wanted in – you said yes.'

'This,' he gestures his hands between the two of them, 'this isn't what I was after.'

That familiar bruise of hurt. It blooms into something else.

'Then what are you after, Nick? Getting your kicks from saving me, huh? You like fucking other men's wives – is that it?'

Quickly, he smashes his open hand onto the edge of the bench. She startles away from him. Astonished.

'Fuck you,' she says, more bravado than she feels.

'Sorry,' he says, sighs, shakes his head. 'Sorry. I'm tired. I'm sorry.'

She has nowhere to go. She wonders if the kids have heard anything. They drink their coffee in silence. She takes his cup and goes to bed.

20

Morning. Waking from deep rocking sleep to Nick banging around in the cabin. Has she missed her alarm? She pushes off the sheet, the sour bed smell of her, warm and clingy.

'Fucking motor won't start,' he says.

She rubs her eyes, wills herself to waking. 'What?'

'There was a noise about half an hour ago, turned it off to check. When I went to turn it back on, nothing. Fucking nothing. Fucking knew we shouldn't have left without the spare starter.'

'Can we fix it?'

He looks at her, scoffs, goes to say something and then seems to swallow it back.

It annoys her. 'Well, tell me if you need a hand. You want coffee?'

He runs his fingers over his hair. 'I'll have to disconnect the battery to work on it. We won't have power for a bit. No water. No autopilot. I'll come up and run you through the coordinates. You and the kids'll have to stay up on deck, I have to pull this whole thing up.'

Resentment curls its fingers in her guts.

'Ess and Sam, you awake?' She knows they are, their closed eyes and curled reposes nothing like the real vulnerability of sleep. 'Come up on deck, we're in charge this morning.'

Essie groans. 'Do we have to?'

She wants to go easy on her, understands the cramping heavy in her daughter, the hormonal strangeness. But it makes her harder.

'Yes.'

'Fine.' Essie throws back the sheet, grabs her book. Sam is already clambering up the steps.

It is hot. She tells Sam to sit in the shadow of the mainsail, hanging limp and useless. The sea barely ripples. The salt-flecked heat begins to solidify around them.

～

They avoid speaking to Nick for an hour but the kids are getting fidgety. She didn't realise it would take this long. They haven't had breakfast even. They're hungry and she needs coffee. She calls out down the hatch, but the stairs of the companionway are still up – that's the only way he can access the engine and there's no other way to get down.

'You want a break? Some food?'

There's no reply, just some thuds and bashes.

'Nick? You gonna take a break? Can I grab some food for the kids, for you? Can I help?'

'What?' His voice is muffled.

'Can you take a break? Kids are starving.'

There is the sound of huffing, clanging of metal on metal, the heavy staircase shifts, and folds down halfway, and Nick is there, face flushed and pissed off.

'Can you make it quick?'

'Yep.' She wants to snap back at him, but she holds. 'Kids, come on, let's grab some snacks.' She waits as Nick clicks the staircase back into place and then hurries down. He turns away to the desk.

Essie hurries after her, slams the door of the head to lock herself away. Shit, she should've thought, tries to recollect her first period, the excruciating strangeness of it. The shame.

Mim grabs a packet of biscuits. She wants coffee so bad. 'Can I put the kettle on quickly?'

Nick grunts.

She has to reach past him to switch on the gas, and he leans away from her, intent on the screen. Arsehole, she thinks, she should have known that there would be some thread of aggression idling away under the surface. There always is.

'Shit,' he murmurs.

'What is it?' she asks forcefully, he can't just shut her out of it.

'Weather coming. I've really got to get this sorted.' He turns to her. 'Things can turn to shit pretty quick.'

'Yeah, I can see that.' She leans back and flicks the switch off.

She knocks hard on the door of the toilet. 'Essie, come on. Nick needs to fix the engine.'

'I am hurrying!' Essie yells, a catch in her voice.

Nick is trying to soften, realising he's being a shit. 'It shouldn't be long, half hour max. Then I'll make you coffee.'

She hears the apology in his voice, but she's ushering Essie and Sam up the staircase ahead of her and back onto the deck. The sound of Nick swearing and muttering is muffled beneath them, the staircase is heaved into the holding position and clicks.

Essie scrunches the plastic wrapper from the box of biscuits in her hands and wedges it between two bottles of water on the table.

'Careful it doesn't blow away,' Mim says.

Sam says, 'This is a funny breakfast.'

A breeze, sly and quick, darts through the cockpit, releasing the purple wrapper, picking it up and swirling it in front of them for a second before it flies up.

'Quick,' Mim says as Sam leaps up, arms outstretched, leaning forward, racing to grab it before it twists up and out into the sea. One step, two, back towards the companionway.

'Careful,' calls Mim, as Sam jumps, the wrapper dancing above him, and he puts his foot on the upturned staircase to lift himself higher –

'Sam, no!' Mim yells. 'It's not –'

He jumps back away, hands on the wrapper, triumphant. She sees the steps shift, hears a heavy whoomph.

'No!' she yells, and the steps fall.

For a fraction of a second there is only the heavy thud, and then a yelp.

Fuck. Fuck.

'Nick,' she yells. 'Nick! Are you okay?'

She looks down the staircase, can't see him.

Then his voice, yelling frantically, muffled. 'Don't touch the steps!' Swearing, a moan.

'Stay there, Sam. Just stay there.' She points at Essie. 'Keep him there.'

'Mum, I didn't!' Sam's face, hand still clutching the plastic wrapper.

Essie holds his shoulders. 'I've got him, Mum. I've got him.'

She has to get down to Nick. Sees the open hatch above his bed. Thinks of her hips, how to wiggle down. 'Stay there,' she repeats, then lowers herself down, scraping her leg. Pain in her armpits. For a second she thinks she is stuck. *Breathe, breathe.* Gets her boobs through, can feel the bed under her toes now. Lets it take her weight, and she's in. Rubs her leg as she clambers through to the cabin, calling his name.

She can't see him, just the staircase down, not entirely wedged into place. She can hear him though, moaning.

'Nick,' she says, trying to be calm now, 'I'm here.'

'My foot,' she hears his voice from under the stairs.

Bending down, she gets her hands underneath the fibreglass lip of the staircase and begins to lift slowly.

'Fuck, fuck, fuck!' Nick yells.

'Shit! What, do I stop?'

'Get it off me!'

Only when she gets it up to her shoulders can she see the blood.

'You got it?' He sounds like there is a vice round his chest, like the words are being squeezed out of him. God, where is the blood coming from?

'Mum?'

The kids peer down from the deck.

'Just stay there,' she barks. They shuffle back, faces white. 'Essie,' she calls out, suddenly realising there is no autopilot, no watch, 'Essie, stay at the helm.'

'Yep,' she hears her daughter call out.

'Just watch the –'

'I know,' she calls back.

The staircase is so heavy, so bulky. 'I've got it,' she says, and she hears Nick move, shuffling, sees one bare foot, his leg, no blood, and then the other.

His foot.

'Don't let it go,' he says and she stares at the bloodied end of his foot. The place where his toes should be.

He emerges, turning on to his arse and shuffling along the floor. His face is white.

'Let it go, now,' he says. Eyes closed.

She bends, lets it fall at the last minute, snatching her fingers out of the way, feels for the latch on the side. Locks it in place. Tests it.

Then she turns around. Nick is on the floor, leaning his back against the end of the couch. His beard seems darker, wiry against the paleness of his skin. Eyes closed, head tilted back, hands spread wide against the timber floor as though to keep him there. Bare legs sticking out of his shorts, unmarked, until the end of his right foot. The big toe looks normal, and the next, but the last three are a mangled mess of blood and flesh, the white of bone.

She reaches to pull a tea towel from the sink, then changes her mind, pulls open a drawer and grabs a clean one. Kneeling in front of him, she hesitates again.

'Just stop it bleeding,' he says.

She nods. Winds the cloth around the foot. Tight, the blood flowering on the faded check immediately.

She can smell him now, something tart – fear, pain – mixed in with the diesel and rust.

'Mum?' Sam's little voice behind her.

'Ice, I need ice.'

'But I can't lift the lid.'

'Sam, I told you to –' but she thinks better of it. 'Come here, it's okay,' she says, 'hold this.' She wraps his hands around the twist of towel. 'Hold tight.'

He nods, his face pinched.

She goes to the fridge, lifts the heavy lid and buries her hand deep down to find the coldest thing. A can. Of course there's no fucking ice. Why didn't she check this stuff, how irresponsible has she been? 'The first-aid kit, Nick.'

'Under the sink,' he says, eyes closed again. Pain pulsing in his jaw.

She fumbles, finds it. Christ. It's as small as the one she keeps in the car.

Her nail catches on the zip, she pulls at it roughly and the kit springs open in her lap. Bandages, silver foil packets spill across her lap.

'Go slow,' Nick says through gritted teeth, but he opens his eyes to look at her now. 'Can't afford another mistake.'

He must smell it on her, this rising fear, see the whites of her eyes brightening with it.

She fumbles with the little bottle of Betadine.

'Hold this.'

He takes it from her as she unwraps the bloodied tea towel.

'Sam, grab another towel,' she says.

'Where from?'

'God! I don't know!' His face crumples at her quick anger. 'Sorry,' she says, 'sorry, Sam. There, in the drawer, just a tea towel.'

The bleeding has slowed, it's an ooze now, enough to see the damage.

They are crushed, the three of them. She fights the urge to gag. He'll lose them all.

Sam is beside her. 'Woooahh,' he breathes out.

'Go check on Essie, see if she's okay.'

He doesn't move for a second.

'Sam,' she uses the warning tone, and then he is quick up the stairs.

She takes the plastic bottle from Nick. It's only fifty mil, it won't be enough.

He sees her hesitate. 'There's bleach, somewhere.'

'All right, we'll do that next.'

She squeezes the maroon liquid out, covers the entire crushed mess of the end of his foot.

'Fuuuuuck,' he whispers, and she knows he needs something for the pain. Antibiotics too. God, what if his toes get infected, what if she has to – *stop*. One thing at a time.

She pulls the gauze bandage from the wrapper. Adds a second one. Her hands are covered in blood, Betadine, she wipes them on her shorts. She can't remember her first-aid training. Does she wrap the whole foot, is it meant to be tight, not tight, open to the air? She begins at the bridge of his foot, holds the feathered end of the bandage with her thumb and gently begins to wrap it around. Already, the skin around the toes is turning purple-black, the blood dwelling under the damaged surface. She loosens off the next wrap of the bandage. Holds it in one hand, while she flicks out the other. At the end of the foot, she's not sure. She decides to wrap firmly, there is still blood oozing but it is tacky, dark. She'll check in an hour. She tucks the end of the bandage in.

She leans her head in towards his.

'It's okay. It's gonna be okay.'

He touches his forehead to hers. It's clammy, hot and cold at once. The sharpness of his sweat.

She scrabbles through the spilled first-aid kit, finds a packet of painkillers, pops four out and gives them to him, gets him water.

He swallows each one.

'Got to get the motor going. The weather,' he says.

'I can fix it,' she says.

21

'It's the starter.'

She waits for him to go on. The statement alone means nothing to her and he knows it.

'One of the bolts was stuck, I nearly had it loose when −' he stops and shakes his head. Winces with the pain.

Mim thinks, *If you say it, if you say that it was someone else's fault, I will push you off your own fucking boat.* He must sense her bristle, because he changes tack.

'You'll be able to get it off.'

'Okay, so talk me through it.'

'You got to get the starter motor out so you can check the terminal, that's the problem.'

Which means the stairs have to go back up. 'Kids,' she calls, 'stay there.'

She undoes the latch, lifts the stairs from the bottom as far as she can, then shuffles her body to wedge her shoulder under, shoving them the rest of the way before hooking them up. A residual smell of hot diesel, metal.

'You're gonna have to climb right in to get to where it is.'

'What am I looking for?'

'Cylindrical piece of metal, bout as big as my hand, two bolts holding it in place. They're pretty loose now. You got to get them undone, lift that cylinder away, and pull the starter motor out.'

'The whole thing?' She leans into the space, there's a little light on the side of the compartment, but as she moves she throws shadow in front of her.

'You see it?'

She breathes out heavily. Her knee is stuck against something, and as she wriggles to move her hip and push further in, there is a sharp cramp in her groin.

'Can you see it?'

'No! Give me a second, okay.'

She hears his huff behind her. She thinks of Ben and all those afternoons before Essie arrived, and then each time the kids outgrew an old bed, and they sat on the floor surrounded by unassembled flat pack furniture and almost wept with their frustration at each other and their respective ineptitude.

There, the cylinder, the two bolts. She leans against the engine with her left arm, it has cooled now, hardly any warmth at all. With the fingers of her right hand she tests the bolts. One is loose enough to wiggle and she twists it out, feeling each satisfying turn before she loosens the whole thing and drags it back. There is nowhere she can put it down so she stuffs it into the pocket of her shorts.

'Found it,' she calls.

'Take the bolts out.'

The second bolt requires the spanner, which she wriggles her arm down to find, and she flexes her upper arm muscle into it, trying to get enough leverage in the small space. The moment when it gives she is elated – simple mechanical success. She twists and pulls and pockets the second bolt.

From there it is more straightforward. Once she pulls the starter motor out of its place, she can bring it back out onto the floor. Under his eye, she can see what it is she has to do, because he dictates it, this, that part, put this here, wipe this terminal, pull this back.

Later, she will know that, technically, it was her hands that fixed the starter motor, and brought it back to life so they could get the engine going again, but she could never feel the total pride that she had done it herself. She was Nick's hands. That's all. She doesn't even know if she had listened hard enough to be able to do it again.

With one hand, Nick can flick the switch, which he does, not even thinking about offering her the chance, a symbolic gesture to acknowledge what she'd done. Immediately it cranks and there is the thrum of it, steady.

'Yes!' she says, grinning.

'Fixed?' Essie calls down.

'Yep!'

Nick slumps back. Sweat beading on his forehead. He nods. 'Let's get that autopilot going again.'

~

Up on deck, Essie is standing tall at the helm. Face determined. The sun is still high and hot, but when Mim turns to see where they are headed, she can see a bank of dark cloud low on the horizon. The first clouds she's seen that are not high and wispy. This is the weather that's coming for them.

'What's it look like?' Nick calls out.

'Black in front of us, right on the horizon though.' She turns back to Essie. 'You're doing a good job.'

Essie nods. Not smiling, but proud, she can see. Doing something important.

Nick's voice behind her, 'I need to be up there.'

She turns quickly. 'What are you doing? Get off your foot, you idiot.'

'You can't do this bit on your own.' He uses his arms to push himself up the step, keep his weight off the foot.

'You have to get off that foot.'

'Move,' he says.

'You've got a crushed fucking foot – you could lose those toes. You need to sit down.'

He moves into her, uses his shoulder to jostle her out of the way. 'Then I'll sit down up here. I'm the fucking captain. You said it. It's my boat.'

She would laugh if he weren't so ridiculous.

He moves past Mim, hopping on one foot, using the surface holds in the small space, dragging the bandaged foot behind. He swings around to sit on the bench behind Essie. He breathes heavily.

'Want me to move?' Essie asks.

'You're good,' he says, and Mim bristles.

Nick leans forward, looking at the nav. She sees him adjusting the autopilot buttons, feels the slight shift as the boat straightens into the wind, into what's coming. The storm is gathering its potential on the horizon. Nick's face, despite its pallor, is set firm. His eyes glisten a little, like he's spoiling for a fight.

He's right. She doesn't know what to do.

'Grab those life jackets for the kids, will you?' he says.

Terror in the pit of her stomach as she gets them out. Knowing that now, for the first time, he reckons there might be a need for them.

'It's too big!' Sam says, but doesn't argue further as she pulls at the toggles, tightens the thing.

'Just ten more minutes, then I want you under. Okay?' Essie nods, invigorated, her eyes on the nav.

～

In the cabin, she tries to distract Sam, gets him to lay out the stale bread for sandwiches. They have to eat something. Empty stomachs will be a disaster if the wind really picks up. She slathers mayonnaise. Sam is quiet. Helpful.

'Was it my fault, Mum?'

'Sorry?'

He lays out the rectangles of yellow cheese, right to the edges of the bread.

'I was just trying to stop the rubbish going overboard.'

'Sam.' She turns, puts her hand on the side of his cheek so he has to look at her. 'Sam, sweetheart, it wasn't your fault at all.'

'Is he gonna be okay?'

'Yep.' She turns back to press the bread, slice the knife through on the diagonal. 'Yep,' she says again, to convince herself. 'If the wind stays, we might even get there tomorrow night. How good will that be?'

'Mum?' Essie calls out.

'You okay?'

'Can you come up here?'

She is up the steps and sees Essie first, behind the wheel, and then Nick, laid out now on the bench seat of the cockpit, one hand covering his face, the white bandage on the end of his foot now vivid red.

Mim hurries to him, crouches down. 'You right?'

'More painkillers.'

'You have to stay lying down.'

'I will.'

She stops to peer at his foot before she goes back down. She'll need to rewrap it soon. By the time she emerges with the rest of the pills, the storm is on them.

It is eerie, how their whole world becomes this new dark, the wind. A moment ago there was sunshine glinting off the water and now there is only inky cloud reflected back in the roiling ocean.

'Essie!' She is frightened by the fear in her own voice. 'Go down with Sam, quick now.'

'But Mum, I can —'

'No! Under. Please.'

The urgency in her tone makes Nick attempt to sit up, his eyes open.

'Shit,' he murmurs.

'What do I do?' she says. 'Tell me. What first?'

'Got to change the sail.'

Mim looks down at the ocean, the bubble of waves, when did they start moving so fast? Spray flickers her face. All around the boat, the sea has come alive. Dark waves peak and trough, frothing and fizzing. The water hisses along the side as they continue to build speed and the sail above her whucker-thumps in the shifting winds.

'Essie, Sam, you okay down there?'

'Yes!' they chorus back.

'It's pretty rocky!' Sam's voice tilts with fear.

'Just stay on your beds,' she yells, and then to Nick. 'What's the safest place?'

He doesn't reply.

'Nick!' Urgent now. 'Where should the kids be?'

Shakes his head like he might laugh if he could. 'They're fine.'

'What happens if we tip over? How do you get out?' All the questions she hasn't asked, the panic, brimming up and over, a flick of sea spray in her face.

'We won't tip over.'

Shouting now, wiping the salt from her face. 'But what if we do?'

'Not worth thinking about.' Nick sits up fully and wedges himself against the back of the seat, leaving his bad foot stretched out beside him.

'Got to get that sail down.'

Not worth thinking about because it won't happen? Or because if it does they're fucked? She remembers her dream, swimming in the upturned hull, knowing the kids were somewhere in the water darkness beneath her. She lurches with the boat, dry retches. Nothing comes up, and she wipes her face again. 'How?'

'I can release it from here, but you gotta get up on deck to the mast and flake the sail down onto the boom.'

'What?'

He points.

She looks ahead to the foredeck. She's hardly been up there. The kids know it's off limits. It's an obstacle course of coiled ropes and rigs and wires that she does not understand. The whole front of the boat tilts against the horizon. The spray arcs up and splashes the deck as the boat shifts and bucks.

'Keep a hold of something – the mast, a sheet, whatever – just have a hand on something,' Nick says from behind her. 'Don't go over.'

Mim turns to him.

'We won't find you if you go over now.'

Adrenaline is crawling across her chest, spidering into her limbs, her breath. It's loud, the noise of the sea and the wind, she'll hardly be able to hear him out there.

'What do I do?' she asks, turning to him quickly.

'You'll see the sail go slack at the top when I release it,' he says. His face is rumpled with pain. He's aged ten years since this morning, and it shocks her. She glances at his foot, the bandage soggy with blood and muck already. It'll have to wait.

'You gotta bring it down and secure it.'

She squints forward, trying to see what it is she must do. The bow is pitching up and down, skewing side to side in the buffeting waves and the boat seems smaller now, yet the front of it appears infinitely far away. Through the companionway, she can just see the kids' feet, they are lying on the bed together. Sammy's leg is tucked over Essie's.

'Okay,' she says, and ducks under the awning, stepping over the back of the seat and onto the foredeck.

The wind whips in her ears.

Under her bare feet, the deck is wet and she has to choose where to place each step. She holds her arms out to the next piece of rigging, pulling back when she feels herself caught by the lean of the boat. She looks over her shoulder and can just see Nick peering out around the side of the awning. He yells something but the wind whips it away. She shakes her head and he points past her, nods.

She looks at the foremast and can see where she needs to pull down the rope. Ten more steps. The mainsail flaps and whacks behind her, the boom shifting from side to side, as far as the taut ropes will let it. As she steps forward, the bow tilts down, and she feels the lift and surge as the boat surfs the front of a wave.

'Yaaaaah!' she yells into the wave, but she is not afraid, not now, it is a rush, exhilaration. She leaps the next steps and puts both hands out to grab the mast as she comes at it hard. She waits for Nick to release the halyard and looks up to see the sail go slack. She wedges her knee against the mast and puts her left arm around it, pushing her shoulder in, her foot, bracing her whole body against it. She bends both knees so she can ride the swell as the deck tilts and rolls. She looks up and she can see the sail begin to drop, now the wind cannot catch its fullness and tip them so close to the surface of the sea. She guides it down, arms above her, trying to hold herself steady, feeling the weight, the awkwardness of all that material bearing down on her. 'Wait!' she tries to call out, but the word is whipped away from her, and she races to keep up, guiding the folds down over the boom like she has watched him do.

Her arms are burning by the time the last fold is down and she is slowing, can hardly get her arms up to wrap the sail with the ties. She lets go of the mast and pushes her hip hard against it, hoping it will hold her if she overbalances.

She can hear her own breath loud in her ears, her eyes sting with the salt of spray and sweat. She holds on to the mast and leans forward, squinting through the spray and flapping rigging to make out Nick's face. She sees his thumb go up.

She is lighter, quicker, as she leans in and around the ropes and the wires, quick-stepping back to the cockpit where she slides in next to Nick, breathing heavy.

'I did it.'

He nods. Face white, a half smile.

'Good. Now the genoa.'

'What?' She feels the adrenaline ebb.

'The little sail. You gotta get that up.'

She shakes her head. 'Can't we just motor through it like this?'

'It'll help keep us steady. Safer.'

She looks back out to the foredeck, the bow careening up and down the waves.

'Mum!' she hears from the cabin.

'You okay?' she calls, rushing forward to peer down the companionway. The kids are standing, holding on, two bottles roll back and forth on the floor as the boat rides the wave down.

'Is it meant to be like this, Mum?' Essie calls up, eyes wide, the edge of panic.

'Just stay down there, close this hatch,' she yells and hears it click into place.

This time, she is quicker, more sure-footed as she goes. Anticipating the fall and the dip of the deck with the swell, keeping her legs wide, the muscles of her core locked.

She recites the instructions. Change the rig. Blue and yellow sheet. Then put the halyard in the winch ready to hoist the sail up as he winds it on.

He shouldn't be doing it. He can sit, he says, and it's true, but she knows his body is starting to refuse, that she needs to check his foot. Things could get bad, and quick.

She is drenched. And the wind is cooler now. Her t-shirt sticks against her back as she works at the sail, flattening and feeding it up, unknotting, pulling it back through, repeating the incantation.

She raises her hand, waves so Nick can see, watches as the little sail begins to unfurl above her. Inch by inch. She puts her hands on the fabric, guiding it smoothly and following it down to check there is no kink, no place for it to catch, like he has told her.

There is a hollow noise and she looks up to see the sail has stopped. She leans forward to try and see Nick. Can just make him out hunched over the winch, jamming his arm. Stuck.

She sees a wave coming from behind the boat, feels the lift and braces herself for the rushing slide as they come down the face of it.

She calls out, 'You okay?' but, again, the words are taken by the wind. She hurries back – hold, dip, feet against the slick deck.

'What's wrong?' she says, leaning in under the awning.

'Fucking jammed,' he spits.

His foot down on the deck now, a smear of blood marring the white surface.

'How do we fix it?'

'Might be the sail, caught on something. Have to check.'

'What am I looking for?'

He shakes his head. 'You won't know.'

'Well tell me.'

'It's not,' he hangs his head, then, with a surge of anger looks up at her, 'it's not that fucking easy! I've done this for years. You can't just – in a couple of days – you can't . . .' He stops and shakes his head. 'I'll do it.'

'You can't stand up.'

'I'll manage.'

She holds on to the rigging with both hands as the boat dips and Nick tries to stand.

'You're a fucking idiot,' she says.

He holds on to the table and shuffles towards the spot where he can get through to the foredeck.

'If you go overboard, what the fuck am I going to do?' she yells over the wind.

'I won't,' he yells back over his shoulder. And then a wave rolls beneath them again and they tilt further. She looks behind her to see the roiling ocean, clamps her grip tighter, looks back at Nick to see him grabbing for another handhold, his weight shifting. Unable to bear the weight on his foot he goes to kneel on the bench and falls heavily, yelping in pain as he twists around to protect his foot.

'Stay there,' Mim says, climbing over him. His eyes are closed and his teeth are biting into his lower lip.

'Essie!' she calls down the companionway. 'I need you!'

～

Later, after the storm, she will wonder what she was thinking. She will berate herself for not weighing up the risks. *I was mad*, she will think. She will imagine a wave sweeping up, imagine the flash of Essie's red t-shirt sinking in the swell, disappearing behind them. She will find herself on her knees in the cabin, hands pressed into the solid floor, gasping for air, not sobbing, not heaving, some foreign land of terror in between, what might have been.

But she will also see her daughter's face.

The way she gripped the mast, one hand clenched, wrapped around the rope, holding the winch in place, then drawing it slowly, slowly, so that Mim could use both hands to test where the jam was, find it, ease it out.

'I'm okay, Mum.' Her voice clear and unafraid as Mim yelled across the roar of the water and wind.

The jubilation in her voice as she yelled down the companionway, 'I fixed the sail,' and Sam's little face looked up at her, awestruck.

And she will press them both to her, forget for a moment about everything else, what's to come, what has been, and will just hold her children's heads to her chest, feel their arms loop around her waist and cling tight, rock with them there as the storm subsides and she will feel a certainty, something finally click into place – 'I will do anything for you,' she whispers into their hair.

22

'We're close,' he says.

'How close?'

'Couple of miles off. Should be –' He inhales sharply, winces and closes his eyes. They'd moved through the storm quickly, it churned the sea in one direction and they sped through with their little sail in the other. She feels high, fuelled by the adrenaline, the responsibility of getting them here. She'd forced Nick to go down under once the wind died a bit, motor chugging along, has left the sail as is. She has checked on him through the hatch. He has dozed fitfully. The pain must be intense, and the double dose of painkillers has made him groggy. When she changed the bandage she was shocked at how swollen his whole foot was, to the ankle. An angry red spreading from the purple-black bruising at the front of his foot. She is tender with him as she touches his foot, his leg. Thankful for the calm she feels now with his skin under her fingertips. Almost maternal.

He needs a doctor. Will need IV. Needs someone to decide if those toes can be saved. But first, they must get there.

She asks Essie to keep watch, takes Nick water, asks him how it needs to be done.

'The cove. It'll be tricky,' he says.

'What do I need to look out for?'

'I'll do it.' He goes to sit up.

'Will you just stop? I can do it. You can't.' She puts her hand on his arm, softening. 'You could lose your whole foot if it gets infected. You've got to keep it up. Keep it clean.'

She squeezes his arm, moves her hand away once he lies back, repeats the question. 'What am I looking for?'

'Deep entrance, but narrow. The current, tide. Got to get it right.'

She knows the way water travels over rock. She imagines the trench at the bottom of this ocean here, the island erupting up out of the underwater mountain range, the way it might fall and deepen, the ridges and valleys. She thinks of the way wind erodes, how it niggles and flows and whips, is trapped and then gusts away. Now she thinks of water.

'What do we want the tide to be doing when we go in?'

'Has to be on the turn. Check the tide chart. On the nav desk.'

She ducks through into the cabin, riffles through the papers on the desk, finds the one.

'Tomorrow morning, early, three o'clock,' he says, decoding the chart after a moment.

'Can I do it in the dark?'

'Not great.'

'You need a doctor.'

He doesn't reply.

'Can it be done?'

'Yes.'

'Okay,' she says, and repeats it, softly. 'Okay.'

∿

She can see the bulk of the island against the horizon as dusk starts to shadow the sky. She gets them into position, faces the boat into the wind, current behind, keeps the motor ticking over. He's said they can idle here while they wait.

She feels sick. A humming adrenaline in her veins that has her buzzing, too high, like she's had three coffees on an empty stomach. Tries to breathe, to slow it down.

She hopes he is right, that they are too far out for customs yet. There's a chance they'll come out to the boat. She can't afford to be seen. It's a risk, but, just in there, there is help for Nick. And in town there are buses, motos, people she can speak to, people who might know Ben.

Ben.

She hasn't thought of him for hours, for a day, since the companionway slammed down. She tries to resurrect his face before her and it's as though he is caught behind smudged glass. Lacking definition. Maybe he has been found. Maybe he is back home, wondering where his wife and kids have gone. Trying to comprehend the shitstorm she has left in her wake. Maybe it has all been for nothing. They might have died last night, taken by the hungry sea, and not a soul would know where they were. Maybe Ben is right now sitting at the kitchen table thinking that she is the one who has disappeared. Perhaps he is grasping at logic and possibilities, hollowed out by his aloneness. Wondering what to do next. She looks at the mass of land rising up out of the sea in front of them, made mountainous by forces deep beneath, by the shifting plates of the continents, by forces that are beyond time and space and control.

Or maybe he is somewhere in there. Lost, held, dead.

You will not recognise me, she thinks, *when I find you.*

~

Down under, the kids are at the table. Essie is drawing intricate patterns in her book. She has done one for Sam and ripped it out and he is carefully, carefully colouring in the tiny shapes she has created. Indigo, then royal blue, then aquamarine.

'They look amazing.' She touches Essie's head.

'Look at mine, Mum.' Sam holds it up, and Mim runs her finger along the indents he has made, pushing the colour so deep into the page that it ruts the thick paper. 'Essie made it for me.'

Essie smiles, flicks her eyes up. Gratitude blooms in Mim.

'So, we're going to be there tonight.'

'At the island?' Sam turns to her, eyes wide.

'Yep. You can see it already if you go up on deck.'

'Cool.' He jumps up, but she stops him, asks him to wait.

'I just wanted to,' she hesitates, 'to talk to you a bit about what'll happen when we get there.'

'Yeah?' Sam says.

Essie doesn't look up.

'We're breaking some rules to be here.'

Sam's forehead furrows. 'What rules?'

'Rules about how you enter a country, how you leave, stuff like that.'

'Will we get in trouble?'

'I hope not.'

'What will happen if we get caught, though?'

'We won't.' She hopes they can't hear the anxiety in her voice.

'But why are we breaking the rules?'

'We had to, Sammy, honey, so we could find Dad. Sometimes,' she reaches out and puts her hand on his shoulder, 'sometimes we have to break the law to do the right thing.'

Essie chimes in. 'There's different sets of rules for different people, then.'

'Well there shouldn't be. But yeah. There are.'

'So we're lying.'

'Sometimes something is against the law, but it's still right.'

'So, the law doesn't apply to us?'

'No. The law applies to everyone.'

'Then what? Because this isn't our country, the law doesn't apply to us?'

'No – it does. It's just a really special circumstance.'

'But don't lots of other people have special circumstances, too?'

Mim takes a deep breath. 'Yep. Yep, Essie they do.'

Essie raises an eyebrow, looks back at her picture.

'Anyway,' Mim says, 'I just wanted to tell you that. So, if anyone asks, we're just on a holiday, okay? Just let me talk. That's really important. You just let me talk.'

~

Later, the moon is full and astonishing on the water. Even after five nights out here, she cannot get over how solid the light is, the quality of it, quicksilver and cold. There's hardly any wind. It's good, means they can drift out here a little, waiting to go in. She keeps checking the nav to make sure they haven't gone too far off course. A cargo ship passed earlier – right on the horizon. She watched it track across the dark, checked the course, that it wouldn't come close. Fifteen minutes, maybe less, that's what Nick said, from the time you saw lights on the horizon to impact. They wouldn't even know they'd hit you, he said. You'd just go down.

A beeping sound. Her alarm. Time.

This is what has to go right:

She has to steer them through the narrow entrance.

They have to go unnoticed.

She has to find a shallow spot to anchor.

She has to be able to inflate the dinghy, get it over the side, get the four of them in it, and then row them in.

They have to find a taxi, or someone in those early morning hours to take them into the city to the medical clinic.

Then, then she can think about Ben.

She checks the horizon. Steps down into the companionway, the cabin inside lit blue with the navigation lights. He is asleep on the bench.

She touches his leg. 'Nick, it's time.'

He groans. She leans over him, touches his face, damp with sweat. He is giving off a bitter scent, fear maybe, or pain, or his flesh starting to rot.

'Nick, I'm gonna do it now. You want to keep an eye on the nav down here?'

'Coming.' He pushes himself up to his elbows, and has to stop. She leans in and gets her shoulder behind his, pulls him up.

'I'm good,' he says, and pulls away. 'I'm coming up.'

'You can't –'

He cuts her off. 'Stop telling me what to do. Okay?'

He struggles to stand against the table, against the faint rock of the boat. But she doesn't touch him again.

He sits on the seat in front of the helm, his leg up, at least.

'You thought of a story if they come out?' His voice is quick, fevered maybe.

'Who?'

'Customs.'

'Should I have?'

'Fuck yes.'

'Right.' She keeps her eyes trained ahead. 'Like what, mine and the kids' passports fell overboard?'

'You would have been on my papers.'

'You picked us up off some remote island? Fuck, I don't know, Nick. Why are you only saying this now?'

'Cos now is when it's fucking dangerous.' His eyes seem wild.

'It's been fucking dangerous the whole time.'

'For you, maybe.'

'Oh, so, now it's dangerous for you, now it's a fucking risk for you, *now* you want me to think of something in case you go down.'

'I can't afford to lose my boat.'

She turns on him, feels her eyes hot in the dark, wishes she could shoot sparks from the tips of her hair, swell the ocean with her fury.

'You can't afford to lose your fucking boat!'

'Bring her round.'

'What?'

'Bring the boat around a bit. Starboard.'

She has to think about it. Doesn't want to give him the satisfaction. Inches the helm around, checks the nav. Notices the flickering red in the corners of her vision, furious phosphorescence. Arsehole.

'Sorry,' he says.

She stays silent.

Quiet schlock of the water, the purr of the engine.

'Hey.' Hand on her arm. 'I'm sorry.'

She nods. Looks at him, his face in shadow, body backlit by the moon.

'They won't come. It's too early.'

'Just trying to get you to the doctor.'

'Yep.'

Lights ahead, dotting the shoreline. Would be almost impossible without the moon.

'Should we turn off our lights?'

'No. But you see anyone coming and you go below.'

'But you can't . . .'

'I'll have to.'

'That the town?' She points to where there is a little cluster of lights trailing back up the mountain from the shore. 'Nick?'

He has lain back, eyes closed.

'Nick! Is this where I come in?'

'Think so.'

'How close can I go?'

'Watch the numbers.'

She looks at the depth sounder.

'How far?'

'If it gets to fifteen metres, you've gone too far.'

'It's eighteen.'

'Soon. Drop the throttle back. Slow.'

She has only seen him do it. The boat feels enormous under her, unwieldy but so sensitive. She is navigating what she cannot see, the vault of water and rock and crevasse beneath her, the shadows

282

hiding in the water ahead, old fishing boats floating close, the black corpse of a tree, rock, chain, tangled ropes and mooring lines, the drowned beaches of the island, the skeleton of a submerged wharf. She can only do it by feel, by careful, breath-holding movement, inching forward till the numbers add up.

'Then what?'

'Anchor.'

'How?'

He swallows. A couple of times, like his mouth is full of sand. She passes him her bottle of water.

'Nick, how? This is the depth, here.'

'Stop the motor.'

She flicks the switch and the quiet storms in.

'At the front. I can —' He pulls himself up, but he is all gritted teeth and no power. '*Fuuuuck!*' he hisses.

'Just tell me.'

'Unhook. Let the winch go. Don't try and hold the rope. It'll take you over.'

She repeats it to herself. Steps out of the cockpit and balances around the edge. She can see better from here, with the sails and the ropes and the shoreline so close now. They must be less than one hundred metres out. She watches for movement on the shore but there is none. She is sweating, can feel the humidity rising out of the jungle just there in front of her. Can smell the green of it, laced through with all the notes — spice, diesel, foetid water — that tell her she is far away from home.

She looks down at the complication of steel and hook and rope, and grits her teeth that she did not ask to learn when she had the chance. She was so willing to be saved. *We fall for that*, she thinks. *How we fall.*

The light from her head torch isn't great, not enough sun to power it today, but she doesn't want to put the deck light on. Imagines someone sitting on shore, watching her clumsy attempts. All the people who might be registering their arrival. She needs to be quick. Needs to get them onto land.

She leans down and unties the hitch holding the ropes in place. The steel of the anchor is heavy. She thinks she can hear Nick calling from the cockpit, but she ignores him. Pulls it out of its spot, positions her feet so her weight is spread evenly. She tries to think logically. Is there a side it should go on? Does she throw it, or let it go gently? How bad can she mess it up? Don't try and hold it, he'd said, it'll take you over. *Get a grip*, she says to herself, *you sailed this thing through a storm, you can drop the fucking anchor.*

When she looks over the side, the light from the torch makes the water green and opaque. A cluster of water bottles and coloured plastic bags, a stretch of palm, is lapping up against the boat. God, she hopes the kids don't have to get in the water.

The chain is looped in a great coil, she checks her feet are clear, moves her hand slightly, the anchor so heavy she can feel the pull in her shoulder. She twists her body, practising the arc it will make through the air when she heaves it over. Counts down. *Do it.* Heaves back, waits until the last moment, feels the knuckles of her spine crunch, protest, and then it's over. *Kickle, kickle, kickle*, the loops of chain whisper and spit as they unwind. It feels like it takes forever, the loops of chain disappearing beneath the surface. She holds her breath as she waits for it to stop, sink in the mud, hold them there.

The sound stops. She looks over the edge, the chain disappearing into the water. Her hands are slick with the humidity as she locks it down, switches off her head torch, lets her eyes adjust to the quick darkness, the slow luminosity of the moon.

'Did you tie it off?'

'Yep.'

'You sure?'

'Nick, it's done. Tell me where the pump is for the dinghy.'

'Under the bench there. Clicks into the generator at the nav desk.' His breath is heavy at the end. She touches the back of her hand to his head. So hot.

⌒

It takes her an hour. Untying the ropes that hold the dinghy to the deck. Unwinding the leads for the air compressor, finding the spots to attach. Essie wakes up when she turns it on, the tinny buzz alien in the quiet.

'Mum, what is it?'

'It's okay, Ess. Just getting the dinghy sorted. Go back to sleep.'

In the half-light from the desk, Mim sees her daughter sit up. 'Have we stopped? Are we here?'

'Yep. I'll wake you up when we need to go.'

'I'm awake now, Mum. I can help.'

'I'm nearly done.'

Essie lies back and rolls on her side and Mim feels instant regret. She keeps confusing the things she should be protecting them from.

~

She wrestles the fat dinghy over to the side and checks the rope is knotted firmly. The moon is lower now and it's throwing white light on the water. If anyone is watching they will see her as clear as day. She feels so close now, but there are still so many things that can go wrong. Get to shore. Get Nick to the doctor. These are her priorities.

Then Ben.

Ben will be next.

The dinghy hits the water, she pulls the rope to get it facing the right direction and walks it around to the stern. She remembers how unsteady she was that first day, certain she'd stumble to the edge and tip straight over. Now her bare feet are sure as she edges her hips past the poles of the canopy, jumps down and ties the rope off at the back. She's not going to put the outboard on, too loud. It's only one hundred metres into the shore, they could swim it if they had to, but Nick, that water. And the gear. She doesn't know when they'll come back to the boat. She keeps leaving places behind without ceremony. It's protective, she tells herself, but she wonders if she is failing to compute.

She's packed the kids' backpacks, and hers. Shoved some clean stuff of Nick's into a bag. Deodorant. Toothbrush. Found all his paperwork in its old leather pouch. It felt intimate. After everything, pulling open his drawer and seeing the t-shirts folded there, so unexpected, as though she had seen something she shouldn't. The soft underskin of him. For a moment, she is back there, skin and stars, and she puts her hand out to lean against the bed. *Steady now*, she thinks.

∽

'Need my passport. The Indo cash.' Nick's eyes are half-open in the semi-dark. He is looking at the packs in her hand.

'I've got it. Your leather pouch, yeah?'

'More cash. In the first book on the shelf.'

'But I don't have any more.' Quick panic, wonders if any of the cards will work. Can't use them. They'll pick her up in a second.

'I've got some US dollars.'

'I can't use yours.'

'You can owe me.' He pauses. 'Your stuff. Bring it or hide it.'

∽

She gives Essie the bag she was going to leave, tells her to find everything that is theirs. Nothing can be left. She flicks through the first book on the shelf, finds the wad of bills there, tucks them into the pocket of her windbreaker, zips it up. Maybe they won't come back to the boat. Maybe this is it. Would he stay, to bring them home? She tries to imagine Ben on board. Feels sick with shame. Not now.

'Getting light,' Nick calls from upstairs.

'Where's Sam?' Mim says to Essie.

'Still on the toilet. He's got a pain.'

'Finish that bag, and grab some muesli bars, yeah? We've got to go.'

She's had all night. But this is how it always rolls, she knows, the last bit of panic before you go.

'Sammy, mate.' She knocks on the narrow door. 'You okay?'

She waits.

'No. I can't do a poo. My tummy hurts.'

'Just stay there a bit. I'll let you know when we have to go. Okay?'

He takes it all in, keeps the smile up, then his body starts to betray him. She knows this, and yet she forgets. She remembers the last term at kinder, when some little shit had started to pinch him, just under the seam of his shorts, or his t-shirt, so the teachers couldn't see the red mark. Every day. He'd explained the bruises away for a bit. It was only when his constipation gave him cramps that made him howl in pain that he finally told her. She feels a flush of shame as she remembers how she'd hissed at the other mother at drop-off, the look of surprise, the realisation that they were the same, really.

She grabs six bottles of water from the store under the floor, stuffs a couple of boxes of protein bars in her bag. Essie is up in the cockpit, looking out towards the shore. She points to a couple of spots of light, moving through the trees above the shoreline.

'Look,' she says, 'someone's awake.'

Sam's head appears in the companionway.

'Success?'

'Nah.'

'You'll be right.'

She wants to haul him into her and hug him, let him snuggle right in, the way he used to. She wants to protect him forever.

'You reckon you can help me row?'

His eyes light up. 'Sure.'

～

They nearly go over, as she tries to help Nick in. He barks at her and so she steps back, and the kids lean out, and the dinghy dips and sways.

'Stay still!' Nick shouts, and in the light from the torches she sees Sam's face fall.

She does not help Nick again. She can see the tension in his jaw, holding it in until he can't anymore and he groans. Moonlight shines on the trails of sweat on his face. He is in a bad way. But she can't think of that now.

'Okay. Ess, Sammy, you share, huh? When one of you gets tired.'

Essie scoffs. 'It's not that far, Mum.'

'Well, I want you both to get a go.'

'I'm first.' Sam, clutching at the oar.

'Bull you are, I am.'

'Stop!' Nick yells. 'Essie goes first.'

They are all pulled up short by his transformation. She tries to think of an equivalent for the pain, surely it's not as bad as child-birth? But she knows she was out of her own head then. A snarling demon. Would have bitten the midwife on the neck to stop her coming close if she'd had the energy.

'Ess, just hold there for a minute while I turn us around.'

It's awkward. The water so heavy but nebulous against the oar, she can't get purchase to turn them smoothly. Water splashes up as she puts the oar in at an odd angle and Sam squeals, 'You got me wet!'

'Sorry. Go, Ess, on that side, that's it.'

She watches Essie's back, how straight she sits, the muscle she is putting into it. The shadows on the shore become clearer as they make their slow, splashing way in. The upturned hulls of the long fishing boats, a crumbling concrete wall set back off the beach. An old shelter, just uprights and palm fronds for a roof. Behind that, the darker shadows of tall palms and squatter trees with fat leaves. The glint of glass and moonlight on tin in a row of shacks set back in the jungle.

Nick angles his face back so she can hear him. 'Check the depth.'

She looks over the side, sees only the moonlight reflected, the swirl of bubbles in the wake of her oar. She hesitates for a moment then realises what he means, shoves the oar down towards the bottom, until her hand is in the water and she can feel it make contact.

'You gotta jump out soon,' he says.

Of course she does. It's mild enough, but she thinks of that line of rubbish up against the hull, thinks of the other couple of boats that are moored, thinks of piss and shit and diesel and sludge.

'Just go easy now, Ess, hand over to Sammy.'

'He won't be able to do it, Mum.'

'Give it here.' Nick takes the oar, digs it hard down and holds them there.

Mim doesn't say a word.

'There'll be concrete, sharp bits,' Nick says. 'Careful. Keep your thongs on.' His voice is hard.

She gets one leg over, can't reach the bottom, water is warm, an oily film to it. She slides down, wet all the way up to her bum. Under her thongs, it is uneven, smooth rock and sharp, she hopes she doesn't cut herself, feels her way slowly, pulling the dinghy behind her.

'Not too far.'

'How are you gonna get in? You can't get your foot wet.'

'Do the kids first.'

She turns to Sam. 'Okay you first, Sammy.' She can carry him still. She loops the end of the rope around her wrist so the dinghy doesn't float away, steadies Sam as he stands.

'Give me a bag too, Ess.'

With the bag on one shoulder, she hoists Sam onto her hip and he shuffles, crablike, round to her back as she wades through the shallows and deposits him on the shore.

'You stay there with the bag and I'll bring the others in.'

Essie is already halfway out when she gets back, Nick still holding the oar in place.

'Careful, Ess,' she says, and then to Nick, 'we'll pull you right up.'

'You can't, you'll rip a hole in the dinghy.'

She shakes her head. 'It's not bad, there's a clear path.'

'Essie, can you?' She turns to her daughter, shows her the handhold, and they begin to pull the dinghy into shore.

Behind them, she hears Nick mutter, and when she turns to check on him, she can see the tension in his shoulders, the furious shame in his face. That he should be pulled into shore by them. She is almost ashamed at the perverse pleasure she feels.

At the edge of the water, he slips his good leg over, and she has to rush back to help, take his weight. He leans into her even as he tells her he's fine, he can do it by himself.

Together, she and Essie lift the dinghy over the rubble at the tideline and tie it off next to the fishing boats.

The sky is getting pale now, the moonlight fading into that predawn blue. There is a rooster crowing.

They sit on the beach. Nick resting against a low concrete wall, eyes shut against the pain, Sam perched on his bag, Essie close beside her. She is rocking slightly, a fluidity to the rocks and sand beneath her and she's not sure how long that will last, but she's not on the water anymore. It's another sovereign land, solid, rock to sand and back down to bedrock. They have made it. Not drowned.

Not stopped by border control. They are here. She has got them here. And with the touch of the earth, she is brought back to her purpose: Ben. The niggle in her guts at the thought of everything that has happened out there, at sea. She pushes it down.

'Okay,' she says, as the morning light cracks the sky. 'Let's find a way into town.'

23

As the morning begins to heat, the smell of the earth seeps up through the dirt, the cracked edge of the bitumen road, the open drains rich with putrid water. The four of them wobble as they pick their way across the rocky cusp of the beach, the earth strangely static beneath their feet. The kids have gone quiet as the roosters ratchet up their chaotic chorus. A useful quiet, but unnerving, as though they have only now realised the craziness of where they are, what they are doing. They stick close to her. She thinks of ducklings, winged by a mother duck. Nick says to look out for the first taxi, a Bemo, a minivan that will take them into the city. They don't wait long, bunched on the corner, before they hear an engine and Mim steps out onto the road to wave the small green van down.

The driver grins widely when Mim pokes her head through the window.

'City,' she says, and the man nods, says something Mim cannot understand, and then laughs along with the passengers in the back.

Mim has to push the kids on through the open side door ahead of her and the women in the back make room, shuffling up with their laps full of plastic bags. She waits behind Nick, hands steadying him as he pulls himself in. The kids sit on the low bench opposite. Nick has to duck his head, the roof is so low. She is aware of the grotty bandage on his foot, but he does not pull it back in or try to hide it.

A woman peeling a green orange and eating the segments, tuts and shakes her head and points at Nick's foot.

'Yes,' Mim says. 'Doctor?'

The woman nods, spits pips over the edge of her teeth, speaks loudly to the driver. There is talk back and forth, and Mim nods, trying to work it out.

Sam's eyes dart everywhere, his mouth slightly open. Essie rounds her shoulders in, aware of their oddness, the fact that they don't belong here. Mim sees the sweat on her upper lip. The smell of the combined body odour in the rising heat.

There are five women, and one of them is drinking something out of a plastic bag with a straw, holding the little handles over two fingers. Bright plastic flowers and cards with foreign words and pictures are stuck above the windscreen and all along the dashboard. The smell is hot and sweet food and spice and sweat. As they round the corner there is the sea again, the silver grey spill of it. If they look back they can see the boat, the *Sandfly*. A lurch in her stomach, it seems so small already as the van climbs higher on the narrow road. Spotted through the jungle are the jagged edges of tin and plastic and tile, the ways in which the locals have clung their lives to the mountain, carved out spots for themselves. As they get closer to the city the foreignness of it flares in her: the rubbish sweepers, the tsunami warning signs, the lines of shops selling engines, bikes, plastics, cigarettes, with signs for Bintang and mobile phones. The clusters of cameras on poles, black and all-seeing under the spaghetti chaos of wires, are familiar. Instinctively, she ducks her head.

The women seem to be seeking consensus, disagreeing with the driver. A younger woman with pink lipstick and a bright blue headscarf looks up from her phone and speaks decisively, and the older women nod. Minutes later, the Bemo pulls over and the woman with the orange leans over to touch Mim's arm, points out the window to a blue cross above a shop a little way up the street.

'Doctor?'

The woman nods. Smiles, ushers them out.

'*Terima kasih*, thank you.' Mim smiles.

She pushes the kids ahead of her, has to help Nick when he tries to get up from the seat and falls back. She hands over some cash, too much probably. The driver smiles and pulls back into the traffic.

The clinic is open to the street. Clean and white and tiled, sandals and thongs lined up at the edge of the tiles. A glass cabinet across the front lined with boxes of antibiotics. Not much she understands. She hopes that someone will speak English. Just not enough to ask too many questions.

The woman at the desk is pleasant-faced but unsmiling.

'Hello. It's okay for me to speak English?' Mim says.

'I speak English.'

'Thank you.' She smiles in relief. 'It's . . .' she pauses, decides quickly, 'my husband.' She feels Essie tense beside her. 'We were on a boat, an accident, he hurt his toes. He has an infection, I think.' She points back to where Nick is sitting, his head leant back against the tiles behind him.

'Passport?' the woman asks, holding out her hand.

'Sorry?'

'The patient's passport. Or yours. You have it?'

Mim scrabbles for the bag. 'His. Yes. Here, sorry.' She hands Nick's passport over. Scratchy skipping pulse.

The woman takes the passport to the back of the counter where there is an old scanner and takes a copy.

'What's that for, Mum?' Sam asks quietly.

'Just a copy, Sammy, so they know who they are looking after. You two go and sit down, huh?'

Any minute, she thinks, any minute and they will give it away.

The woman slides a laminated sheet across the counter. It is a list of fees. Traveller consultation, it reads, twenty-five US dollars.

Sailors must maroon themselves here often enough, broken or bitten or burning up with tropical fevers.

'Yes, of course.' Mim hands over the cash, a silent thanks to Nick. The beginning of a ledger she does not know how or when she will repay.

'He can come now,' the woman says, gesturing to Nick.

'Right.' Mim turns to Nick, to the line of locals who are sitting against the wall, some swipe screens, an older man rests his head on the shoulder of a younger man, his son, perhaps. A young woman holds a small child in her arms, a saline line taped to her little wrist, snaking up to the clear bag on the silver pole. The woman wheels the pole as she walks up and down.

Mim hesitates. Straight to the head of the queue. Promises herself she will make up for her privilege at some other time. By fuck, she will use it now.

'Through here,' the woman says. She is impatient and Mim feels as though she is being punished.

Nick stands slowly, and Mim goes to him, allows him to lean on her. She tries not to make eye contact with the others who still sit there. Waiting.

∽

It is a small room and Mim and the kids squish up against the wall as the woman gestures for Nick to sit on the bed. A man, the doctor, nods his head and they exchange words. Mim wonders if she is saying 'Stupid fucking foreign sailor. With cash.'

She leans back, wishes there was more air than the whirring fan.

'Mum, I'm hot.' She passes Essie the water bottle.

There is a smell. Ammonia, the nose-crinkling scent of gauze, just unwrapped, the sweet of the pink handwash. She is acutely aware of how they all must smell. Thinks back to the last wash, the deck shower, the sun, my god, all that has happened.

The doctor helps Nick put his foot up on the bed. Gently unwraps the bandage to reveal the damage beneath. He leans in, pokes his gloved finger towards the toes. What is left of the toes.

'No good,' he says and shakes his head. 'Hospital.'

'You fix it,' says Nick. 'I have more cash.'

The doctor frowns, shakes his head again, says something to the woman in Bahasa.

'The injury is too bad. He must go to hospital,' the woman says. 'There is a private one here, in the city. I will get you a taxi.'

'Fuck,' Nick mutters under his breath.

'Mum?' Essie looks at her, speaks almost under her breath. 'What about Dad?'

'Shhh,' she says, touching Essie's hair, pretending not to notice the woman's eyes flick up. 'Let's just get this sorted, huh?'

～

The hospital is at the top of a winding street, narrow with street vendors, silky bunting hanging from low, tiled roofs. Bikes weave slowly, schoolkids bunch in their uniforms, little backpacks strapped on their backs.

A woman in a pale peach shirt with a green logo embossed above the breast comes out to meet the taxi as they pile out of the car. Nick is wobbly and weaker now from all the movement.

A young man brings out an old wheelchair and Mim lets them take Nick, help him to the chair. He lets out a soft oomph and she is momentarily pierced with embarrassment, it seems like something an old man might do.

Inside, the hospital is bright. Yellow walls and cartooned posters showing handwashing, covering your face when you sneeze. There is movement, bustle, just like any hospital at home, except this time they are the foreigners; there are curious glances, smiles, quick nods. Some of the signs are in English, so the hospital must have a few travellers, ex-pats maybe, as patients, but they are rare enough to be of interest. She feels grubby, wants to explain herself. Is suddenly weary to her very core. 'Just a little bit longer, then we'll go and clean up,' she says to the kids, but it isn't as if they care. They wait in a small room with Nick until a doctor comes and says they should wait in reception. She touches Nick's shoulder as she leaves. 'I've got your stuff,' she says.

He nods, catches her eyes, tries a smile, but he looks so tired now. Part of her wants to stay and look after him, the him of before, of that first cracked smile back at Eagles Nest where she was tethered to memory. She also wants to leave him now, he is complicating things. She feels a part of her sloughing off. The bright steely autonomy of what might be underneath.

They pile their gear on a seat in the reception area, and Mim tells the kids to sit while she goes out to the vendor she can see through the window. She buys soft drinks for the kids, Nescafe in a can for herself, bread in a packet, a knobbled green fruit which the female vendor presses on her, smiling, nodding.

They wait. The same young woman in the uniform brings her a form to fill out.

'For your husband,' she says, and Mim nods, smiles, takes the board and pen.

There are words in Indonesian, the English translation beside. She scans the page and realises how little she actually knows about Nick.

'Do you have many Australians come here?' she asks when she hands the form back, the niggle of possibility.

'Not so many,' the woman says and smiles. 'Sometimes, sailors, but also Americans, English, Italian.'

'From the project?'

The woman cocks her head.

'Golden Arc. The mine?'

She purses her lips. 'They have their own medical.'

'On the island?'

'Of course.' The woman nods her head. 'Much money, China. But sometimes, if an injury is very bad, maybe . . .'

Mim leans forward, a pulsing at the corner of her eye, exhaustion, feels a headache building. 'Do you – sorry . . .' She turns and grabs her wallet from the bag, pulls out the photo of the four of them and shows it to the woman. 'Have you ever seen this man?' She points to Ben's smiling face.

'Your family?' the woman asks, and takes the photo, peering intently. 'Your children are very beautiful.'

Mim smiles quickly, but presses her, 'Have you seen him?'

'Your husband, no?' The woman is frowning, looking at the man in the picture who is so clearly not the man Mim has come in with.

She breathes sharply. 'No – not my husband – have you seen him though?'

The woman shakes her head. 'I don't think, I'm sorry. He works for Golden Arc?'

Mim nods.

The woman shakes her head. 'Bad news there lately. They say there was an explosion. People were hurt, maybe, but they keep to themselves. We wouldn't know.'

An explosion.

'How many people were hurt?'

'They don't say, it is rumours only.'

Mim nods. 'Thank you, thank you anyway.'

Essie rounds on her when she sits back down. 'What were you showing her?' she demands.

'Nothing, it wasn't . . .' Mim trails off. She looks out through the streaked window, the mayhem of traffic, Bemos, motorbikes, bicycles, the street vendors up and down the road, the cars weaving in and out, all the way down to the harbour. What if he's hurt? Worse? And they are trying to cover it up? An acidic trickle burns in her gullet. Where are you, Ben?

⁓

After a while, the same doctor comes out, ushers them into another room where Nick is sitting up on a bed, his foot stretched out in front of him, clean at last. Next to him there is an IV drip lacing down from a tall metal pole and into the crook of his elbow. His head rests back on a pillow and he opens his eyes as the doctor begins to talk.

The doctor is a tall man, young, belt cinching at his hips, white shirt smoothed and tucked, immaculate.

He explains that Nick will need to stay a couple of days, needs antibiotics to stop the infection spreading. They got here just in time, he says, he could have lost his toes.

'He won't though?' Mim asks quickly.

'No, we will do surgery this afternoon, repair what is damaged. He will keep his toes.'

'That's good.' She smiles. 'Isn't it?' she says to the kids, and they nod at Nick.

Nick attempts a smile. 'Go get a hotel. Come back tomorrow.'

Mim feels a lurch in her gut at the thought of leaving him. No, not leaving him, but being on her own, with the kids, in all this strangeness.

'It's okay, we can stick around.'

The doctor coughs quietly. 'There is a hotel right next door. I can ask reception to help you organise a room there. You will be very close.'

Nick nods at her. 'Go on, go have a shower, get some food, then you can come back, if you want.' He levels his gaze at her. 'You'll be okay,' he says.

She moves forward, grips his hand quickly, then lets it go.

'Your husband is in good hands,' the doctor says and Mim thanks him quickly, ushering the kids out of the room before they can say anything.

24

The air outside is wet. She thinks of the autumn dry she usually hates back home, when the air feels like it might shatter at your touch, nothing like this damp fug. She wants to towel her skin until it flakes away. She needs to find a phone shop, a network, some way to send a message to her mother. Tell her they are alive, okay. But first – god, yes, when Nick said it – first she wants a shower.

⁓

The man at the hotel reception is sweet, young, his smile cracking at the kids as he rushes to help them with their bags when they come in through the glass entrance.

She's had better hotels, but this will do.

His smile slips away when she says she does not have a passport she can hand over.

'We are sailing.' She laughs nervously, her hand going out to touch Essie's shoulder. 'We came straight to the hospital, there was an accident.'

'No identification, madam?' he asks again. 'I am sorry, but to check in . . .' he trails off. He is nervous, she thinks, young. Trying to follow the rules.

'My husband is at the hospital, his passport is there. I can get it tonight.'

He smiles widely. 'Yes! Yes, that will be okay. I will tell my boss.'

⌣

The kids have been appeased with the sweet green welcome drink the boy from reception has brought up. Their screens need charging but there is an old television in the corner that screams some kind of music, the chaos and bang of cartoons. She leaves them to it, half-hoping they fall asleep with the heat, the madness of it all. She has no idea what time it is and tries to count back the hours. Was it only this morning they arrived on the beach? Could be mid-afternoon by now. She wonders when it will get dark. Must get some food into the kids, must get back to check on Nick. Must find her husband. Shakes her head, grabs the towel from the cheap bedspread.

Under the pounding heat of the water, she puts her hands up against the tiles, one against each wall, feels the strange sensation that they are swinging and rocking beneath her touch. She tries to fix her eyes on the taps to hold herself steady, but the walls appear to bulge and tilt and she has to go with it, moving her body like she did when the kids were young, rocking and rocking, that constant motion. Her body wants to be back on the boat. She turns off the shower reluctantly.

There is a mirror – the first time she has seen herself for days.

Look at yourself.

Shoulders pink and scaly, the skin shrunk with sun and salt. The white of her boobs, not swollen with sex and want like she'd imagined them in his hands, his mouth, the dark of that star-plucked night – just ageing skin. She leans closer, self-loathing curls her bottom lip. A dark hair above her nipple, she tries to pinch it between her thumb and forefinger, can't, tries again, pulls hard and spitefully. The sting of it coming free, tears in her eyes.

She bites down. Below the lip to skin, so that she can really feel it.

Imagine Ben fucking someone, she says silently to the woman in the mirror. *Go on, imagine it. How does that feel you shameless bitch? You selfish, horrible person.*

She presses her hands against the mirror. Black mould in the corners where the glass has chipped.

What have you become?

She feels deceived by her own body. Towels herself hard with the thin fabric. Punishing herself. *Forget,* she thinks. A moment of madness. This is what is real, now. Ben. This is what is true.

∽

When the three of them step outside the hotel doors, pushed out by growling stomachs, the sky bulges with dark monsoonal clouds. The air is soupy, a haze of bugs linger around Sam's head. She wants to go into the hospital, but the kids both whinge that they need food.

Her nerves flicker as she looks down into the maze of streets. She needs to find some Aeroguard – there could be malaria, dengue, who knows what strange diseases are sprouting in this overheating quagmire? God, what would a travel doctor have advised them to have shots for? Add it to the list of her parenting fails.

'C'mon, Mum!' Sam calls, and she grabs Essie's elbow and follows him, so she doesn't have to make the decision herself.

It is a blessing really, that it's so overcast. She imagines full sun with this wet heat and thinks they would not even be able to venture out in it. They step over the cracked concrete of the sidewalk, swerving over little mounds of moist dog shit, splattered bags of brightly coloured muck.

'Hello! Hello!' A young man on a becak slows to ride beside them. 'You want a ride to the market?'

Mim smiles, waves him away, but Sam tugs at her sleeve. 'Can we? Mum, please?'

'No problem!' the man says, smiling, placing his feet down. 'You jump in?'

Mim smiles apologetically, shakes her head at Sam. 'No, mate, we have to keep our money, it's good to walk.' Sam's face drops. 'No, thank you, *terima kasih*,' she repeats to the man.

'Okay, okay!' he calls brightly. 'For free! I'm going that way.'

'Mum! Please!'

Mim throws up her hands.

'Where you from?' he asks as he brushes down the short bench seat in the small, canopied buggy behind his bike. It is perfectly clean already, pale blue vinyl, a string of lights around the scalloped edge of the roof, but he wipes it down anyway, holds out his hand in invitation.

'Australia,' says Sam enthusiastically, as he scrambles up and shuffles along. Mim and Essie squish in next to him.

It takes a couple of moments for the becak to take off. The young man stands on the pedals and bears down hard. Mim reaches forward to get his attention. 'It's okay,' she says, embarrassed. 'We're too heavy, it's okay!'

The becak driver laughs, does not stop. 'Okay!' he says and they begin to build momentum. The traffic surges and drifts chaotically around them – other becaks, bicycles, motos with entire families, polished SUVs with darkened windows cutting in front of everyone else. The squat concrete architecture of the buildings seems brutal, ugly, but it is softened by the curlicues of vines, flowers, the blossoming pattern of mould, almost growing in front of their eyes in the humidity.

'Look! Mum!' Sam points to a balloon seller on the corner. Hundreds of colourful foil characters swaying in an enormous net above his head. The pulse of the city all around them. She wonders if they will ever travel through a place just to see it again. Whether the kids will ever wander, wonder, like she and Ben did once. Marvelling at the differences, eyes grown wide with culture shock, the thrill of it all.

Essie holds her screen up: a trolley filled with square cakes, a shopfront open to the street bulging with straw brooms, cascades of purple shampoo sachets, a child crawling on the tiles, laughing at a cat. Her face is bright with it all.

He lets them out at the edge of the market, thronging with people and noise. She tries to pay him, but he waves her hands away. 'My gift,' he says, 'enjoy!'

'Wait,' she grabs at her wallet, 'have you seen him?' She holds out the picture of Ben. 'Have you seen this man here?'

He looks closely, shakes his head slowly, then raises his eyes to meet hers. 'Your husband?'

She nods.

'He is here?' he asks in surprise, hand gesturing to the streets, the madness around them.

She takes a deep breath. 'Maybe. The mine,' she says, 'he was working at the mine.'

The man frowns. 'Bad news, Golden Arc.' He leans away from her and pushes down on the pedals. She watches him as he rides away.

Next time, she will not mention the mine.

～

She must ask fifty people inside the stuffy, crowded aisles of the market. Holding out the photo, the head shakes, the women, especially, who look at her with something like pity, something like satisfaction. She feels inept to have misplaced her husband.

Essie observes it all with her screen. Framing and watching and hiding behind it. Sam ducks under the hands that reach to touch his hair, to fondle and marvel at the shocking blond of it. He smiles at first and then starts to grumble, to hide behind Mim. She buys them fat maroon lychees, squat yellow bananas and they scoff them as they walk. Finally she spots a place with internet and she buys them all drinks, sweet coffee and ice for her, lurid cans for the kids, and hands over cash for them all to have a screen.

'Only ten minutes,' she says, 'you can play what you want.'

She rests her hands lightly on the keyboard. She has to concentrate. Has to be careful.

The connection is fast, then slow, and she waits for two minutes with her search term frozen in the box.

Heidi Fulton.

Finally it loads, but there is nothing new. Academic papers, university contact details, nothing about a house fire, no death notice.

But the absence of anything chills her. *The Chronicle* would have a piece if the local vet was in a house fire, if anyone in town was in a fire.

She types in *house fire* and *NSW*.

This time it is faster, but when she scans the first two pages of results, she knows that there's nothing about Heidi there.

Now she finds *The Advocate* site. Glances behind her to check if there are cameras. She can't see any, but hunches over the screen all the same.

Quicksilver adrenaline rippling through her.

She follows the process, almost familiar now.

Medallion Hotel.

Going out tmrw.

She presses send. Closes the screen down. Stands quickly and hurries the kids out, shushing their protests.

⌣

The kids just want to go back to the hotel, but she bribes them with promises of ice-cream and says they'll be quick. She needs to see him.

She needs to see him because, now, she cannot do, she cannot be, both.

Something has to give.

It's not going to be her.

The same woman is at the hospital reception and she smiles at them, bows her head. It is comforting, the sounds of the hospital, the same everywhere. People striding purposefully, an air of authority. She feels as though someone else is looking after everything here.

Nick is sitting up in bed and looks up when they enter. His face is not as flushed now, but his expression is tight.

'What is it?' she says.

He keeps his voice low. 'Immigration have been.'

Pressure like a clamp in her chest. 'Who? Department?'

'No,' he says, 'local. Indonesian.'

She exhales, ushers the kids to the spare bed in the corner. Essie huffs but leads Sam with her.

'What did they say, what did they want?' she says, low and urgent.

'My papers. To know why I didn't check with customs.'

'What did you tell them?'

'The accident. My foot. Had to come straight in.'

'Do they know about us, the kids?'

He cuts in. 'I don't think so. They got a tip on the boat, they said. I didn't tell them anything.'

'What happens now?'

He shrugs. 'They did the paperwork. Tourist visa. I paid a fine. And some extra. That seemed to work.'

She is breathing easier now. Sits on the edge of the bed so she is facing away from the kids. Nick moves his hand so it is close to her thigh. She hesitates, then puts her fingers over his.

'You find something to eat?' he asks, not noticing.

She nods. 'Went to the market.'

'Kids like it?'

'Yeah.' She smiles. 'We took one of those bikes. They liked that.'

'Good,' he says, leaning back and closing his eyes, 'that's good.'

She cannot leave him like this. It is her fault that he is here, that he is in hospital. It can wait. 'You're wrecked,' she says, moving her hand. 'We should go.'

He grabs at her fingers. 'Don't,' he says. 'Not yet, five more minutes?'

His need for her is satisfying. Fingers laced together again. Carefully, making sure the kids can't see. His eyes still closed. Smiling.

'I'm sorry,' he says suddenly.

'For what?'

'For being a prick. When I was hurt. My foot. I'm sorry.'

She smiles. 'Yeah, you were.'

'You did good,' he says, opening his eyes. 'That was pretty rough, that weather.'

She flushes with pleasure. 'Found my sailing legs.'

'Maybe you should spend more time on boats,' he says, and then, quietly, 'on my boat.' His expression now is too much and she looks away.

~

She is sixteen. They are lying next to each other on his bed, the curtains don't block the summer glare and there is a triangle of fierce light on his cheek. He is looking at her, she knows, his finger tracing lines between the freckles on her shoulder. She is still clutching the sheet across her chest, feeling vulnerable, so vulnerable to all of it, to the bigness of it, to the feeling that every one of her nerve endings is jumping, vibrating. And she knows, can hear the words he isn't saying, thinks it's so odd how all the movies get it wrong. It's not *I love you*, that's not the expression that fizzes on the end of the tongue, what wants to be said. It's not that many words. Just *you*. That's what it is – astonished and breathless and confused and possessive all at once. *You.*

~

313

Now she must move her hand. Before she says something. Before she cries.

'I have to find him now.'

His fingers press then pull back. 'I know.'

Behind her, Sam's voice, 'Don't! Stop, Essie!'

'You two!' she hushes, then turns back. 'And you! You've gotta get home. Back to your mum, to your boat.' She tries to laugh, to relieve the levity of it all. 'To the dream.'

He looks away. 'You reckon?'

'If you stay, I'll . . .' The pause is just long enough. She wonders if the inside of his mind looks the same as hers right now. Sun on a deck, salt-flecked skin, the horizon clear and far away.

A fantasy.

She focuses. 'I've got to get out to the mine island, see if I can get a local to take us.'

'Well, you've got a boat if you need it.'

She laughs. 'That won't sail without you, though, will it?'

'You don't need me, you sailed us in just fine.' He reaches out and holds her arm. 'Take the boat.'

Behind her, the kids' squabbling rises and falls. 'Two more minutes!' she calls and turns back to Nick. 'What?'

He is leaning forward now, insistent. 'The *Sandfly*. Take it, I'm leaving it here for you. You're gonna need a Plan B. Sell it, sail it, doesn't matter. It'll make it easier for me to go back if I know you've at least got that.'

'You can't give me your boat. You're selling it, the cash for your dream boat.'

'Other ways to make quick cash.' He shrugs. 'Think of it as a long-term loan. Maybe I can check in on her from time to time?'

Possibility. Enough to warm herself on when she is doubled over with regret later.

'Your foot, though? How will you –'

'Hey,' he says, puts his hand on her arm. 'You don't have to look after me. I'm good, huh?' He smiles.

She closes her eyes for a second. 'How are you gonna get back?'

'There's a flight back to Jakarta tomorrow afternoon, then home from there . . . easy.'

'Do you need money?'

'All good, some woman gave me a bunch of cash to take her sailing.' He smiles and she could change her mind, she could.

'Thank you,' she says. She lunges forward, enfolds him, or he her, she isn't sure. He is beginning to smell like the sea again.

'Anytime, huh,' he says and pulls away.

She takes a deep breath, calls for the kids to come.

He rummages in the pocket of his backpack, finds something and places it in her hand.

The keys for the galley door.

'Like I said, it's just a lend, yeah?'

She closes her eyes. Nods.

'You gotta go,' he says, closing her fingers over the keys, pushing her gently away from him.

She nods. Turns. Walks away.

At the hotel reception, she asks the man if there are any messages.

He looks up from his device and shakes his head.

'Nothing?' she repeats.

He smiles, although she knows she has pissed him off. 'Nothing for you, madam. Is there anything I can assist with?'

It is not the same man as this afternoon, this one is beautiful and aloof, not as eager to please.

'No, thank you.'

He smiles with his mouth only, goes back to his screen, unfreezing the face she glimpses there.

'Actually,' she says, leaning back on the counter, 'can I place a call to Australia?'

The man sighs, looks up slowly and points to the old desktop in the corner of the lobby. 'You can log in over there.'

'It's just,' she says, reaching into her bag for her wallet, 'I'll only need a moment, but I can't have the call traced to here.'

The man raises an eyebrow. Showing interest now. 'You could use this app I have. If it's just a short call? End-to-end encryption. Can't be traced.'

'I'd be so grateful,' she says, sliding notes to him beneath her palm, aware of the blinking camera in the corner. She ushers the kids up to the room with the card key and tells them she'll only be a minute. She takes the phone when the man offers it and moves away from the counter, turning her back to him.

She waits for a moment, rehearsing scripts, planning what she will say if Steve answers.

But it is her mother who picks up, the voice sounding so near it unnerves her. 'Mum?'

There is a silence. Then quiet, careful. 'Are you okay?'

'Yes.' And now, finally, the relief. Like a wave over her and the tears are unexpected. Her mother's voice has loosed them from her. 'Yes, we are okay.'

'I don't need to know where.'

She realises her mother is being deliberately careful. That she knows they will be listened to. Admiration blooms in her. And guilt.

'It's okay. We're okay.'

A choking sound. 'Good,' her mother says, 'that's good.'

'Mum, I don't know when –'

Her mother interrupts. 'It's okay. It's okay. This is enough. For now, this is enough.'

Mim nods, cries, will hurt later for the moments she did not speak, the moments she wasted. She has to ask. 'Heidi?'

'The same.'

Mim gasps. Better than dead.

Or worse, she imagines Heidi saying, wryly.

'I visit,' her mother says. 'I visit all the time. I'll tell her you called.'

'Yes,' Mim says, 'yes, please do that.' She knows her time is also up. 'I'm sorry, Mum, for all of this.'

'Don't. You did what you had to. Off you go then. Big love. To the kids, okay. Big love.'

'Love you,' Mim says, but her mother is gone.

〜

After Essie was born, Mim had asked her, just once, to stay.

'I didn't realise, Mum,' she'd said, looking at her mother's face, 'I don't think I can do it.'

'Of course you can.' She'd held her palm to Mim's face for a second, cupped the other around her granddaughter's head as Essie snuffled and sucked at Mim's breast.

'It is the hardest thing in the world,' her mother told her, 'and the simplest. You just do it. You just do each day.'

She had pushed it. 'But some days, you must wish,' she had said to her mother. 'Some days we must disappoint you, you must think it isn't worth it?'

She remembers the flint in her mother's face, the pain and the strong of it.

'You do what you can,' her mother had said. 'You do what the books tell you and what your friends tell you and what your sister-in-law tells you, and you try, sometimes, to do the opposite of what your own mother told you, and you just hope, you just hope that you're doing it right, even when you know that you must be doing it wrong. And then – and then you realise that it's so beyond you. Sometimes, despite what you do, despite everything you do –' at this her mother had stopped, could not go on, Michael's name like a solid thing between them.

'Mum, sorry, I shouldn't have –'

But she'd interrupted her. 'And sometimes,' and she'd taken Essie from Mim's arms, scooped her over her shoulder, rocked slowly side to side. 'Sometimes, despite everything you do, you turn out something miraculous.'

~

Back in the room, she can feel sleep coming for her, the wipeout of exhaustion.

'You done a wee, mate? Before you go to sleep? Your teeth?'

'Yes!'

'No you haven't,' Essie bites.

Mim sighs. 'Sam, c'mon, it'll just take a sec.'

He grumbles, but gets up.

Mim closes her eyes.

His little voice triumphant, from the bathroom. 'My poo's coming!'

Essie laughs.

Mim smiles and calls out, 'That's great, Sam, take your time!'

She hears him begin to sing. Something uncoils in her chest and she opens her eyes.

'You okay, Ess?' she asks gently. 'Have you stopped bleeding?'

Essie makes a noise like a huff, doesn't look up. Mim waits.

Sam's voice rises and falls from the bathroom.

'Kind of,' Essie finally says.

'Do you need more pads? We can buy some tomorrow.'

Essie shakes her head. 'It's just kind of − I don't know.' She squirms with embarrassment and Mim wants to go to her.

'Not like blood? Just a weird colour?'

'Yeah,' says Essie, shoulders dropping in relief.

'Yeah, that'll happen for a few days. Or maybe you'll start bleeding again earlier than you think. It takes a while for your body to sort it out.'

Essie keeps her eyes on the page, scribbling, but she is alert, Mim can see it in her body.

'It's stupid. I hate it. Why do we have to have it?'

'Well, because it's your body getting ready –'

Essie interrupts, quickly. 'God, Mum, I know all that.'

'Right,' she says, pressing her lips together.

'I mean, why, as in it's not fair. That this has to happen to me every month until, until I'm like old. *Every month*, Mum. How do you put up with it?'

She wants to laugh in solidarity with her daughter but she is so earnest, so intent, she knows that it will break this precious equilibrium.

'I hated it, too,' she says. 'I did, and then, eventually, when Dad and I decided we wanted you, I realised how brilliantly lucky I was.'

'But I don't want to have kids.'

Essie has always said this. Has always been averse to even the cutest babies. It twinges sometimes, in Mim's chest, the thought that her daughter might so vehemently reject the thing that she herself has chosen.

'Well, maybe you'll –'

'Don't say it, Mum. Don't say I'll change my mind. I won't. It's irresponsible. To have a baby in this world. You're only doing it for yourself.'

Mim nods, is quiet. How did all the children get so wise?

Sam's voice trills, the sound of a flush.

'That's exactly what your uncle used to say. But look, I got you, huh?' She touches Essie's hair. 'Anyway, it doesn't matter about the baby stuff. You choose whatever you want.' Essie is looking at her now, she only has a moment before Sam is back. 'You are stronger and braver than you know. You are.'

Essie holds her gaze for a second more. 'Okay, Mum,' she says and looks away, scribbling again.

But Mim knows, she knows she has planted it. Sometimes, just sometimes, she feels like she gets it right.

Sam throws his arms around her neck. Squeezes. 'That was *such* a great poo, Mum!'

'That's great, darling,' she says, squeezing him back. 'Love you both, sleep well.'

'Goodnight, Dad,' she hears Sam whisper. 'See you tomorrow, I hope.'

Her heart crunches. The bed ghost-rocks around her. She waits for the oblivion of sleep.

25

Knocking on the door. Not frantic, but insistent. Weak light of early morning through the curtains.

She rolls over. *Let me sleep*, she thinks.

The rhythmic knock continues. A soft voice. 'Miriam?'

Swimming up through the sediment of sleep. Who would call her by her name, here? She rolls, rubs her face, feet on the cool floor.

'Yes?' she says, sharply, attempting to sound competent, in control.

'Miriam?' The voice muffled through the wood. 'I need to speak with you. It's Raquel Yu.'

Raquel Yu? The journalist. Here. Outside her room.

When she pulls back the door, the woman who stands there is short, compact; her upper arms tight with the grooves and dips of someone who works out. Dark hair pulled back in a ponytail. Hard to tell how old she is, thirty maybe. Malaysian background, maybe.

'Can I come in?' Raquel says quietly and inclines her head towards the room.

'What are you doing here?'

'Please,' Raquel says, 'let me come in and we can talk.'

Mim steps aside, letting Raquel past. She smells freshly showered and Mim runs her tongue across her front teeth.

'The kids are asleep,' she says and Raquel nods, moving towards the window, away from the beds.

'You're all okay?'

Mim scoffs, shakes her head once. 'How do you define "okay"?'

'Any leads on Ben?'

'Have *you*?' Mim is struggling to understand how the journo on the other end of her messages has materialised in front of her. Now. 'Is that why you're here?'

Raquel is brisk. 'Got in last night. A couple of hours ago I got a message from our cyber team confirming a window of time we can contact Ben.'

'He's alive?'

'If it's him, and we reckon it is, then yes, he's alive.'

He's alive.

And she doesn't realise how great her fear was, that this would not be so, until she lets the relief wash through her. It thrums in her body, unlocking her knees so that she must put her hand out to the windowsill to steady herself.

'I had a flag on the location,' Raquel says. 'We found a bunch of hits indicating an asset was to be extracted from here. Given the rumours out of Golden Arc about the explosion, I figured it was worth a trip.'

Asset.

Extracted.

What the fuck is this? What has he done? If he's alive why hasn't he contacted her?

She looks at Raquel in the pale light seeping in through the curtain.

'Why are you here?'

Raquel looks at her squarely. 'Your husband has something of great value. Information, evidence, I don't know. This is my chance to get at it before he, and whatever he knows, disappears again. We don't know who it is – the UN, a terrorist org, a company, another government – but if I don't get the story out now, it may never get out at all.'

'Why is this so important to you? How the fuck can you find my husband when the fucking Department can't?'

'Maybe they're here already, I don't know, that's why we need to act fast. Their cyber teams are likely to be working on the same comms data we discovered.' She pauses, runs her index fingers under her eyes as if to wake herself up. 'I've been working on this story for six years, Mim. Golden Arc needs to be shut down. It doesn't matter how many stories get out about environmental devastation or the displacement of local landowners or government corruption or health impacts on children – at best it's a tiny story in independent presses that gets a few hits; at worst it never gets published, and a source ends up with their house burned to the ground or their head kicked in, or dead. No one gives a fuck, Mim, unless it's a big old conspiracy that threatens geopolitical stability in an entire fucking region.'

Mim feels sick. 'That's what you're hoping for?'

Raquel does not flinch. 'Hope isn't the word I'd use. But yes, it would help.'

'Have you called the number?'

Raquel shakes her head. 'The pattern they picked up shows the window on this number is for ten minutes at six am. And maybe it's not him, or someone else will pick up, or they'll cut us off immediately. But he's more likely to stay on the line if he hears your voice.'

Mim's jaw aches from gritting her teeth, and she releases them, letting her chin drop and feeling the blood rush back.

'What if we put him in danger by calling? What if they're tracking him and then they come and find me? The kids?'

'I don't know,' Raquel says, stepping towards Mim as though she is approaching a skittish animal. 'But the way I see it, we've both travelled a long way to find him. You've risked your life – your kids' lives. It's got to be worth a shot, right? And you are my best shot at getting him to talk.'

Mim turns to look at the sleeping forms of her children. She shakes her head. She has run out of trust. Of hope. After all of these days, these kilometres, that she would suddenly have this opportunity handed to her. It's too unbearably easy to be true.

'You came here to find him, Mim. One call. If it's not him, if you hear something going down, you hang up. What have you got to lose?'

Mim walks to the window, hooking a finger in the curtain to draw it back slightly. The city is waking up, the street below filling with people and bikes and bells; she wishes she were out there, away from the choices she has to make.

'Mum?' Her daughter's sleepy voice, muffled by the sheet.

'Can the kids talk?' Mim says, quick and low, before she turns around.

'Just to say hello,' Raquel says, nodding. 'We haven't got much time.'

～

Sam needs no convincing to wake up once he hears the word 'Dad'. It is only slightly troubling to Mim that neither of them baulks at the stranger in their room, and once Mim has explained that Raquel is there to help, they both shrug and make space for her on the edge of the bed.

Raquel checks the time again. 'Here,' she says, handing Mim a small square of a phone and an earpod. 'I've put in the number. Remember, you haven't got long. Your Department agents, they could already be here, on his trail – and yours.' Tenderly, Raquel tucks back Essie's hair to place a small white pod in her ear, then neatly inserts a final one for herself.

Essie turns to Mim, her hand at her ear. 'We get to talk to Dad?'

Mim breathes, smiles. 'Yes. Yes, but just, you don't have long. Just to say hello. Don't tell him where we are – the hotel, the boat, anything like that. It's really important,' Mim says. 'To keep him safe. To keep us safe.'

Essie and Sam nod.

'We can run interference for five minutes, that's it,' Raquel says, 'after that we risk them picking us up. One of those minutes is mine.' She looks up from the screen. 'Okay,' she says. 'Now.'

Mim cannot press the button.

'You okay?' Raquel asks, briskly. 'There isn't time.'

'Want me to do it, Mum?' Essie takes the phone, presses the green icon, hands it back.

A long tone. Repeated. She frowns, shakes her head at Raquel, then a click. A voice. 'Yes?'

'Ben?'

'Who is this?'

His voice. Opening up that crack inside of her. Everything before. Everything since.

'It's you.'

'Mim?'

The relief of it. 'Yes, yes, it's me, we're here.'

'*Here*? Jesus, Mim. The kids? Why are you here, where – ?'

Essie has her hand to her ear. 'Dad!'

'You there, Essie? Sam?' he says, fast, frantic.

'We're here, Dad,' Essie says.

'*Dad!*' Sam yells, pressing his face up against Essie's so he can hear the tinny voice through the pod.

Essie begins to cry.

'Where are you?' Ben asks, voice splitting with panic.

'In a hotel,' Sam yells, 'on the island.'

Essie hisses at him, 'Sam, shh.'

'Quick, you two,' Mim urges, 'you'll see him soon, let me talk.'

'Dad? Love you, Dad.'

'Love you, Essie, love you, Sammy.'

Mim's throat tightens as she hears him begin to cry.

'Here,' she says, gently scooping the pod from Essie's ear and moving away as she protests.

'Ben,' Mim says. 'Where are you?'

There is silence for a moment. 'I can't,' he says.

'We're here now, we can come for you, it doesn't matter what's happened.'

Silence.

'Ben?'

She hears him breathe.

'I fucked up.'

'Why didn't you let us know where you were? God, Ben. What have you done?'

There is quiet. The seconds tick.

'They say there was an explosion? Are you hurt?'

'I didn't have a choice, Mim.'

'What?'

And then, like he will burst with it, the words all jangle and tumble over each other. 'I was trying to buy some time. To get word out. The rebels – locals against the mine – they'd tried to get me to help them before – I had a contact – it wasn't meant to blow like that – no one was meant to get hurt.' His voice breaks.

'What do you mean, Ben? What did you do, where are you now?'

Quieter now, calm. 'I found something no one was meant to see, plans for the mine. I realised what they were doing.'

She waits. Feels like her neck will snap with the tension.

'Post-extraction plans. The final project phase is being run by GeoTech for the Department. Meant to be a clean-up, environmental rehab, only it's not. The plans showed more tunnelling. Enormous cavities, deep under the mine. A huge network.'

'I don't understand.'

'It's for storage. Burial.'

'Of what?'

'Nuclear waste.'

'*What?*'

'They're dumping all that fucking nuclear waste they couldn't bury at home.'

'But that's fucking insane, it's on a fault line. The disposal theory never held.'

'The plans are clear, Mim.'

'But, even if it worked, it could be catastrophic, the risk, the fault line could blow. It would –'

'Destroy the entire region.'

Mim is suddenly aware of the sound of Raquel breathing fast. 'But why?' She can't make sense of it.

'Security measure? Insurance? If shit goes down in China, Russia, anywhere fucking north of us . . .'

'But it could take out us as well,' she murmurs.

Ben scoffs. 'Well, only the top half — it's a well-calculated risk.'

Raquel points to her phone, rotates her hands, urging Mim to move quickly.

'Where are you? Near the mine? You said someone was hurt?'

'We needed time, to get the plans out. I managed to get a copy, but then, they said it wasn't enough.' Ben halts, a moment of silence.

'Ben! We don't have much time!'

'The organisation we contacted, they wanted more than the evidence, wanted to be clear whose side we were on. It was only meant to blow one rig, block the tunnel —' His voice has risen, but it drops again. 'I miscalculated. Didn't realise how destructive it would be.'

She waits.

Almost a whisper. 'It killed three people.'

You killed three people.

But there is no time. 'How did you get away? Where are you, Ben?'

'It was too big, I was knocked out. One of the rebels dragged me out of there, hid me in the village. Five days before I woke up. When I tried your number, it was disconnected. You were gone. And by then, it was too dangerous anyway. The plan was already in place. I couldn't risk it.'

Complete stillness in the hotel room. Raquel, rigid with listening, the kids' faces as they try and read her own.

'We had no idea where you were,' she says blankly.

Silence.

She wants to hurt him.

'Did you think about us?'

'Every day,' he says. 'Every minute of every fucking day.'

'Before! Before, Ben.' She feels the heat rise in her. 'Did you think about what would happen when the Department found out what you'd done? When they listed you as a terrorist, charged you with treason? What would happen to us?'

She hears him start to weep. 'I had to do something. There was no time, I had this one chance, to *do* something,' he says.

She interrupts him. 'Do you know what it has been like? Can you even fucking imagine?' She raises her voice now. 'I've brought our kids across the fucking ocean to find you!' She is crying now, furious weeping.

Essie is beside her, takes the earpod back, gentle but sure. 'We nearly drowned, Dad,' Mim hears her daughter say through the line. 'We didn't know where you were. Mum didn't know what to do.'

'I'm sorry, I'm sorry, I'm so sorry,' he is saying. 'I fucked up.'

Mim thinks about the sway of the boat beneath her feet, the slip of it in the storm, how she steadied, how she held her nerve. She didn't fall.

Raquel's hand on her wrist. 'I need to talk to him.'

Mim takes the pod from Essie as she speaks. 'We are coming to get you,' she says.

'You can't.' Finality in his voice.

'Why not?' she says.

'I'm getting out. I can't take you with me. They're extracting me tonight.'

Raquel is holding out her hand, but Mim shakes her head.

'Extracting you to where?'

'Europe, somewhere, they won't say. To keep me safe, then once the investigation is done, they say I can send for you and the kids, new identities, twenty-four-hour security, a new life.'

But she has stopped listening.

Her voice is loud and surprising. 'Fuck you!' She's going to choke on it, her anger, tears. 'We came so far, Ben. We've come so fucking far. We risked everything. The kids could've been killed.'

She rips the pod from her ear, cannot bear to hear his voice any longer. Raquel moves away, her voice quiet and sure. Mim turns to her children, their faces white with shock, and takes them in her arms, shhing their questions, so it doesn't have to be real. Not yet.

26

Raquel has her hand on Mim's shoulder. Her mouth is moving, but Mim cannot make sense of what she is saying. She shakes her head until Raquel grips her firmly.

'The Department could be here already. Go to the airport. You got a phone?'

Mim nods and Raquel rummages in her bag, handing Mim a card.

'Here's a new SIM. He's going to share the files with me. That's smart – they're his insurance. I'm only here until I receive them, then I'm gone. Another hour, maybe. Give me the phone so I can put in the number.'

Mim nods as she reaches for the phone, inserts the new SIM, feels like she is on autopilot.

Raquel grabs it quickly, thumbs flying over the keys. 'They will be looking for you,' she says, shouldering her bag and heading for the door, her eyes flashing already with the enormity of the story she has.

Mim watches her leave and tries to jigsaw the moments of the last hour together so that they make sense. They don't seem to fit.

Extraction.

Nuclear burial.

Europe.

Ben's voice.

～

Essie sits beside her with a glass of water, smoothing her hand back and forth over the stubbled flesh of Mim's knee. Sam has his back curled against hers, his face, fleshy with crying, is hidden in the sheets and she can hear from his breathing that he is sucking his thumb.

Anger has burned her out and there is nothing left. They came all this way for nothing. Risked it all. Did he really think he was going to change anything? Make any fucking difference at all? That his heroics would close the mine, that he'd run through the jungle like a movie star and save the world by the closing credits?

Yes, she too would be livid if she'd unearthed the plans. The difference was she didn't have time to be a hero, because she was doing school drop-off instead. Because she was responsible for two children. But wasn't he, too? A new wave of fury pulses through her guts and she stands up to loose the adrenaline before she screams.

Ben may be safe, but Mim and the kids are not.

'Fuck you!' Mim hisses, spitting the words at the window. *Fuck you!*

'What are we going to do now?' Essie says.

An alarm begins to clang.

Mim looks out the window, trying to work out where the sound is coming from, outside or somewhere inside the hotel? It's an old-fashioned sort of a ring – *klang-klang-klang-klang* – perhaps it is the hotel's fire alarm? But then she notices people pouring into the street below.

Sam sits up behind her. 'What's that, Mum?'

Underneath now, horns, sirens, a cacophony of warning.

'Mum?' Essie says, 'Mum?'

'Must be a drill,' Mim murmurs but the people scattering on the street below do not look like the organised calm of people following a drill. They look panicked. Streaming out of doors and through the lane next to the hotel, out into the street and up the hill.

Up the hill.

You're fucking kidding me.

'Tsunami alarm!' she says, turning to pull them up from the bed. 'Quick! Go!'

Sam screams and Essie is moving, pushing her brother. Mim grabs the backpack, knows the cash is there, the phone – that's all that matters.

'Go! Go!' she yells behind them as they charge down the stairs, voices shouting, 'Evacuate! Evacuate!'

'Hold his hand, Ess!' Mim calls as they race through the front doors and are swept into a crowd of people jostling and calling, motos, a Bemo, all moving up the street towards higher ground.

The noise is outrageous – the sirens, voices, a buzz of pings and music as people hold their devices up, filming, looking wildly around them.

She looks back to see the crowd below them, moving en masse up and away from the sea which still looks eerily calm, gleaming its silver petroleum sheen under the clouded sky. So many people.

'Keep going!' she shouts as she turns back, and realises she has lost sight of the kids for a moment.

'Shit,' she says under her breath. They know to stay close, especially in a crowd, and this is pure chaos. She pushes ahead, ready to grab them both back and demand they hold her hands if they can't stick together.

But they are not just ahead.

'Sam! Essie!'

Heads, bodies, shoulders, colours, bikes, backpacks, faces turning, moving, running.

But no Sam. No Essie.

Chest seizing. Breath hammering against ribs.

They were just here, right here in front of her.

'Essie! Sam!'

Fingers scrabbling at air, at t-shirts, at other people's shoulders, hair, pulling, twisting.

'Where are my kids?' she screams.

People turn, look away, one woman points, 'Up the hill, up the hill,' she calls and urges Mim on.

But Mim cannot see her kids.

They are gone.

'Where are they, where are they, where are they?' She careens in and out of the snaking column of people and vehicles and noise. Stops, hands to mouth. She heaves, splutters, heaves again, but there is nothing but dry coughs, emptiness.

Look for his hair, blond hair, one lucid thought cutting through her panic. She runs again. And she can smell it, smell Sammy's head, the piquant sweet at the end of the day, can feel the soft thread of it between her fingers.

'*Sammy!*' Her scream is hoarse now, but still she cannot see him. She pushes hard up the hill, her calves cramping, head reeling.

Up ahead, where the road turns back up the mountain, a crowd is gathering on what looks like outdoor volleyball courts. *There, there, they will be there.*

'Please, please, please,' she murmurs, eyes darting above the heads, registering young people and mothers with children and men on bikes but not her children.

She is stupid, stupid, stupid. She should never have let them out of her sight. She should never have been allowed to have them in the first place. She has always been unfit for this job. Since the beginning. This will be her punishment, to know, forever, that she lost them. It was her job to look after them and she lost them. She lost them. It is her fault. All of it. Heidi, Ben, she has broken everything.

Hands on her knees, folded at the waist. She sucks in air, can't get it past her chest, feels like a punctured vacuum.

Someone pushes her, pulls her up. 'This way, this way,' they call and she is jostled back into the crowd. She twists to look behind her, perhaps they got lost and went back – of course, that is what she has always told them to do, *Stay where you are*. She must have gone past them. She begins to push back against the throng, fighting her way to the edge, to the cracked tiles of the shopfronts, where women are feverishly pulling down roller shutters, pushing piles of shoes, plastic buckets stacked high, back inside to keep them safe from whatever is coming.

She can see the hotel doors, the man from reception, she yells out but her voice is lost in the mayhem. Running the last fifty metres, scanning the crowd, searching for that blond head that should be a beacon to her.

But they are not there, not anywhere.

The receptionist turns to her in surprise when she grabs him.

'Have you seen my kids?'

He shakes his head, eyes wide. 'They are still inside?' he asks, making to undo the lock. 'But, I checked all the rooms.'

'No, no, they were with me, I lost them in the crowd. I lost them.'

He frowns. 'They know it is a tsunami warning, they must go to higher ground?'

'Yes, yes,' she says, 'they know, but I lost them.' The side-splitting pain that curls her over again, to even have to speak the words.

'They will be at the evacuation zone. Come, I will take you, we will be there quickly.'

He motions for her to follow him to the neat line-up of motos and grabs a helmet from the back, handing it to her, straddling the bike and kicking the engine into life.

'Please,' he says, gesturing for her to get on behind him.

But what if she misses them, what if she goes too fast and they pass each other, what if – ?

She jumps on the bike and he swings out into the madness. Leaning back as far as she can without throwing the balance, she darts her head left to right and back again. Calls their names over the noise of the engine. God, all these people, how far will a wave come, where will the water go, how high? An image, of a hospital room, stairs, panic, unable to walk – *Jesus, Nick* – but she can't think of him, she can't. The kids, she only has space for them. Nick will be okay, he's always okay.

The man accelerates, mounts a gutter and turns into a tiny lane, calling over his shoulder, 'Quicker!'

She grips his waist, sure she will leave bruises, the signature of her fear.

He slows for a moment as they swerve around a hole, a puddle, then surges forward again, a steep incline, ducking under low hanging cables and then emerging into space, the volleyball courts, the crowd beginning to assemble. She is off the back of the bike before he has stopped.

A lap of the perimeter, hoarse now from calling their names, inconceivable that they are not here, not waiting for her, not where they should be. God, she will kill them, she will never let them out of her sight again.

Oh fuck. Oh god.

In the centre of the space, a man in the khaki uniform of the army. She runs at him but stops herself from grabbing his arms.

'Please,' she says when he turns to face her, surprised, 'my children are missing, somewhere here, in the crowd.'

'False alarm,' he says, offering her no more and turning away.

'Sorry?' she says.

When he frowns at her, she asks again, 'Please, my kids, they are lost.'

'No tsunami, the warning system went off by accident. Computer error. That's why the alarm has stopped. Wait until the crowd goes home, you will find your children.'

The man from the hotel is beside her. 'It is a false alarm, okay? Your children will be fine, we will find them.'

There is no relief that her kids won't be swallowed by a giant wave. She just wants them here, now, their flesh under hers, solid and safe.

'They are not with your friend?' the man asks.

Mim looks at him blankly.

'The woman who came to the hotel this morning?'

Mim scrabbles in her bag for the phone. Call Raquel. Get Ben. He will find them. He will fix this.

She dials the number on the screen, praying it will still work. Almost cries with relief when she hears the woman's voice.

'The kids are gone. You have to help. You have to get Ben.'

Raquel is reluctant, nervous, asks again and again if Mim is sure, if she really has lost them.

Mim wants to scream into the phone. 'Please,' she says, 'please call him, tell him they're gone, that he has to help me.'

'Wait there. It'll take me ten minutes.'

⌣

A shopping centre. Sam strapped to her chest, still so young that Mim is in the breast-leaking, sleepwalking zone. Essie slips from her, ducking under an arm and through a couple to see something glittering in a window. It is five seconds, that is all, and Mim feels herself rupture, glimpses the parallel dimension where children do not come home safe, where each morning holds the nightmare of remembering reality, of losing again. Essie's face as she gripped her hands so tight, her nails dug into her daughter's soft skin – *Never do that again, do you hear me, don't you let go of my hand.* Instant remorse at Essie's shock. Anger at the old woman who tutted at them; either she'd never known the feeling, or time must erase the fear.

⌣

A sheen of sweat on Raquel's forehead when she arrives.

'He's coming. But don't freak out when he comes. He has minders with him, and they're armed.'

Mim is walking in rapidly frantic circles. She is well beyond freaked. 'Where is he? Where the fuck is he?'

'Coming. He made them come. But they're worried it's a set-up.'

'They're his fucking kids!'

'Just be careful. If they get spooked, anything could happen. I need that evidence to get the story out, to help finish what Ben started, to make it worth it.'

'It isn't worth it.'

'You'll find them.'

'How? Where?'

'He should be close now. I told him to come here, to the evacuation area. Hiding in plain view.'

'The officer said it was a false alarm. Computer error.' Mim keeps scanning the crowd for Essie, Sam, and now Ben too.

'It'd be easy enough to hack the system,' Raquel says, 'maybe someone needed a diversion for getting a dirty load off the docks.'

Mim's hand at her own neck, pulling in air. How fucking stupid is she? She murmurs, tries to say Raquel's name.

'What?' Raquel turns.

'They aren't lost. They were taken.' Certainty setting like concrete in her guts.

'*Mim!*'

And there he is. Thirty metres away. Like an illustration of a man she used to know. He is wearing a shirt she has never seen before and yet relief courses in her. Ben is here. Ben will fix this.

He goes to move towards her, but is held back by a man beside him. There are two of them, tall, militaristic, each of them with a hand at his belt, and a weapon.

Ben turns to them, appears to be talking, convincing; his hands splayed out as if to say, just wait, wait.

She begins to run across the road, hears Raquel's voice behind her, but fuck it, fuck them, this is her husband and the kids are gone and they must fix this.

His hand is up now towards her, telling her to hold, to wait, and they are looking at each other and not at the white van which suddenly screeches up between them.

Everything happens so fast.

'Mum!'

Sammy's blond head at the window, Essie's face beside him.

'Sam!'

And then two figures spilling from the back of the van, each extended at the arm with the flat black shine of a weapon.

She is running at the van, at the window where she can see the children, their faces terrified, screaming for her.

'Stop!'

One of the figures, a stocky man, is pointing a gun at Ben; the other, a woman in black, at her.

Time slows. She looks at Ben and he shakes his head. *Don't move*, she almost hears him speak into her brain. The men, his protectors, have disappeared. Where are they now with their guns?

The woman speaks. 'You can make this really simple, Ben.'

The accent is unmistakable, and even though they aren't in uniform, it's clear who they are. Who has sent them. The Department.

There is a beast howling inside of Mim. *'Give me my fucking kids back!'*

The woman smiles. 'You can have them back. As soon as we get what we need.'

The man who is pointing the gun at Ben speaks. 'Him.'

Mim thinks she might faint, sound muffles and warps in her ears as though she is underwater, as though she is drowning. Ben raises his hands and begins to walk towards the man.

'Wait! Ben!'

He stops and looks at her but she directs the next question to the woman. 'How do I know you'll let us walk away once you have him? How do I know we'll be safe?'

'Once we have him, we don't need you or the kids. Although I wouldn't suggest going home. Or contacting the embassy. At best, no one will believe what you have to say; at worst, we'll decide we have to keep you quiet and your children will go to BestLife.'

Behind the windows, Essie is pale, her arm around her little brother. Sam's face is crumpled with fear. Can they hear?

'The kids first,' Mim says.

The woman nods. Calls something back to the van, and the door slides open, the kids rush out holding each other, yelling for her.

'One of you go to your mother,' the woman says.

Sam and Essie look at each other, then Essie pushes Sam.

'Go to Mum!' she yells and watches as her brother sprints across the space.

Mim grabs him. High moan in the back of her throat. Trying not to smother her son as she grips him in her arms, keeps her eyes locked on her daughter, her fierce, brave daughter who is still standing next to the van, next to a woman with a gun.

'You!' the man yells, motioning for Ben to move forward.

Ben looks at Mim, as if he has something to say. But there is nothing to be said.

She nods and he raises his hands and walks towards them.

'Slowly,' the man calls, 'keep your hands up.'

But Ben rushes the last few steps and grabs Essie's hands, folds her into him. The man is yelling, 'Hey! Hey!' Mim screams. The woman waves her gun, pulls Ben back.

Essie clings to her father for a moment more, her face pressed against his chest.

Sam squirms in Mim's arms.

Then Ben is pushing Essie away and she is flying across the asphalt towards Mim, her face already collapsing. Mim's arms stretch out over Sammy's head so she can grab her daughter and envelop her.

She's got them back. She presses their bodies into her own and looks up to see Ben being led into the back of the van, the two Department heavies pushing him in, so he is facing away from her.

A blur of movement out of the corner of her eye.

'*No!*' she calls out before she even realises what she is seeing.

Ben's minders, the men who were protecting him, raising their arms in unison.

The figures at the van turning, Ben's face in profile.

Two shots.

The red bloom across his chest as he crumples at the knees. The woman yells, pressing her hands against the crimson spread.

Knowing she must hold the kids' faces at her chest. Knowing they must not see.

Raquel's voice, frantic, 'You've got to go! Now, quick!'

Raised voices over her shoulder, the army officers, attention she must escape.

'Mum?' Essie's muffled voice, her chin scraping against Mim's collarbone. 'What was that, what's happening?'

And now Mim is saying it too, 'We have to go, we have to go *now*,' turning the kids around, protecting them with her body, urging them away, away from the van.

'*Dad!*' Sam screams, but Mim forces him forward.

Raquel is beside her. 'Get out of here. I can't help you. *Go!*'

As they race down the street, Mim can only nod at Raquel, watch her peel off and begin to disappear into the crowd.

'Wait!' Essie calls, pitching after the journalist. Mim cries out, but Essie runs to Raquel, clutches at the woman's hand, shaking it once and then pulling away.

Raquel looks down in astonishment, her fingers unclenching enough to reveal the slim black rectangle in her hand.

Mim looks at her daughter, then back at Raquel, but she has already vanished into the crowd.

'C'mon!' Essie says, pulling at Mim.

Don't leave him, must leave him. She looks back once over her shoulder, but the van is already beginning to move. She must hide them. Get away. To the water, to the boat. The silver sea glints at the bottom of the hill.

The sea.

'Quick!' Mim says, pointing to where a moto is parked at the edge of a lane. 'There!'

And before she can think, before she can question or worry or second-guess herself, she has straddled the bike, pulling Sam on in front of her and directing Essie to hang on behind and she is someone else, someone from before, someone who knows how to roll start a motorbike, steer it until the engine coughs. Someone who can get her children down a mountain, weaving through the crowd all the way to the harbour.

27

The water is only lukewarm and the detergent doesn't soap up. It won't clean the bowls properly, but she uses the moment to flick the rim of scum from beneath her thumbnail. It's a little low, the sink, she wonders how he ever put up with it. There is a constant ache in the small of her back. Everywhere, actually. Her body feels ten years older, the way her knees crack with the constant balancing, the bruises on her hips, her elbows. The tap's leaking too. She'll add it to the list of questions when she calls him at the next harbour. It's a long list.

'You okay up there?' She leans back and calls up through the hatch.

'All good, Mum,' Essie's voice rings back, loud and clear and strong.

She dries her hands on the damp tea towel, turns from the sink and reaches out to touch Sam's hair. 'Nearly finished?'

The black lines of his drawing are intricate, careful. Figures running and flying, speech bubbles squished in above.

'Which chapter are you up to?'

Sam doesn't look up. 'Ninja Boy and the Storm Chasers.'

'You want to show me?'

Sam sighs. 'It's not ready yet.'

'Okay,' she says, 'half hour, yeah, then bed.'

She leaves him, bent over the paper, the tip of his tongue resting pinkly at the edge of his upper lip.

'Mum?' he says and she pauses on the first step. 'Will there be a postbox at the next stop?'

'I don't know, maybe, why?'

'I want to send this one to Dad, or maybe to Nan if we still haven't got his address, can I?'

She doesn't turn around so he cannot see how she closes her eyes, stills.

'Can I, Mum?'

'We'll see, my love.'

And it is enough, for now, even though she knows it won't stay that way.

Raquel hasn't been able to find out, either way, and maybe that's for the best. Mim's holding it at bay – the possibilities, the grief – just for a little while longer.

She emerges on to the deck and to Essie at the helm. Her daughter's hair flicks around her face in the breeze and she looks taller or older or like someone Mim might want to be when she grows up. Because even though these sailing aches make her feel older; inside, she feels eleven again. Fifteen. Twenty-five. As if the stratigraphy of the rest of her life has been ground back, worn away and her past is the utmost layer again. 'How's it going?' she says as she moves to stand beside Essie.

'Wind's picked up a bit.'

'That's good, keep us under sail a little while longer.'

'Where are we going?'

Mim glances at the nav to check the coordinates. 'It's there, Ess, Turtle Island, that's what we're following –'

'I don't mean that.'

Ahead of them, the horizon is all lit up. The kind of equatorial sunset that folds and glows with colour – peach, grey, gold. The wind whipper-snaps around the mast, the wires.

'I don't know.' Mim pauses, honesty making her throat raw. 'But we're going to choose. Together. We'll decide.'

Essie nods – long, thinking nods – without taking her eyes off the water ahead. 'You think it can be somewhere that has a soccer team?'

Laughter in Mim's throat, sudden and loud and sweet. 'Yes. I reckon it can.'

She reaches for Essie's hand, holds it tight; the weight of her daughter's fingers pressing back against her skin.

Acknowledgements

I acknowledge the Traditional Owners of the lands and waters this book was researched and written upon and recognise their continuing connection to Country that was never ceded. I pay my respects to their Elders, past, present and future.

This book began with a scribbled *What if* at a time when the Australian Government closed our borders to people seeking asylum. Over four years, while our border policies remained, the book changed trajectory but at its core remains a question about how we treat people who ask for help. At a time of global crisis, it's worth remembering the paradox of what we would do to protect the people we love at the same time as we punish others for doing just that.

I was told Pippa Masson was the best agent in the country and I'm still pinching myself she took me on. Thank you, Pippa, for your astute guidance, warmth and for organising conference calls while

I stood on hills in remote WA – calls which ended in this book finding its perfect home. My thanks also to the team at Curtis Brown, especially Caitlan Cooper Trent, and to Alice Lutyens in the UK.

Thank you to my indomitable publisher and editor Fiona Henderson whose enthusiasm, intellect, laughs and doggedness to make things perfect have taken this book to the next level. I wish exceptional editors Siobhan Cantrill and Deonie Fiford could accompany my words everywhere in everyday life. Dan Ruffino, Anabel Pandiella, Anna O'Grady, Elissa Baillie, Anthea Bariamis and the entire team at Simon & Schuster in Australia, thank you for championing this book from the beginning. And to Phoebe Morgan and the team at Harper Collins UK, thank you for bringing Mim across another ocean in such splendid fashion.

Thank you Sandy Cull and Daniel Lint for the incredible cover, and to Erika Wells on a steamy Darwin night who first showed me Daniel's work.

Toni Jordan is a novel whisperer who first said 'Maybe just kill him?' and opened this book out into something new. Penni Russon was my first and treasured reader. Aviva Tuffield gave me the confidence to dive in. I would never have held my nerve if it were not for Charlotte Wood who guided me and this project through the very shittiest part and back out again. I am forever grateful.

When I began, I had never set foot on a yacht. Thank you to all those who assisted with my sailing education: Leigh McLeod first let me take the helm, Sharon Mullins, Di & Bernie Mcgoldrick and Jane Courtier shared tales and books, Chris Wells answered endless questions, read 'the boat bit' and is never reticent in telling me where I get things wrong. That said, any sailing related errors are my own.

I had a mad idea to crew aboard a yacht from Darwin to Ambon, Indonesia, and Captain Neville Gill was kind enough to take me on. To Neville and the crew of *Finally*, Neil Brown, Pete Smith, Ray Jarrett, Matt Wilson, Joy Eggenhuizen and everyone involved in the Darwin to Ambon Yacht race 2018, my heartfelt thanks. I could not have written this book without you and those four days at sea. Neil – I stole your story of the whiteout in the Banda Sea. I hope you don't mind. Thank you to Adjeng Hatalea and the people of Ambon I was lucky enough to meet.

On geology, I am indebted to Dr Susan White, Dr David Steart and Philomena Manifold for answering my many questions.

To all the mothers I know, and the ones whose stories I read, your experiences – myriad as they are – are the backbone of Mim's story. Thank you. Solidarity.

Thank you to my writers group Meg Dunley, Katherine Collette, Kim Hood, Emily Brewin, Nicky Heaney & Venita Munir, especially for our magic retreats at Musk where so much of this book was written, deleted and written again. Thank you Cathy and Peter for allowing us somewhere to retreat and create. Thank you Meg, for keeping me accountable, and Katherine, for the joy and craziness of our podcast adventure. To my coven, Penni Russon, Zana Fraillon and Penny Harrison, thank you for sharing the splendid chaos of our writing and real lives and all the ways they crash up against each other. I'm so lucky to have you. Kelly Gardiner, thank you for your wise counsel always. To the RMIT PWE crew, thank you. Please don't kick me out. I promise to finish one day. To the Class of 2016: Mark Smith, Mel Cheng, Rajith Savanadasa, Michelle Wright, Mark Brandi – here's to our seconds (and thirds and fourths, you overachievers!). Thank you Alice Robinson, Angela Savage, Sally Piper, J.P. Pomare, Karen Viggers, James Bradley & Kris Olsson for your generous early support. The beauty of doing this second time around is that my circle of writing colleagues has grown enormously; to all those I drink with, study with, interview for the podcast, chat with over twitter, thank you for sharing the strange wonder of this writing life.

I'm grateful for a Creative Vic grant and for residencies at Varuna, The Writers House and Bundanon where I had time and space to write. Susie and Paul at Point Hicks Lighthouse let me write on the balcony for two glorious days over the 2018/19 summer and talked to me about Indonesia. Thank you.

Booksellers make the world go around and I thank them for their passion and tireless devotion to books and stories and authors and readers. Our words would not go anywhere if it weren't for you.

Thankyou to my girls: Eri, Shay, Tess, Mel, Amy, Julia, Polly, Katja, Jess, Bee – the best fan club ever in work and in life. Eri, Mont, Ash & Leroy shared (another) adventure of a lifetime, one that involved being in phone reception at strange times in remote places for bookish things. Thank you for sharing the thrill and Eri, for everything, always.

To my family who make life happen in ways big and small; my in-laws, especially Graham, who saw this started but not finished, and who would have been 'powerful proud'. To my sister, Maggie, and Mum and Dad, for everything but especially for kid wrangling, unconditional love and razor-sharp reading eyes – thank you.

To Adam, who says writing is my job and gives me space and time to do the work, thank you. You are a good man and I love you.

To Gracie and Etta. Thank you for understanding that I am your mum and a writer, both. For sending me off on writing retreats with hand drawn signs that say, 'You can do it, Mum!', for the fierce tousle of the heart and mind that is every day of being a parent, for teaching me what it's all for. I love you.